Chinese Whisperings: The Yin and Yang Book

Chinese Whisperings
The Yin and Yang Book

Edited by
Paul Anderson & Jodi Cleghorn

Written in collaboration with

Jen Brubacher, Christopher Chartrand, Carrie Clevenger,
Jason Coggins, Rob Diaz II, Laura Eno, Annie Evett,
Jasmine Gallant, Tina Hunter, Lily Mulholland,
Emma Newman, Tony Noland, Claudia Osmond,
Richard Jay Parker, Dan Powell, Dale Challener Roe,
Icy Sedgwick, Paul Servini, Benjamin Solah,
& J.M. Strother.

An Imprint of eMergent Publishing
www.emergent-publishing.com

PUBLISHED BY eMERGENT PUBLISHING
Brisbane, Australia & London, United Kingdom
All rights reserved

ISBN 978-0-9807446-9-9

First published (electronically) in Australia, 2010

Typeset in Adobe Garamond Pro 11/15
Headers Chow Yum

www.emergent-publishing.com

Contents

PROLOGUE..1

THE YANG BOOK..9

Three Monkeys
  Paul Servini 11
Three Rings
  Christopher Chartrand................................25
Dogs of War
  Tony Noland..39
This be the Verse
  Dan Powell...51
Providence
  Dale Challener Roe...................................63
No Passengers Allowed
  J.M. Strother..77
Thirteen Feathers
  Rob Diaz II...89
One Behind the Eye
  Richard Jay Parker..................................101
Chase the Day
  Jason Coggins..111
Somewhere to Pray
  Benjamin Solah......................................121

THE YIN BOOK..133

The Guilty One
  Emma Newman.......................................135

Excess Baggage
      Carrie Clevenger..........147
Where the Heart Is
      TinaHunter..........159
The Other Side of Limbo
      Claudia Osmond..........171
Freedom
      Laura Eno..........183
Cobalt Blue
      Jasmine Gallant..........193
The Strangest Comfort
      Icy Sedgwick..........205
Lost and Found
      Jen Brubacher..........215
Kanyasulkam
      AnnieEvett..........225
Double Talk
      LilyMulholland..........237

EPILOGUE..........251

Foreword

This anthology was slated as *The Jade Book*. Obviously plans changed, between completing *The Red Book* and beginning this one (our cover artist Lucas Clevenger didn't miss this though!) With most things *Chinese Whisperings*, a lot of what appears, when you look back at the end project, happens by pure chance (accident). This anthology is no different.

Sometimes I imagine Paul and I garbed up as mad scientists, leaning over our latest creation with a set of jumper leads.

"What do you think?"

"I reckon it will work?"

"What the hell."

"Yeah, nothing ventured, nothing gained, right?"

Then there's a worldwide black out…

In reality it is far more mundane, involves sleepwear more than white lab coats and epic, long distance Skype sessions rather than a shared lab and continual supply of electricity (which I'm certain all our neighbours are quite pleased about).

Paul returned to drawing and painting at the start of the year. Amid the landscape and portraits three conceptual book covers, experimenting with the idea of Yin/Yang, came through.

"What do you think? Two anthologies. You can edit a male anthology and me a female one. Yin and Yang. The covers separate and combine like this…" And in a nanosecond of joint creative fission, the unimaginatively titled "The Yin and Yang Book" (known as #yandy in the Twitterverse) came into existence. But this was just the beginning.

I got overzealous and invited too many male writers, forgetting Paul and I needed spots on the anthology. We both wanted to keep the integrity of the ten story anthology, so what to do? Who did I kick off the Team Yang? The last invited? The last to accept? It was another lesson in nothing is a mistake... simply a boon you haven't yet realised.

In the end we came to a compromise, two anthologies of ten stories, with a shared prologue and epilogue. And this is where it got really interesting. A shared prologue and epilogue implied a connection between the two anthologies. Could we do it? Could we create a 'mated anthology' (a term coined by Tony Noland as we struggled to explain just what we were pitching) where each story stood alone, each anthology stood alone, but reading both anthologies gave the entire picture... and a bit more. The Red Book was based on a circular principal. The Yin and Yang Book a fusion of spider web and sliding doors.

A mated anthology required shared space. Paul and I considered a wedding and a funeral but somehow we ended up in an airport. We ruled out weather, a strike, terrorist attack, computer malfunction and a few other scenarios. This was in January, months before Eyjafjallajökull sent worldwide air travel into a tailspin.

I pitched an airline collapse. My sister had been on the final Compass flight out of Melbourne in 1991. It happened mid-operation, on a Friday evening and four days before Christmas. Australia only had two other domestic airlines at the time. Luggage was seized as part of the bankruptcy proceedings and it took months for it to be returned. The court case surrounding the grounding of the Compass went on for years, making its way to the High Court of Australia for a ruling.

Paul wasn't immediately sold on it as an idea... until he hit on who forced our fictional airline into receivership and why. I wasn't sold on it as an idea, but as a compromise Paul said yes to an airline collapse and I said yes to who collapsed the airline. The rest is jaded *Pangaean* history.

I was both excited and daunted once we'd finalised the details of the premise. Finally we would get the opportunity to test the sliding doors concept in a Chinese Whisperings anthology. But we'd grown from 8 writers to 20. Paul and I wouldn't be editing together. I was comfortable with the creation formulae of The Red Book and felt a spider-web approach was much too wide-open a creative space. After all, how do you create a literary web with the complexity and clarity needed to engage and hold the reader through 22 stories?

You know how—you get the hell out of the way and put your faith in the intrepid writers who, throwing their lot in with you, trust you. No pressure!

This year I learnt pushing boundaries opens the floor for experimentation. Putting an untried concept on the table gives writers permission to do something different. Add editorial support and writers will push the short story structure, their writing skills and ideas to the absolute limit. Nothing ventured, nothing gained, indeed. It hasn't always been easy, and there were moments when I honestly thought we'd bitten too much off. But here we are!

I didn't intentionally set out to create a dark, aggressive, gritty and for the most part nasty or cringe-worthy 'Yangiverse'. After all, the yang half of the symbol represents 'light'… unless you come to play in the world of Chinese Whisperings. Even though I had a totally hands off approach to any kind of connective theme, one emerged as Paul and I line edited the final manuscript. The Yangiverse characters are, to a greater or lesser extent, being 'done over' (except of course poor Calvinsweetheart who wishes he was). Be heartened though, in the dark glimmers of light always abide and in the maelstrom of the worst of humanity, the best shines through all the brighter.

Jodi Cleghorn
Brisbane, October 2010

If *The Red Book* was the stunning debut album by a young and slightly raw new band, then *The Yin and Yang Books* were the difficult second album. The one where cracks begin to show in the band, what was exciting before is now tedious and creative differences rear their ugly heads.

Nonetheless, beautiful music gets made.

This anthology was tough. Far tougher than the last time. We had twice the number of writers to deal with than last time, with a story arc far greater in scope and infinitely greater in complexity. Add to that the dogged determination of our old nemesis, the CW Fairy, to plague the writers and editors alike with illness, injury, bereavement, unemployment and legal problems, and you realise just how draining an experience it was this time around.

I think the authors who forged the 'Yiniverse' had an easier time of it than those in the Yangiverse. And that wasn't necessarily a good thing. My usual 'hands-off' approach went a little too far this year, to the extent some times weeks would elapse between an author submitting a draft and the actual editing taking place.

We got there in the end though. I was blessed to be working with ten authors who had infinite reserves of patience, both with my somewhat irregular editorial interventions and with my ideas for 'improvements' to their stories. Sometimes those improvements required a complete overhaul of the structure of the story. Sometimes it was nothing more than the odd word here and there.

The airport of the Yin and Yang Book occupies two different, but parallel, realities. Some events happen in each, others are unique. As each story was written, this dichotomy widened, meaning that whoever the unlucky sod was who had to write the epilogue to tie both anthologies together, well… Oh yeah, that unlucky sod was me!

Even accepting the airport is in two parallel dimensions, there is still a question of when and where (roughly) the airport and the events of that day take place. The 'when' is fairly simple. Now. The collapse of *Pangaean* occurs in the present day. The 'where' however is a little bit more difficult. The airport bounced all over the globe, from Dubai to Singapore to Moscow to London. At one point it was an ocean away from Paris, but still only three hours from Brussels. It may be London, but if it is then it is Parallelondon. If you read the stories you'll find as many things that suggest London as things that suggest against that.

And while you're distracted with that, a thief is making off with a priceless work of art. So perhaps we should turn our attention to this theft, and let air traffic control wonder where exactly the airport is.

Paul Anderson
London, October 2010

An airport is a place somewhere between heaven and earth, where answers wait for questions and their asking.

- Anonymous

PROLOGUE

I grit my teeth, push the ancient suitcase across the taxi seat and follow it, slamming the door behind me. The worn jeans and cotton shirt feel like a tailored suit of steel and sandpaper against the bruises blooming over my body and the lacerations tightening with dried blood. The driver turns and I smile, ignoring the pain.

"Where you going?"

"Airport."

The taxi does a u-turn, headlights cutting a swathe through the fog. I close my eyes and hope the driver refrains from assaulting me with a one-way discussion of whatever the shock jocks are polluting the airwaves with this week. I need this ride to unwind and rest in safety.

Exhaustion ebbs and flows with seasickness motion. I look at the window, distracting myself from the bone-shattering tiredness, thinking of the future rather than the past.

My mind wanders to the comfort of the scuffed Doc Martens and how good they feel after two years in designer shoes; Christian Louboutin, Jimmy Choo and Dior, as dictated by the role of Keely Jackson, personal assistant to John Hildebrand Junior, CEO of *Pangaean Airlines*. The last pair I wore, and hopefully I will ever wear, abandoned in JJ's bedroom. The rest lined up with military precision, in Keely Jackson's overpriced studio apartment.

A place I'll gratefully never set foot in again.

I wonder if JJ will find the Dior platforms? The housekeeper certainly won't. Her only act of defiance is to not vacuum under his bed.

JJ insisted I keep the platforms on, bending me over his dressing table, one hand jammed between my shoulder blades, the other hand grabbing at my hipbone, his fingers digging into the tender hollow. It replays behind my eyelids, his face looming in and out of the mirror with the rhythmic pounding, grinning with narcissistic delight.

Sex which pushes boundaries is something I've always sought, but there was nothing to relish about sex with JJ. I only got off because I knew the man with his head buried between my thighs stood to lose his family's most prized possession... to me. That, and only that, allowed me to orgasm, howling and writhing in genuine ecstasy.

1

I faked it from that point on, my body obeying, subservient, while I disassociated. In this fashion two years of sexual fantasies unravelled for JJ, his hidden cameras throughout his penthouse capturing every minute and nuance of his brutality.

Hours on, in the bosom of a heavy sedative, JJ slept, his perfect mouth slack, a silver line of saliva pooling on the silk pillow case. I corrupted the security system, disabling the cameras, wiping the archives and backups. Dressed in one of JJ's business suits, with his trademark black fedora pulled low over my forehead I unlocked the safe and took what I'd been waiting two years for.

With a single upmarket department-store bag in hand, I slipped out the fire escape to the car waiting below.

"Domestic or international, Miss?"

The question pulls me back to the present. The driver's eyes meet mine above the tacky pine tree deodoriser swinging from the rear vision mirror.

"International, please."

My body protests when I stretch, but I push aside the pain. I don't regret kowtowing to JJ's sadism, every second worth the agony.

Skin heals.

Plastic surgery removes scar tissue.

He fucked Keely Jackson's body, and I'm not her now. In the end, JJ was the one fucked, good and proper.

It is 6.05am when the taxi eases into the chaos of the drop-off zone. Sleep-deprived travellers tumble into the cold, hitting the ground just ahead of me, clutching luggage and staggering towards the automatic doors. A group of people gather to the left of the doors, out of place in the human tide. Heavy coat collars turned up. Words hang midair in white frosty clouds. None have luggage. A few stamp their feet. My heart skips until I see the flash of a familiar uniform and remember the strike by a rival airline.

"Bloody unions," the taxi-driver mutters. "You flying with them?"

I shake my head and concentrate on finding the correct change, then worry about moving myself and the suitcase out of the cab.

Out in the cold, I let the pain fall from my body, winding my scarf around my neck to keep out the chill and prying eyes. I'm early. With time to spare, I haul the suitcase to the smoking area, pull a packet of tobacco from my pocket and roll a cigarette. I hate smoking but it is a good excuse to kill time without being obvious.

The striking employees wait for breakfast TV cameras to arrive to provide sensationalised fodder for the brain-dead masses. I stretch the life of the rollie, knowing I won't inadvertently be in a background shot broadcast into millions of homes. As the cameras arrive, I grind the butt into the ground, bend stiffly to retrieve it and bin it with the tobacco and matches.

Inside a leather backpack I find a bottle of bergamot body-spray and a packet of mints. I mist the air around me and pop a mint into my mouth. The intense citrus scent settles on me and the transition from Keely Jackson to Medae Newman is complete. I swing the backpack over a shoulder and pick up the suitcase, walk as casually as possible toward the automatic doors sucking away the last bitter traces of nicotine and the last two years.

The line up at the check-in counter is twice the length now. Fifteen minutes and one cigarette is all it takes to be in the best position in the queue. When it is busiest, people pay you and your luggage only the briefest attention. Checking in becomes a production line with a smile and a personalised tick list of all the dangerous goods you are not carrying. X-ray security behind the scenes keeps everything moving to avoid a delay.

The line coils six times through the temporary barricades, squeezing the most people possible into the small space. I join the line behind a woman carrying an over-sized garment bag arguing loudly on an iPhone with someone named 'Louise'. Her bag is big and heavy enough to be transporting a dead body, though if she's trying to hide anything she's making a sham of it. Further ahead, two nondescript businessmen with slip-on shoes and equally unremarkable black laptop bags. One is whistling in between taking verbal swipes at his travelling companion.

Every few minutes the queue moves, like an anaconda devouring a large mammal. My body recognises the check-in two-step and shifts to accommodate the new beat. Down-up-shuffle-shuffle-down-up. The brainless repetition relaxes me.

When it is time to move again, my hand lingers atop the suitcase after I place it down. I'm not usually attached to things, but both the case and contents represent significant investments of time and patience.

Rising to the top of my profession didn't happen by being impulsive. Everything is done slowly, incrementally. Luck plays no part. It all comes down to planning and patience. The fact it took me two years to steal from the Hildebrands is testament to my ability to wait.

You could say I was born a thief, though I didn't officially steal until I turned nineteen. Anyone can learn to crack a safe, disable a security system or hotwire a car. Anyone, with a reasonable level of intelligence has the ability to learn to hack a computer, procure illegal identity papers, master another language or charm the unsuspecting. Few, though, have the patience required. That's what separates those in prison from those of us still plying our trade.

Given the opportunity, I'd happily stand in a check-in line for hours. People-watching in an airport never raises suspicions. Plus, people in transit often let their masks slide, exposing sides usually hidden from public life.

Medae Newman hit my radar while waiting in line, playing airport bingo to pass the time. Travelling as Keely Jackson, to take up the position with JJ, she checked in ahead of me. She wore a long, classic-cut suede coat, with old jeans and a soft white shirt, red hair cut short and choppy. A very old leather suitcase stood by her side. Her perfume attracted my attention first. I guessed Estee Lauder's *Sunflowers*, one of the squares on my airport bingo card.

Of course, I have no idea if she'd been christened Medae. I wheeled my Samsonite suitcase past her, hearing the clerk greet her as Ms Newman. That's when I realised the *Sunflowers* square on the bingo card could not be marked off; she was wearing bergamot oil.

I play airport bingo to pass the time, not find my next identity. The card is always the same and under normal circumstances, no identity associated is considered assumable. Medae Newman was an anomaly—the trick of her perfume.

It has been a long time since I last filled a bingo card. Scanning the check-in queue I feel lucky.

Six ahead of me is the disgruntled corporate type, his body trying to escape the ill-fitting, pin-striped suit. He's the overworked executive of a company too cheap to fly him business class, who spends the entire flight thumping away on a laptop, using the paper napkin supplied with the meal to mop his brow, the ectoplasmic flow of fat from his side breaching the arm rest delineating your seat from his.

Several families stand around mountains of luggage, parents hissing threats at restless children. After a time I find the woman travelling alone with the over-active child. He's dressed in a Thomas the Tank Engine parka and trying to swing from the industrial tape separating her part of the line from mine. He's the kid who'll want to say hello to you from the seat in front, a small snotty face popping up between the head rests.

I see several likely students and finally locate one with a lip piercing and purple foils, oblivious to anyone beyond Charlaine Harris's Dead Before Dawn and her iPod.

Moving on, a couple at the head of the line can't stop kissing. In the middle of the line, a woman in a sky-blue raincoat tries desperately to put distance between her and the guy who shoved through the line to join her half an hour earlier.

The line shifts forwards, and I'm one, two coils closer to the end.

I smell *Sunflowers*, spy a purple Samsonite suitcase and then a fake alligator one.

I round another bend. And another.

A bald man. A woman who thinks she's beautiful.

A Canadian Flag sewn on a backpack.

I'm close to the head of the line and filled with the thrill of finishing the first bingo card in years.

A commotion to the rear of the line distracts me. A crowd of dishevelled men in matching blazers try to push their way through the line, an airport representative between them and passenger revolt. They're not the type of traveller I'm interested in.

Yves Saint Laurent's Jazz wafts my direction compliments of a male flight attendant stopping to chat to a brunette clerk.

BINGO!

And I'm the head of the line.

"Good morning," the same brunette says motioning me to her counter, the tail end of laughter clinging to her face as the male flight attendant walks away with a list in hand. She pushes a strand of hair behind her ear. "Travelling through to Paris this morning, Ms Newman?"

I nod, putting my backpack on the counter to look for my passport and travel documents. Once I've handed them over, I ease the suitcase onto the conveyor belt. The digital numbers on the counter stop at 32kg.

"Spot on." The brunette prints a baggage tag and sticks it around the wooden handle, then loops on a weight warning. "You don't see many cases like this."

"Family heirloom," I say, trying not to pay the suitcase more attention than it warrants. "My great-grandmother was an artist too."

She nods her head in an absent way born of repetition rather than interest and runs through the list of items I'm forbidden to transport.

"I don't have any of those," I say, waiting for her to hand over my boarding pass. The conveyor belt lurches to life, taking my case and the Hildebrands' painting from me. My heart picks up pace watching it disappear. Then, for the first time this morning, I relax and smile.

"Boarding through Gate 46 at 8.45am." She hands me my boarding pass. "Please clear customs as soon as possible to enable you to board on time. Have a safe trip and thank you for flying *Pangaean Airlines*."

"Thank you," I say, with a little too much emphasis on the 'you', euphoria flooding my system. I put my travel documents in a secure inner pocket, my hand brushing the cover of the diary as I do. Hidden in the safe with the painting, I can only speculate on its contents until I find a quiet place to sit and read.

I zip the backpack and look up. Suits cut through the swarm of passengers on the concourse, headed straight for the *Pangaean* counters. The one heading the pack wears fashionable glasses and a well-cut jacket, leading with an open ID wallet. Adrenaline surges through me and I search for an escape route, the space between him and me closing.

The easiest is off to the left, through First Class check-in, from there, a clear path to the taxis, but I hesitate, and it is not just the thought of abandoning the suitcase. He pushes past me, standing at the counter I've just vacated waiting for his posse to file over the baggage scales and behind the counters before stepping up, raising a hand for silence.

"Ladies and gentlemen, your attention please. As the representative of *Rourke International Administrators and Liquidators*, I regret to inform you that as of 6.30am *Pangaean Airlines* was put into involuntary administration. All operations are now suspended. All *Pangaean Airline* flights, including this one, are cancelled. Anyone still wishing to travel today will need to find an alternate airline."

"All *Pangaean Airline* assets are under the control of Rourke International as administrators. Checked-in luggage will be held by the administrators pending inspection to ascertain they are not assets of the company. We expect to begin returning luggage in the next 24 hours. Your cooperation in this regard is appreciated."

Beyond him the main baggage conveyor jerks to a stop and I freeze. Those behind me still have their luggage.

THE YANG BOOK

Three Monkeys

Paul Servini

"Airport. Now!" Typical Suze.

Two words. No explanation. No niceties.

"Sal, forget about the second coffee, love." I wave my phone at her.
"HMV!"

His Master's Voice.

Sally christened Suze that when I first started coming to the café.

The GPS leads me quickly through the maze of anonymous side streets.
Waiting to turn onto the slip road leading to the bridge, I switch the GPS
to radio mode. The unmistakeable tones of Big Bop Nouveau fill the car,
my fingers relaxing around the first Camel of the day. In my head it's me
playing.

The time signal.

Eight o'clock.

The news. And bang goes any hope of trumpet practice.

"*Pangaean Airlines*, one of Europe's major airlines, has gone into liq-
uidation. Details are sketchy but…"

11

Daydreams end as my foot hits the floor.

Sixteen minutes and ten seconds later, I pull up at the departures terminal, hazard lights blinking. The security guard is too busy controlling a rowdy group of strikers picketing *Freedom Air* to bother about my illegal parking.

Inside the main concourse, a group of passengers look displaced, chess figures waiting for the players to arrive. Uniformed officials are conspicuous and, in the middle of it all, stands Rex, arms flaying like a child on the verge of a tantrum. Sweat beads across his receding hairline.

I walk straight up to him; the sight of me exacerbates the panic in his face.

"Where's JJ?"

I thrust my key ring, with Dad's three monkeys swinging from them, into the operation manager's sweaty hand.

"Your guess is as good as mine. Why don't you be a good boy? Go park the car."

Upstairs in JJ's office I flick on the screen. Suze appears, after a few seconds of snow.

Reclining in his leather chair.

Unlit cigar waving.

Trademark smile on his lips.

"Fenix, at last. So what do you think of my little machination?"

I stare back at him. He couldn't mean…

His mocking laughter fills the room.

"There's one thing you've yet to learn, Fenix. And until you do so, you cannot hope to succeed. Nothing, not even the tiniest detail, is ever down to chance. If it happens, it's because you make it happen. You think your warnings about John Junior have come back to haunt me? Nothing could be further from the truth."

He lights the cigar.

"The company folded because I wanted it to."

He leans forward and pushes a button.

"Your warnings weren't entirely fruitless. I've been keeping a closer eye on JJ."

A video clip appears in the corner of the screen, time stamped 2.17am. I click to enlarge it.

A young lady removes a painting from the safe in JJ's bedroom wall. White cotton gloved hands. Face hidden from the camera. She's an expert, freeing the canvas from the frame, then rolling and slipping it into a long tube.

"I told that good for nothing his screwing around would be his undoing." Suze sucks hard on the cigar. "That painting cannot see the light of day. But I don't need to explain that to you, do I Fenix?"

"No, sir."

"Right now, her case is under lock and key in our baggage area and she can't do a thing about it. That, my friend, is why John Junior's little company folded. Oh, I know, it's a shame: the employees, the passengers, the chaos. Makes me grateful I'm not flying anywhere today."

Suze is obscured by smoke.

"Do whatever it takes to get the suitcase. I can depend on you, can't I, Fenix?"

Of course he can. I'm not JJ.

I smoke my second cigarette of the day and watch the video again. There's something familiar about her... I can't quite put my finger on it.

The fax whirrs with the press statement and it is time to go.

A barrage of questions accompanies the stutter of flashes when I appear with the press release. I hold my hand up for quiet and stare at the paper, sticking to the script.

"Ladies and gentlemen. With great regret it is my duty to inform you of the demise of *Pangaean Airlines* due to circumstances beyond our control. Our company chairman is cooperating fully with the authorities and we apologise for the inconvenience."

I dare to look at those present now that I've read the statement: officials nonplussed by the drama, journalists baying for my attention, passengers running the gamut of emotions. They don't just want explanations—they want to be heard.

That is not my job.

❧ ❧ ❧

Rex takes a long look at the monkeys, and then me, before handing back the keys. The monkeys weigh heavy in my hand.

The temptation for another cigarette needles me, but I make my way down to the baggage area. A few lame excuses for wanting access go through my mind. It's obvious I'm a company employee, so I don't insult the guard's intelligence with them. He tells me there'll be no call to his supervisor if I leave now.

There's one way in and the pawns are guarding it.

I need to think.

Coming up the stairs, I exit through the emergency door out onto the concourse and then up to the second floor balcony. I'm out of breath when I light up. Things are busy below. Passengers arrive at regular intervals. I pay little notice to the individual travellers. My mind keeps going back to the woman on the video. I replay the scene again and again. What is it about her?

Shouts go out.

The picketers try to stop colleagues from entering the terminal.

Poor beggars.

Their chairman's probably as corrupt as…

I pull myself up. I can't believe what I'd come close to thinking.

Another cigarette does little to calm me or bring clarity. There has to be a way to retrieve the suitcase. I look down onto the main concourse through the glass.

If the suitcase is still here, so is the girl. Someone who goes to the trouble of stealing a painting doesn't walk away. The opening moves have been made—pawns moving out. From here I don't know what to do.

I see Dad's face as my mind goes back.

Patience, son.

Patience. That's something Suze's never had. Everything is always too late for him. One of his many… I have to force myself to think the word 'weaknesses'. Any other word would stink of disloyalty, after all he meant to my father and has done for me.

The familiar Blue Mitchell notes—Dad's favourite song—pierce my musings and I flip open my phone.

"Fen, it's Rex. You'd better get down to the baggage locker. There's a problem with the luggage."

I smile thinking it is my lucky day after all.

"They keep bringing in new luggage. The baggage guys say it's coming from *Ganda* but they've got our tags. The suits have no idea what's going on. And the guy in charge just collapsed."

I end the call and take the steps two at a time onto the concourse.

She has made her next move.

Now to counter.

There are long lines at the check-in desks everywhere. *Ganda Airways* has an emergency check-in queue bulging with irate *Pangaean* passengers and a solitary clerk in tears. Cutting across the front of those waiting to check in, I go straight to the girl, handing her my folded handkerchief.

"Thank you," she sobs, pressing the monogrammed linen into her mascara stained eyes. "First, Ms Sheridan went running off and then the other girl just vanished."

I look across to the next counter and see a suitcase sporting *Pangaean* labels for our Paris flight, a bewildered couple looking on.

"Who was the other check-in clerk?" I glance at her name badge. "Mary?"

"I don't know. I've only been here three days."

Only now do I recognise where her attack is leading. My queen is cornered leaving the king exposed.

The Blue Mitchell notes harass me again.

Rex.

I let the call go through to the message bank.

I've never failed Suze and I'm not about to start.

I'm not JJ.

Rex collides with me on the stairs.

"Answer your bloody phone," he says, shoving a small but elegant briefcase into my chest. "This was handed in at the desk for you."

I prop the briefcase on my knee. It's unlocked and inside a white blouse is folded neatly, Mackenzie Sheridan's security badge pinned to the lapel; a ticket for *Pangaean's* Paris flight, and an employee card, revealing her identity. It explains why I thought she was familiar.

I ring Suze immediately.

"Keely stole the painting."

Suze doesn't seem surprised when I explain. She's going to try to reclaim her suitcase with the mislabelled *Ganda* luggage and escape via Belgium. I push my pieces forward to enclose her.

Too late.

"Ladies and gentlemen, this is an announcement for passengers travelling on *Ganda Airways* flight GA7563 to Brussels. Would the following passengers please present themselves at the *Ganda Airways* desk in the departure area immediately? Louis van Berten. Coralie Hewson. Mary-Lyn Jones…"

I head toward the departures lounge, then stop. Security will refuse me entry without a ticket and a passport. And the staff ID tag promised by JJ is, of course, in the mail.

My phone again.

"You're off to Brussels on my private jet. You'll arrive well before the *Ganda* flight. I want you there when they disembark."

"But…"

"Are you telling me you can't pick her face?"

"Of course not."

"Don't ring until you've got the painting… and Keely."

I arrive in Brussels shy of 11.00 am and make my way straight to the short-haul arrivals lounge.

I glance up at the board.

I've made good time.

I feel elated.

The feeling I get when I promote a pawn. With my queen restored, my chances are far better.

I nip out for my last cigarette of the day before the *Ganda Airways* flight arrives, an hour later than scheduled. Opposite the exit gate, amid the other bystanders, I watch.

First out is a young boy in a wheelchair, pushed by a flight steward.

Next, a group of elderly ladies, clutching coats and handbags.

Behind them, a young student in jeans, scuffed Doc Martens and carrying an old leather suitcase, chattering away merrily to a Marco Nightwish look-alike.

The trickle of people exiting turns into a stream and I strain to examine each person as they pass through the automatic doors, moving out into the open. Keely must be hanging back; trying to catch me off guard.

There's no other exit but doubt sets in.

The doors open again.

Two nuns walk out. A lady in a Gucci suit follows.

I move forward to intercept her, but she's immediately swept off her feet by a tall, well-built man in uniform. She has no check in luggage, just a laptop bag and a small suitcase on wheels. I'm caught as to whether or not to follow.

The Tannoy booms, directing me to the main information desk.

I hesitate.

The woman and her uniform walk out onto the concourse and are swallowed by the crowd.

Public announcements are not Suze's style, but when I look at my phone it is still turned off. I slip it back in my pocket.

A man, immaculately suited, presents himself as I approach the desk.

"Mr Fenix? I have orders to take you straight to your hotel, sir."

I've worked for him since high school and never remember him booking me a hotel. He's a tight bastard.

But rules change.

Someone is one step ahead of us.

The suited man directs me to a waiting car, and I get in.

Compliance is my only strategy right now.

I'm dropped at a small, stylish hotel, not far from Brussel-Zuid train station.

"Welcome, sir. We were expecting you," the middle-aged hotel clerk says when I present myself at the concierge desk. "You're in the south wing, room 379. Your key and the envelope the young lady left for you."

"Young lady?"

"Yes. The young lady who made the reservation. She said you would be arriving within the hour. She was most emphatic you have this the moment you arrived."

He hands me the large padded envelope and I thank him.

I stand out from the other hotel guests because I have no luggage. The porter leads the way to my room and is less than happy with my scanty tip. Doubtless I'll be the curse of the porters' beer fraternity tonight. But that's the least of my worries.

Nothing seems right.

It's as if I've strayed onto a different board.

Someone else is calling the shots.

I don't like it.

I sit down and open the envelope. It contains several photos of the stolen painting. An attached note on hotel stationery says:

Café Brocante—6pm.

I check the envelope again. My fingers make contact with more paper. The newspaper on the outside is an article about art treasures stolen during World War Two. Folded inside are excerpts from a personal diary in JJ's handwriting. They have been chosen very carefully, to whet my appetite without revealing too much.

Like father like son?

My father's face appears and I let him stay. What would he think of all of this? Suze had been his friend, and Dad's last wish was for him take me in. Dad couldn't have known. His credo was simple and I've carried it with me my entire life.

Three monkeys.

Never close your eyes to any injustice for the sake of convenience.

Never let an ugly word frequent your lips.

And the third… the one I struggled with the most as a kid. Don't linger where evil is broadcast from.

"It's not my fault if people say bad things when I'm there," I used to argue.

Have I become the sort of man he would have wanted me to be? Or have I become the sort of man Suze demands?

I've closed my ears to the evidence for years, lingered even when the evil was shoved in my face. A journalist once tried to convince me Suze wasn't clean and I threatened to hit them. I pack everything back into the envelope and hide it under my mattress. I'm about to throw the newspaper article in the bin when my eye falls on the words Menschikow Manuscript. I read on in a trance…

> *The infamous Menschikow Manuscript has been lodged with Christie's auctioneers on behalf of an unnamed client and will go under the hammer next month in what historians have labelled a sacrilegious act of consumer greed. According to our sources, the client is not related to Dr Menschikow himself who was executed during the last weeks of the Communist regime in East Germany.*
>
> *Believed lost, the manuscript is thought to expose the power struggles at the heart of the Kremlin during the Cold War. Leading historians argue it may also explain how a number of top-secret documents came into the possession of Western security agencies in the mid-1980s.*

Suze swore he destroyed it. On this very point he'd assured me I would always be safe.

More lies.

And how did Keely know I was a Menschikow?

I can't stay inside. The atmosphere in my room is oppressive.

There's still three hours before I can hope for any answers. My first thought is to distract myself with a visit to the Musée des Instruments de Musique. They have a Dizzy Gillespie trumpet. I've always wanted to see one.

Once in the fresh air, I can't face the thought of being cooped up again and head for Jubilee Park. Walk until the memories return.

I see Dad in his workshop, bookshelves lining the walls and surrounded by leather bindings; stitching signatures together, gluing them to the bindings with care before placing them in the press. I imagine the secret visits, the manuscript changing hands and the dilemma. If caught, it would cost him his life. He must have known that. I hear the Staatspolizei, their boots thudding on the stairs, breaking down the door, the cries; from my room I see the car racing away, Dad inside, then Suze—the comforting voice contrasting with his terrible explanations. The manuscript is gone and so is Dad. But I am safe.

The chimes from the Maison Cauchie Horloge float across the park.

Five o'clock.

I'm drawn to the *Café Brocante*.

Can't wait any longer.

Flip open my cigarette packet; third time that hour. Same result—daily ration used up.

As I cross the road in front of the café, a bundle of newspapers whizzes past my nose into the hands of the waiting vendor.

"Sorry!"

I nod in reply and am brought up short by the billboard in front of his stand.

LOST MASTERPIECE RECOVERED

I grab a copy, throw a €5 note on the top of his new pile and vanish without waiting for change. The front page tells all: an anonymous donor handed an unspecified masterpiece into the offices of a Paris insurance consortium just before three o'clock that afternoon. This isn't the first work retrieved in this way. It is suspected the consortium has hired a professional thief.

I start thinking.

She must have gone straight from the hotel to Paris once she had reserved my room. It figures. The famous jingle echoes around my head.

Ding, ding, ding… the SNCB: Europe from heart to heart in under 90 minutes.

❦   ❦   ❦

The café is empty. Too late for afternoon tea, too early for returning office workers. The cigarette machine beckons. When I get there, no damned coins. I think wistfully of my €5 note in the news vendor's pocket and wander back via the bar but think better of it.

My mind goes back to the article in the envelope; far different from Suze's version of events. I can't help wondering what would have happened if we hadn't fled.

I no longer trust Suze. I'm beginning to doubt everything he ever said to me.

A young lady comes in and sits down at the table next to me. It's five to six.

I wait for her to say something. She reads the menu then starts to file her nails oblivious to my existence.

Wrong woman—again.

When the waiter comes up to take her order, she declares she's waiting for a friend. I take a good look at her.

Shoulder length, auburn hair, curled around her face. A complexion as fresh as any top model. Sky-blue, knee-length skirt and white blouse, the top button undone, permitting the imagination to go further. The barman is also giving her the once over.

I watch from the corner of my eye for ten minutes as she works on her nails. She gets up and heads towards the ladies carrying a Gucci bag. A few minutes later, out comes the same carrier-bag, in the hands of the young jeans-clad student who had struggled with the massive suitcase this morning. She goes to the counter and orders, pointing to my table.

I can't believe this is the same Keely Jackson who is—was—JJ's personal hound.

"Fenix Walsham," I splutter, ridiculous given she knows who I am.

"Fenix? Zeus's henchman, right?"

21

I look away.

"Alex…" She knows my real name; my king teeters. "If we are to work together, no more lies."

No one had called me Alex since I was a kid.

"You obviously have the better of me on the matter of names, so what am I to call you?"

A sliver of playfulness flickered in her eyes. "Call me Medd."

"Welsh?"

"My mother was Welsh. She called me that because it reminded her of the meads, where my grandfather's bees gathered the honey. 'My little honeyfield,' she always used to say."

"Nice story. Did you rehearse that one on the train back?" I push the evening paper over to her. "Why?"

Raised eyebrows. Nothing more.

"Little girls don't dream of growing up to be art thieves."

"Don't they?"

I drag the newspaper back.

"What makes you want to break the law?"

"You assume what I am doing is illegal."

"Isn't it?"

She laughed. "That's rich coming from someone so tight with John Hildebrand Senior."

An uneasy silence follows, unbroken until she asks: "What was your father like?"

I eye her carefully. I've never spoken to anyone else about Father. And I'm not sure the woman sitting across from me is the right person. In way of an answer, I take out my key ring and lay it on the table. She picks it up and smiles.

"A man of simple but profound moral integrity." She hands them back. "Do you know what was in the manuscript?"

"Something important enough for Father to risk his own life. But not mine. Suze lied and said the manuscript was destroyed."

"You consider it your father's legacy?"

"I don't know. Maybe."

"Why take up with Suze?"

"My Father begged Suze to take care of me, to take me out of the country. Suze was his friend and confidante."

She looks straight into my eyes.

"I visited my Father in prison, just before we left East Germany. Suze arranged it. I took my chessboard. For years I thought…"

The unrelenting stare.

The waiter brings two large milk coffees and I look away. Focus on the coffee. On anything but the woman across from me.

"I started stealing art to make money—to impress my father."

I look up, momentarily startled; unprepared for her talking, much less to be privy to her confession.

"Money talks, but he still ignores me. I'm worth twice as much as him and now I steal paintings only from those who do not own them. Suze's painting was looted, taken from France during the Second World War."

She reaches across and takes my hand. Senses what I'm going through.

"I'll steal back your father's manuscript." She lets go of my hand and reaches into her bag and pushes a slim diary to me. "If, you agree to help me take down Suze and JJ. Or I'll just walk out of here and blend into the crowd… leave you with your father's three monkeys."

"Checkmate!"

Three Rings
Christopher Chartand

It is funny what sticks in your mind. I remember collapsing behind the wheel, kicking off my pumps, rubbing my feet and deriding myself for how soft I had become. Five years out of the military and I could barely handle eight hours on my feet. I remember thinking for the thousandth time, what a small price to pay to protect Bradley from the type of childhood I had. The final argument with my father replaying like a bad movie in my head—him furious because his two best field agents were leaving and me angry because he'd never had the balls to sacrifice anything for me.

I remember staring at Bradley's picture on my phone, thinking my father's ire and sore feet were worth it. We were safe.

"Hey Karen, it's me. I'm leaving work now. Tell Bradley sorry I'm late but–"

Loud beeping, cutting my words off as the line picked up.

"Mackenzie Sheridan?" A deep male voice, unfamiliar and out of place. "We have your son."

"Who the hell is this?"

"There's a mobile phone in the top left drawer of your roll-top desk. We'll call at 7.00pm with instructions. Let it ring exactly three times before answering. And Mackenzie… if you want to see your little boy alive, keep your mouth shut. No cops."

    ☯   ☯   ☯

I pull myself back to the here and now. Passengers for the Belgium and Paris flights are lining up, and there's only Mary and I who haven't called in sick.

"Good morning, welcome to *Ganda Airways*. How may I be of assistance?"

How many times have I spewed that line with false sincerity and a smile pinned in place by my company-required hair bun? Assisting untold numbers to leave this God-forsaken city, always wondering how many of them would be unfortunate enough to return. How many live here, like me, because they have no choice? Divorced, yet tethered for the sake of the child.

This morning every word, every action chips away at my soul.

"Paris," says the man dressed in a loud golf shirt. "The missus and I are off on a three-week holiday."

They're both grinning from ear to ear.

"It is our first trip overseas," she says. "We're so excited."

Oh, lovely. Planning on visiting The Louvre no doubt. Please tell… I'm so interested in your plans. Have I mentioned my son was kidnapped from my apartment a week ago and I've done something I swore I'd never do to keep him alive? But it's always about you, isn't it? I hear the Eiffel Tower has quite a view.

"Tickets and two forms of ID each, please. How many items of luggage?"

"Two."

"Three," he corrects, wedging his golf clubs between them.

I switch to autopilot and finish their check in. The trained enthusiasm and memorised lines keep me functioning while my son is God-knows-where with monsters.

❧ ❧ ❧

"Where's Bradley? What have you done with him?"

"Three rings Mackenzie. I expected better."

"I—"

"Disobey me again and you'll spend the rest of your life wishing you'd paid more attention. We'll call Sunday with a set of instructions. Follow them exactly and your son will be returned unharmed."

❧ ❧ ❧

I welcome the next in line.

"Paris," she says tersely and thrusts her paperwork at me.

The flashbacks keep hitting me.

What have I missed?

…wishing you'd paid more attention … wishing you'd paid more attention.

The kidnapper's voice changes into my father's then back again. Over and over, until they're a single voice. The words twist with memories, dragging me beyond last week. Back to places I don't want to go.

Gasping for air in a dark room with the Big Men. Terrified I'm going to die. Yelling. Them demanding I tell them how to open my father's vault.

They're water-boarding my baby. Oh, Bradley.

No, stop it. He's OK. They want something from you, not him. Bradley's just leverage.

The woman clears her throat, jolting me back to the present. I hand her the boarding pass and baggage claim ticket then launch into my scripted speech; saved again by the monotony of this job.

Angry shouts spread through the terminal. My desk phone rings and I jump. It rings three times and I answer.

"*Ganda Airways.* Terminal eight," I say into the heavy old-style handset.

"*Pangaean* just went under," says my manager, his voice sweaty and

27

nervous. "There's a shit-storm happening over there and it's coming our way. How much space is left on our Paris flight?"

I open a new screen and run a query. Damn these antiquated terminals. I miss the military's cutting edge technology. My manager's sighing and nervous wheezing is my hold music for almost two minutes.

"Twelve."

"Brussels?"

"Ten."

"Offer those seats up at the base price. Stand-by rates less ten percent for anyone else with a *Pangaean* ticket today—good PR that we're not profiteering from *Pangaean's* fuck up."

"I'll handle it sir. Mary can continue normal check in."

"Good. Quick as you can. We can't afford to delay other flights for this."

"Right," I say. "No problem sir."

Jesus, does this have to happen today?

My boy…

… Stay focused.

☯   ☯   ☯

"Dad, it's Kenzie, don't hang up…" His silence cut deeply. "It's Bradley, he's been kidnapped."

"I told you—"

"For Christ's sake Dad, now isn't the time for an I-told-you-so speech."

"What do they want? Money?"

"No, not money. Corporate sabotage."

"Why call me?"

"I dunno. Thought my father, the General, would want to help rescue his fucking grandson."

More silence.

"I'm risking everything calling. You of all people should understand. If they find out they'll kill him."

I chewed my bottom lip as the brutal silence deepened.

"They may kill him anyway."

"Him, Dad? His name is Bradley, your grandson."

"I'll call William?"

"No—not William."

"Bradley's his son too, Mackenzie. You can't just—"

"Please Dad. Find another operative. Can I count on you?"

        ❧   ❧   ❧

I ready the counter for the impending rush of displaced travellers then brief Mary on the situation.

"I'm lucky you're here, Ms Sheridan," says Mary, shifting from foot to foot like a nervous child. "I feel more confident knowing you're here, ready to help. Funny how things work out."

Yeah, hysterical. Like the one about the girl who was kidnapped only to grow up and have her own child kidnapped? It's a real knee slapper. The part where they shave the little girl's head will have you doubled over.

"Yeah, lucky... here they come."

An angry detachment of *Pangaean* customers advances like a scene from Braveheart. The fastest of them jostles into line and I beckon for him to step up.

"*Pangaean?*" I ask and he nods. "You are in luck; we're holding the departure of our Paris flight."

The aging businessman hands over his Gold Amex.

"Thank you, Mr Snell. Let's book your ticket."

There's an odd feeling on my thigh.

"I'll also need your *Pangaean* ticket—"

There it is again. Oh God, the kidnapper's phone is going off in my pocket. Not now. There's the third ring. Only seconds to answer.

...wishing you paid more attention.

I grab the phone and turn my back on Mr Snell.

"Hey," he yells. "You haven't finished processing my ticket. Lady! Don't any of you airlines know customer service? LADY!"

I keep my back turned.

"Hello, Mackenzie." It's the same deep voice as before.

"Bradley?"

"He's safe."

...They may kill him anyway.

His voice muffles for a moment, as though he's talking to someone off phone. "You did well, MacKenzie."

"Bradley?"

"He likes to play hide-and-seek, right? One... two... three..."

"Where's my baby?"

"Close by." He starts to laugh. "Coming, ready or not."

The line goes dead.

I'm tempted to hurl the phone against the wall but slip it back in my pocket. Mr Snell is glaring at me when I turn around.

"Rude," he says, jabbing a stubby finger in my face.

"I'm sorry, sir," I say in my best the-customer-is-always-right voice. "Perhaps you would be happier waiting a day to fly with a different airline, or, if you'd like, I'd be happy to shove that fucking finger of yours into the nearest power socket."

I swat his bloated, liver-spotted finger from my face with a satisfying slap and turn to Mary.

"Sorry kiddo, it's time for your training wheels to come off."

I walk off to a chorus of angry shouts and am immediately penned in by a teeming mass of possible suspects. I find myself frozen; unsure how I should proceed.

What's your malfunction Mackenzie? Bradley needs you. You can't start seeing kidnappers in every face.

My head clears and I start thinking like an operative, identifying and prioritising steps to rescue my son.

Step one—secure tactical assistance.

The airport is too large an area to cover alone. I need to call for help, but I don't trust my phone.

Moving with the current, I scan ahead for an easy mark. The orange coat of an airport employee jumps out among the milieu. As I close in,

I see there are two of them—the x-ray boys everyone calls Rocky and Bullwinkle.

I saunter over, making eye contact well in advance, turning my fake smile back on and tossing in an extra eye-batting or two.

"Do either of you handsome gents have a phone I could borrow? Mine's out of credit."

"Sure thing, love," says the larger of the two, puffing out his chest. I catch a brief glimpse of a hot-pink silk hanky as he retrieves his phone from a pants pocket.

"Thanks."

Turning, I take a few steps away and punch in a number I swore never to call again. I get the standard greeting designed to confuse non-operatives.

"Royal Flooring. Luxury floor coverings at a peasant's price."

"This is Jade. Give me management."

There's no response from the secretary. The phone goes dead then clicks over and rings three times.

"Mackenzie?"

"They've released Bradley. He's somewhere in the airport. Dad, he's—"

"I anticipated this. There's an operative on-site."

"The rendezvous point?"

"The passenger lockers closest to your check-in desk."

A swarm of people block my view.

"Operative's name?"

"William."

I freeze.

"Son of a bitch."

"Stow it, Mackenzie. I didn't train you to run ops off your emotions." Then he's gone.

You know he's right. Suck it up. You have work to do.

I toss the phone back and run to the passenger lockers. William is there, dressed in a nondescript dark coat. His smile gives me butterflies as he makes his way towards me.

"Hello, Mackenzie."

31

After all this time, all the pain and shit he's put me through, that damn smile still floors me. I realise it's how Bradley smiles...

Bradley? Oh God...

...You don't have time for this. Stay focused.

"I've been briefed on the situation."

The situation! We're talking about our son. Can't anyone say his name?

"Airport security is aware and working with us."

He hands me an ear bud and a small rectangular ID card, the price of Dad's help.

You've already broken promises to yourself, what's one more?

"The ear piece is tuned to the airport security frequency. We'll know the second they find him."

I remove the SIM card and thrust it into William's hand before tossing the kidnapper's phone and my *Ganda* employee badge in the bin.

"Have the techs run a trace on this. I want to know where the incoming calls originated," I say, as I pin on my military ID.

"Later, I'm not leaving you again, we–"

"William, I need tactical support. We'll cover more ground separately. Just like old times. Me on the ground and you watching my back behind the scenes."

"I'll upload the data from the car to my techs. They'll phone through the results."

He leaves, moving efficiently through the crowd, and disappears. I switch the ear bud on.

"Unit 12, station house... station house, go ahead... we've spotted a male child fitting the description... copy that unit 12. What is your location...We're outside *Starbucks*, Concourse A..."

Everything fades as I run for the nearest security checkpoint and the tram to get me to Concourse A. I slide to a stop at the security area where a mountain of a woman demands to see my travel documentation.

"My name is Captain Mackenzie Sheridan, that's my son they're talking about."

The guard looks as though I've just asked her to swallow a Volkswagen.

"What the hell are you talking about?"

I point to my ID badge.

"Hold on," she says, picking up her radio. Her voice blends with the hollow sounding radio in my ear, as she calls for confirmation. Apathy drains from her face as she whips around to the security guard a few feet away.

"Martin, get your arse over here and man this post. Now!"

She turns back to me clipping her radio to her belt. Her hand drifts to her nightstick, picking it up a few inches and letting it drop into its holster—the unmistakable mark of a trained officer.

I follow her as she runs away from the tram.

"Where are we going?"

"We ain't taking the tram."

She moves back through the terminal with a speed and agility that do not match her size. I fall in step directly behind her. She's fast but I want to move faster.

"Station house to all units. Be advised, we have an ID on kidnapper. A Mr Warren, travelling *Pangaean Airlines*. Suspect believed to still be in the vicinity of the *Pangaean* check-in counter. Suspect is…"

It takes every ounce of self-control to keep following the guard and not turn back. He was right under my nose.

Let William get the son-of-a-bitch. Focus on Bradley.

We stop briefly as the guard unlocks a steel door to a part of the airport I've never seen. A few seconds later we are outside in the frosty air. We clamber into the nearest squad car, and the guard hits the lights and sirens as she jams her foot on the accelerator.

"We'll be there in five minutes, love," she says, just missing a baggage car. "Hold on."

"Thank you," I say, staring ahead.

"I'm a mother too, Cap'n Sheridan. Got a daughter, and there ain't nothin' could stop me from getting her back. You just sit tight."

There's a lone security officer waiting for us.

"We've got the boy in protective custody," he says, opening the door. "Says his name's Thomas."

"Thomas? No, his name's Bradley." Panic strangles my voice.

The security officers are talking but I'm too dazed to hear them. My breath catches when the door opens and I see a small, milk-moustached boy in a green jacket, sitting with a half-eaten bag of crisps.

"That's not my son."

A rage crackles up my body, like a summer lightning storm. My inner switch is thrown. Mackenzie the customer service rep is gone. I'm Mackenzie the soldier and I'm ready to rip this place apart with my hands, find my son and kill the bastards who have done this.

"What's your name?" I say to the officer who drove me here.

"Barbara," she says.

"Barbara, I need your radio." She hands it to me and I change the frequency. "William. It's not him."

"I heard. I'm back on Concourse C. I have visual on the suspect."

"Get him, what the hell are you waiting for?"

"Easy, Kenzie. I'll radio in when I have him."

I choke down my desire to bolt back through the airport. Barbara eases me down in a chair, pressing a cup of lousy coffee into my hands.

There's talk of extra cameras and local law enforcement. I sip the coffee waiting for William's voice.

Is five too old for a white coffin? I'll never forgive myself—it's all my fault. Is that why Mother shot herself? Thought she'd failed me?

I slam my walls back up. This psychoanalytic bullshit won't help. I am not my mother and Bradley is not me. I came out of it alive and so will he. Mother was ill; it had nothing to do with…

Barbara taps me on the shoulder and hands me her radio.

"Kenzie." William's disembodied voice fills the room. "You better get over here."

"Bradley?"

"No."

The walls tumble for a moment and I see a white coffin and the handgun from my nightstand.

❧ ❧ ❧

William is waiting on the other side of the holding room when I arrive. He's not smiling. I need him to smile.

"Bastard won't talk."

"Maybe not for you," I say and walk towards the holding room door.

"Before you go in," he says gently placing his hand on my arm, and leading me out of earshot of the officers. "The phone. I had the techs run the data again to be sure. Mackenzie... the calls came from Management."

"Management? That makes no..."

wishing you paid more attention... three rings...

...I told you something like–

My throat closes as the world folds in on me.

I'm twelve years old. I can't breathe because the Big Men are dumping water on my head.

"What do you mean you don't know the combination? You better remember quick or you'll be wishing you had paid more attention."

Pain shoots through my knees and I realise I've fallen on them.

Daddy, you knew...

...Mummy

Focus.

...Mummy.

Focus, Mackenzie. The man in that room knows where your son is.

William helps me stand but doesn't let go of my hands. My head swims as I'm brought back to the present.

"You don't have to do this," he says.

"That's a hell of a thing for you to say to me." I straighten my crumpled shirt. "Do you remember Bosnia?"

He nods. "Wherever this goes, whatever happens, I'm with you. No judgments this time."

I open the holding room door and look William in the eyes.

"Right then."

William walks over to tell the security officers to power down the cameras. The door shuts behind me. The smell of antiseptic makes my nostrils flare as my eyes adjust to the bright, interrogation lights. There are two folding chairs and a metal desk bolted to the floor. He's younger than I expected, cuffed to a large metal hoop in the middle of the desk. I take the seat across from him.

"Where is my son?"

He puts on a cocky grin in lieu of an answer.

I'll slice your fucking face!

"Understand," I say, pulling out my hairpins and laying them out on the table in front of me. "I'm not a cop."

I hold a pin up at eye level, flick off the protective tip with my thumb.

"I'm not airport security."

I grasp his wrist tightly.

"I'm a woman whose child you stole."

I flatten his hand and place the pointed metal pin at the tip of the man's finger just below his nail.

"And I want him back."

"Go fuck yourself!"

I shove the pin under his nail and wiggle it back and forth. He screams and looks for a moment like he'll pass out. A small dribble of blood follows the hairpin out from under his thick, yellow nail.

"Bitch!"

His screams feel good. I want to do more. I want him dead. I want him alive. I want him to hurt forever. I shove the pin under another nail.

Can't kill him… need him alive… have to make him talk.

"Go fu—"

I slam the hairpin as hard as I can into the top of his hand. It stands straight up in a growing pool of beautiful crimson. I hope I hit a vein. His scream lasts longer this time.

"Next one goes in your eye," I say with my customer-service smile.

"Jesus Christ. All right!" He's staring at the pin impaling his hand. "Some guy hired me to take him. He's in the woman's bathroom outside the bar. My girlfriend left him tied up and drugged in one of the stalls with an out of order sign. For the love of God lady, I'm sorry!"

I rip the pin from his flesh.

"God's got nothing to do with it." I wipe the blood in an 'x' pattern on his shirt to the left of his heart. "Pray he's okay."

I slam the hairpin in the centre of the 'x'. Not a fatal wound but he'll never forget me.

I look through the one-way glass and nod. A pale-faced guard opens the door. William's at the door and Barbara's screaming into the radio. People scramble to get out of our way as we barrel through the concourse to the woman's bathroom outside the bar. I knock a woman out of the way as she wanders out of the stall next to the one with the out of order sign.

"Bradley?"

"Mummy?"

It's him. That's his voice. That's Bradley.

William kicks in the door and I topple to the floor drawing Bradley to me.

He's alive, thank God he's alive.

Tears stream down my face as William helps me up with Bradley in my arms. He's heavier than I remember but I know I could hold him forever. William moves in and I allow him to hug the both of us. It feels so good to have his arms around us. Around me.

"I dreamt some big men told me you'd gone away," says Bradley groggily, through scrunched up lips. "But I knew you wouldn't."

I put him down and he holds fast to my hand.

"Can we go home now? I don't want to play here anymore."

"No baby, we can't go home. It isn't safe for us there."

"Where are we going to live then?"

"Daddy and I have some very special friends." I look up to William and he nods. "You're going to stay with them for a while."

"But you're coming? I'm scared."

"Daddy will take you, baby. I'll be there soon."

First I have to visit Grandpa.

Dogs of War

Tony Noland

"You ever been to Paris, kid?"

"Vince, I'll make a deal with you. If you stop calling me 'kid', I won't start calling you 'Grandpa'. How's that sound?"

The older man trilled out a whistle, as though in admiration. "Ooh, pretty touchy, aren't you, Gene? What's the matter, kid? I hit a sore point? It's okay, you can tell old Uncle Vince. Oh, I got it. You never been to Paris before and you're nervous, right?"

"I've been to Paris, Vince."

"On vacation, maybe. But you've never attended one of these Euro-zone division annual meetings. Or did I read your file wrong?"

The younger man turned his face away and looked out the cab window.

Vince chuckled. "There's a first time for everybody. Yeah, this is a high-powered group, a bunch of real bastards who'll rip you a new one if you screw up, but so long as you don't make any mistakes, it's just another wine and cheese party."

"I won't make any mistakes, Vince."

"Naturally. A young hotshot like you doesn't make mistakes; that's why you're in the company's Succession Management and Reallocation of Talent pool, right? Because you're a SMART-arse?"

"Knock it off, will you? I didn't pick the name of the leadership training program, I just applied for it."

"Sure, kid. Just make sure you don't slur your accent."

"Slur my accent? What do you mean?"

Their cab stopped in front of *Pangaean Airlines* in the international terminal. Gene paid the driver and the men got out. The two men took several steps apart as Vince moved directly to the terminal doors while Gene headed for the curbside baggage check station. "Aren't you checking your bag?"

"What, are you crazy? Never check a bag, kid." Vince patted his carry-on laptop bag. "If you can't travel light, don't travel."

"But we're in Paris for a week."

Vince laughed. "See you inside, kid."

Gene checked his bag, thanked the porter and went into the terminal. Vince was tapping at his phone's screen. Gene waited a moment then said, "Well? Are you ready?"

"Hold your horses, kid, boarding won't be for another two hours. Let me just... and then... there! Okay, let's go."

As they walked toward the *Pangaean* line, Gene said, "Hey, what did you mean back there in the cab, about not slurring my accent?"

"During your presentation. If you slur your French they get all *ne vous comprends pas* on you. It's all an act; they understand you just fine, but they can make trouble for you, so just remember to enunciate clearly."

Gene stopped, his face paling. "Enunciate... in French?"

Vince turned to look at him. "Of course in French. Unless you want to try Chinese. Maybe Portuguese?"

"But Mr Glover told me everything would be in English."

Vince looked surprised, then grinned. "He did, did he? Really? Well, ain't that a bowl of rattail stew. Look, Charlie Glover hasn't moved his arse out of his corner office in fifteen years, so I guess he didn't know what the score is. Ah, don't worry about it, kid. Go ahead and tell 'em you don't speak French. What else can you do? If they want to get insulted, just stare 'em down. To hell with 'em, right?" He started to walk, turned back. "Come on, kid. You okay?"

"I, I took some French in high school, maybe I could…" Gene tapered off and stepped forward to join Vince.

Vince nodded, as if considering. "Yeah, good idea. This evening's meeting is what, thirteen hours from now? Plenty of time to learn French. Get yourself a phrasebook, knock the rust off, no problem. At least you'll be able to say *excusez-moi, je ne parle pas le français* with a straight face. That'll win 'em over."

They joined the line of passengers snaking its way up to the *Pangaean* counter, Vince whistling through his teeth, Gene swallowing hard and looking sweaty. In silence, they held their laptop bags and moved forward a few steps at a time.

Twice, Vince nudged Gene and nodded, once to indicate the older, professional-looking woman in line in front of them, and again towards the younger, intense-looking woman immediately after them. Both times, he waggled his eyebrows and twitched his lips, apparently trying to communicate something complicated but obviously lurid. Gene scowled. Vince smiled and resumed his whistling.

The line moved forward. After an age, an agent beckoned them forward to an open spot.

"Hi there!" Vince said, his voice chirpy and sweet as he showed his ID. Gene drew a deep breath and did not roll his eyes. "Vincent Guerrero, I'm on the 8.30 to Paris. I checked in through the website; I don't need to do anything else, do I?"

The pretty blonde bit her lip while she typed. After a moment she said, "Ah, Mr Guerrero, we're always happy to have our Gaia Club Platinum members flying with us. No, it looks like you're all set. It says here no baggage to check this morning?"

He grinned and said, "Nope, not a thing. It's like I always say–" he made an obvious production of leaning forward to peer at the nametag on her left breast, "–Allison, if you can't travel light, don't travel."

She smiled back. "That's a good way to go, if you can manage it. Do you need a boarding pass, Mr Guerrero?"

He waved a sheet of paper. "Printed it off this morning. I like to make things easy for you folks." He winked at her. "You have a good day, now, alright?"

She smiled at him and turned to Gene. "Can I help you, sir?"

Amazed, Gene watched him stroll away. Twelve minutes later he stomped over to Vince. "What was all that about? I didn't know you could check in over the Internet."

"No? Well, I guess they don't teach that stuff at Harvard." Vince shrugged. "As long as you're a Platinum Gaia member, you can do it 24 hours before flight time. *Pangaean* even has a check-in app you can download; that's what I was doing on my phone while you were screwing around checking your bag outside."

"So why the hell did you make us wait in line? Why didn't you just tell me about the website check-in deal? We could have skipped all that nonsense!"

"What's this 'we could have'? Not 'we'. Just me. I get it because I'm Platinum. When you've flown half a million miles with *Pangaean*, you can be Platinum, too. I promise." Vince shrugged. "Since I had to wait for you anyway, I thought I'd do you a favour and make sure you didn't get lost on the way to the check-in counter. You need all the help you can get."

Gene's reply was cut off by a phalanx of suits pushing past them, headed toward the *Pangaean* counter at a good clip.

"Come on, kid, I need some breakfast," said Vince.

He walked toward the security screening station at the gate. Gene moved to follow, but stopped when the man who ran into him started speaking in a loud voice back behind the counter. Gene listened, then took a couple of quick steps back toward the desk so he could hear better over the rising noise from the crowd of passengers.

"Vince," he called over his shoulder. "Get over here! Something's going on with *Pangaean*—they cancelled the flight!" Gene turned, saw Vince continuing to walk away. "Vince!"

Vince turned at the shout. He stood where he was, so Gene had to run over to him.

"Something just happened with *Pangaean*," Gene said. "It just went bankrupt or something. The flight's cancelled, Vince; the whole airline is shut down."

Vince whistled, said, "Well, good thing they did it before we took off."

"How are we supposed get to Paris?"

Phone already in hand, Vince grimaced, as if in pain. "We get another flight to Paris on a different airline, and we do it fast before everybody else tries to do the same thing. Jesus, kid, use your brain, will you? Did you get your bag back?"

"Oh my God!" He turned and ran back, joining the shouting mass crowding the *Pangaean* counter.

Vince tapped rapidly at his phone. As the noise at the counter grew, he looked up and watched Gene try to elbow his way forward, working to get someone's attention. Other people in the crowd were willing to push harder and shout louder; Gene's attempts were blocked repeatedly. He finally reached the front, as the mob broke away and descended on the food service carts that suddenly appeared, grabbing free sandwiches and soft drinks. Now at the desk, there was no one left to ask; every *Pangaean* employee had been forced away by the men in suits. Vince cocked his head to one side, thoughtfully. As Gene ran back, Vince cleared his expression and focused on his phone's screen.

Gene was sweating. "They won't give it back! They say it's been declared an asset of the airline, but it's not. It's mine!"

"Doesn't matter, kid." said Vince. "Nobody knows what's what in all that mess, so they seized everything just to be sure. It'll probably take months for you to get your bag out of the legal limbo." He kept tapping his screen.

"Go to Paris with no luggage? No clothes, no shoes?"

"I told you not to check your bag, kid. That's the voice of experience talking. But, if you don't want to listen to it, that's fine by me."

"Vince, if you don't have anything helpful to say, will you please just shut the hell up?"

"Don't speak to me in that tone, you little snot. I've just burnt my hard-earned frequent flier points with *Etruscan Skyways* to get us replacement tickets on their 10.45 flight. However, if you're going to stand there and do a crybaby 'boo-hoo' over a simple bump in the road, I'm happy to cut your sorry arse out of the loop and leave you behind. Now are you gonna cowboy up or not?"

Gene, flushed and angry, said nothing. He took several deep breaths before speaking slowly and evenly. "I'd like to be in Paris for this evening's meeting."

Vince looked him in the eye. "Say please."

Gene's lips turned white as he pressed them together.

"Aw, hell, I'm just yanking your chain, kid," Vince said and started to walk off to the *Etruscan* counter.

"But what about my bag?"

"What about it? Buy some new stuff. That's why they put shops in airports, to take advantage of poor suckers like you. Get a bag, a couple of shirts, some socks and underwear, you'll be all set for a week in the city of lights."

"Doesn't any of this bother you at all?"

Vince shrugged. "If you wanna run with the big dogs, you gotta get off the porch."

"Ah." Gene was silent for a moment, then said, "Alright, I give up. What does that mean, exactly?"

"It means I've earned a goddamn drink for saving our arses, that's what it means."

Together, they shuffled forward in the *Etruscan Skyways* ticketing line, Gene scowling and biting his lower lip, Vince whistling and tapping away at his phone.

An hour and a half later, they entered *O'Malley's Pot O' Gold Authentic Irish Pub*, one of the larger restaurants open for breakfast in the international terminal. Over Gene's shoulder was a black carry-on bag, sales tags still attached. His lips moved slightly as he whispered phrases to himself from a French–English dictionary, the closest thing the airport bookstores had to a phrasebook.

"Hey Gene, keep mumbling to yourself, and you'll end up looking like that guy."

"Eh? What guy?"

"That squirrely little guy that was in front of us in line at the *Etruscan Skyways* counter. You know, the one with the wife who wouldn't shut up, who kept nagging him and calling him sweetheart."

"Um, I think that was his mother, actually."

"His mother? Damn, that poor bastard must be crazier than I thought. Grow a pair and cut the apron strings, for chrissakes. Although, maybe you disagree? She was pretty hot for an old lady, huh, Gene?"

"Vince…"

"Oh, come on, you'd do her, right Gene-sweetheart? Or maybe take her and her little boy, maybe get a three-way going? He looked like he coulda used a little action, don't you think?"

"Vince, goddamn it, people can hear you!"

"Ah, your problem is you got no sense of humour. Go grab us a table," said Vince. "I'll score us a couple of Bloody Marys."

Gene sighed, and moved toward a table in the back. Once seated, he returned to flipping pages and mouthing French phrases.

The woman behind the counter was sour and slow moving. "Good morning, sir, what can I get for you?"

"I'd like a large Grey Goose Bloody Mary please, a triple, and a Virgin Mary, same size." Vince set a twenty on the bar and dropped another twenty into the tip jar. The bartender's mood and speed improved instantly.

She was more than generous with three vodka shots into one of the glasses. Vince took both drinks back to the table. Behind him, the bartender rang them up and pocketed the change, along with the twenty she lifted out of the tip jar.

Vince set the Bloody Mary in front of Gene. "Well," he said, lifting his glass, "here's to Paris." Gene put the dictionary down and lifted his own in response. Vince drank deeply, and Gene did the same.

"Pffaugh!" said Vince, "These airport bars, they always make them so damned weak, don't they?"

Gene swallowed and then coughed. "Hmm, you're right. I can barely taste the vodka at all." The waiter arrived to take their orders; when he left, Gene took a deep drink, then spoke in a serious voice.

"Vince, I'm the kind of guy who's interested in self-improvement."

"Oh? I never would have guessed."

Gene nodded. "I am. I've been thinking about how you reacted when *Pangaean* imploded. Frankly, it was impressive. You handled things much better than I could have."

"You could say that, yeah."

Gene bobbed his head again. "The fact is, one of my faults is that I tend to be so goal-oriented that I get, well, maybe more inflexible than I should be. Basically… Vince, I'd love to learn your technique for staying calm in a changing operational environment."

"Ah, that's a lot of buzzwords for so early in the morning, but yeah, I know a few tricks for keeping a level head."

"Vince, I don't like to admit this, but frankly, I'm little rattled by this meeting being in French. A level head is exactly what I could use right now. If you have any suggestions to offer, I'd be grateful." Gene was looking at him with an eager and open expression.

"Kid, did somebody teach you how to do that kind of junior executive suck-up, or is that something you figured out yourself? Oh, calm down, Gene, it was just a joke. Look, you wanna know my secret? I'm the best damn field guy this company has ever seen. Tons of guys would kill to get my territory. I don't tell my secrets to just anybody. But you? I look at you and I see myself, twenty years ago. I like you, kid. You wanna know my secret?" He fished into his jacket pocket and withdrew an unlabelled bottle. He set it on the table. "There's my secret."

Gene looked at it, puzzled, then astonished.

"You mean… drugs? Your secret is drugs? You mean, like amphetamines or tranquilisers or something?"

"Come on, kid, I thought you were smarter than that. These are a combination of beta-blockers to improve mental focus, Ritalin to heighten concentration, high doses of malic acid and vitamin B12 to enhance language-processing function, aspirin and caffeine to improve capillary blood flow in the brain. All that stuff is legal as iced tea. All the top dogs in the company take these, and you bet your sweet arse our competition does, too. I took 'em this morning."

"I... I just can't believe that everybody is taking drugs."

"Don't get moralistic. We're not talking uppers or coke. Look, Olympic athletes take performance enhancers, and who gives a rat's arse about one gold medal every four years? I'm out there busting my arse every day. I bet you'd give your left nut to boost your mental faculties right now? Huh?"

Gene held the pill bottle, staring intently at it. "Are they safe?"

"Sure, you can even take them with alcohol. Here, watch." Vince picked up his glass and drained it. "There, see? When I really need to kick arse, like when I have a tight deadline for a big assignment, a couple of these babies with a nicotine patch or two and I can go full-bore for twenty, thirty, even forty hours at a stretch."

"Vince..." Gene turned the bottle over, end to end. "If I don't get this French under control, I'm sunk."

The older man drummed the table and finally said, "Well, just this once. After this, you can go get your own prescription. I'll give you the name of the doctor the company guys go to." He looked up and saw the waiter coming over with their food. "Take three, with plenty of fluids."

Gene opened the pill bottle and shook three red and white capsules into his hand. One by one, he washed them down with a big swig of his drink. By the time the third capsule was gone, so was his drink.

He handed the bottle back to Vince, and said, "This is really gonna save my life, Vince. Thanks."

"No problem, kid. What are friends for?"

For the next ten minutes, Vince watched Gene's movements grow progressively less controlled. When his fork and knife started trembling in his hands, Gene seemed to become aware that something was wrong. He shook his head, as if to clear it. He leaned forward and started a belch, but clenched his lips at the last moment. He swallowed, hard.

"I... I don't feel so good. These aren't doing... I... I... gotta piss..." Gene tried to stand, slipped on the edge of the table, and went thudding down hard on one knee. He didn't seem to feel it.

"It's okay, kid, I got you," said Vince. He was out of his chair and helping Gene to stand, grabbing his own laptop bag before he did so. Arm around Gene shoulders, Vince manoeuvred them around the tables to the men's room. Gene stumbled in toward the first urinal, having trouble undoing his fly.

Turned sideways, Vince already had his phone out and up near his ear, waiting.

"Unh... unh! Oh God, unh!" Gene was yanking at his crotch in frustration. His mouth fell open as he took a deep breath and he jerked as his mouth filled with vomit. He staggered away from the urinal toward one of the stalls. Four feet from the door, he tripped and went down. Vomit exploded forward, a flood of Bloody Mary and bile carrying half-digested pieces of omelette and toast onto his chest. Four big gushes came up; after that, it was just foam and spittle. Convulsing on the floor, Gene dry heaved again and again, barely conscious.

Vince kept his phone up until Gene's bladder let loose and the pool of urine spread across his lower body. He waited a half minute longer before pressing the <STOP> button on the screen, then <PLAY>. In the small video, slightly off-centre, but perfectly focused, Gene was perfectly recognisable as he groped himself at the urinal. Vince stopped the playback after a few seconds. Laptop over his shoulder, he walked out of the men's room and out of the restaurant, leaving Gene's carry-on bag and laptop still tucked under their table.

Walking down the concourse, Vince watched the video in its entirety, twice. He emailed it to one of his anonymous Gmail accounts, with the subject line, "Gene Thompson—insurance—for YouTube". Then he brought up his contact list, selected a number and dialled it.

"Hello, may I speak with Mr Glover, please? This is Vincent Guerrero, with the Eurozone division? Yes, I'll hold. Good morning, sir. Yes, I'm fine, sir, thank you. I just wanted to give you an update on the Eurozone divisional meeting, in Paris? Yes sir, it starts this evening. We were scheduled to fly *Pangaean*, but... oh, it is? No, sir. No, no problem. I booked seats with *Etruscan*, boarding in about thirty minutes. No sir, I used my frequent flyer miles. That's what they're for, right? Absolutely, I couldn't agree more. Nothing more than bump in the road, sir. Oh! Well, thank you… Charlie."

Vince smiled. It lent a buoyant spirit to his voice as he walked.

"Mr Thompson? No, he's not with me. I'm supposed to meet him at the gate. To be honest, I'm not sure where he went. He said he needed to get something to calm his nerves. He was pretty unhinged by *Pangaean* folding. Do you happen to know if he's travelled much? Really? Really? Well, the way he was acting you'd never know it. No, I don't know. Well, for one thing, he'd somehow gotten it in his head the meeting would be in French. No, he didn't. Yes, sir. Sorry, I mean sure, Charlie, I told him it would be in English, but he wouldn't listen. I'll be honest, I don't know him that well, but he's certainly got what you might call a strong personality."

At the gate, Vince stood, tapping his foot as his listened for a long time.

"I will. No matter what, you can count on me. And I wouldn't worry about Mr Thompson. He knows how important this meeting is. He'll pull himself together. Well, thank you, I appreciate the vote of confidence. I will. Yes, I will. Right. I'll email you from Paris. Right, goodbye, sir. Oh, hell, I'm sorry. Charlie! I'll remember from now on. Right, goodbye, Charlie."

He pocketed his phone and took a seat opposite a pale woman with dark hair who was nursing a baby wrapped in a Cookie Monster blanket. Vince sat quietly for a moment, before opening his laptop bag and tearing off a page from his *Pangaean* itinerary. On the blank side, with a 14K gold pen he reserved for special occasions, he wrote:

Nobody tries to take over my territory and gets away with it.

Nobody, but NOBODY fucks with Vincent Guerrero.

His expression was calm, almost serene as he looked over what he had written. He drew a deep breath and held it for a long, long time.

He let the breath out and relaxed. With firm, precise movements, Vince tore the paper up into small pieces and dropped them into a nearby trash can. Taking out his phone, he started whistling as he settled in to get some business done before the boarding call for First Class.

This be the Verse

Dan Powell

Calvin wanted to lose his virginity.

In the café , staring at the departure board updates, he could think of nothing else. His right foot, resting on his left, jigged and flicked with nervous energy, stopping for a few moments every now and then, only to begin once more. Every part of the trip, from flights, to the city he would be staying in, to the location of the hotel, was a cog in the machine designed to propel him into the realm of the sexually active. Every part except one.

"Calvinsweetheart, I asked if it was time to check in?"

Calvin pulled his eyes away from the screen to look at his mother. She arched her eyebrow.

"Calvinsweetheart?" She always said it as one word. "Did you hear what I said?"

"Yes, Mother."

"Well, is it time?"

Calvin checked his watch.

"There's still a few minutes," he said. "Finish your tea, then we'll take the bags over."

"Didn't I tell you it was worth leaving a few hours early dear? This

51

way we get to relax before the rush of check-ins and boarding calls. When I flew with your father, Godresthim, we were always running late for flights. Did I ever tell you about the time we…"

Calvin stopped listening and watched her mouth moving. Over the years he had grown adept at shutting out her droning. He nodded now and again but let his thoughts drift back to the trip. If he could just get Mother settled in the hotel, she might well have an early night. He could still get away, explore a bit before putting his plan in motion.

Forty-two was quite old enough to still be a virgin. For goodness sake, there were Hollywood movies lampooning the sad state of his personal life. Something had to be done.

Calvin originally booked the trip for one, but was forced to plump for another ticket when Mother, during a search of his room while he was at work, found his holiday stash.

"There must be no secrets between us," she had said. "Don't you want your old mum to have a holiday too?"

He shook his head just as he did when a child.

"That's settled then. I mean, who wants to go on holiday on their own?"

Uncomfortable on the hard plastic of the airport café chair, Calvin cringed at the memory of his spinelessness.

"Are you okay, Calvinsweetheart? You don't look well."

Calvin shrugged. "I'm fine." He shook his head to clear it a little. "We should go."

He stood and took his mother's tweed travel jacket from the back of her chair, waiting as she checked her purse, stood and smoothed down her skirt.

"Thank you," she said as he helped her into her jacket. "Such a good boy."

She stretched up to kiss his cheek. Calvin felt his teeth grit.

"You're welcome, Mother."

In the check-in queue, Calvin waited while Mother rummaged through her purse. He put a hand to his pocket and retrieved the tissue inside. He unfolded it carefully, mesmerised by the signature scrawled across the soft paper surface. Ava Scott. Film star. Ingénue. Glamour model. And wasn't she recording an album of show tunes soon? Calvin's thoughts filled with the image of her signing the napkin. Again he was struck with how his Cilla managed to capture some of Ava Scott's look, at least in her photos.

"Put that away, Calvinsweetheart," Mother said.

As he slid the napkin gently back into in his pocket, Calvin noticed the two men standing behind him. One kept glancing around nervously, but the other looked right at him, eyes cold, mouth grinning as if enjoying a private joke.

"Here we are, Calvinsweetheart."

Calvin, glad of the excuse, turned back to Mother. The man behind him laughed then started whistling, as Mother handed Calvin the tickets and passports.

"Now don't go losing them. I want them straight back when the lady has finished looking at them."

Calvin nodded and wheeled their trolley forward a few inches with the movement of the queue. His fingers rested on his only piece of hand luggage, a laptop bag strapped over his shoulder and across his chest in case anyone should try to snatch it. His laptop, a necessity in his line of work, was his only private space. Mother's unfamiliarity with modern digital devices allowed Calvin a retreat where she could not follow. Nor could she argue over the time he spent on it in his room.

"I have to work," he told her when she tried.

The laptop made the trip possible. The planning, the booking of tickets. Most importantly the abundance of social networks helped him find Cilla. Calvin could barely believe she was waiting for him. Only a short plane flight between them meeting in the flesh.

"Passports please." Calvin looked up. He was at the head of the queue.

"Give the nice lady the passports, Calvinsweetheart," Mother said, nudging him forward.

Calvin handed over the passports, a frail smile breaking over his lips.

He hefted his suitcase onto the conveyer.

"Did you pack the bag yourself?"

Calvin nodded. The check-in rep stared at him.

"Yes I did," he added, nodding harder.

"And, your wife?"

"Oh, she's, oh she's, oh oh…" Calvin stuttered.

"I was never lucky enough to marry, dear. Calvin's father passed away suddenly during our engagement." Calvin's mother gave his cheek a squeeze with her chubby fingers. "This is my beautiful son."

Calvin felt something knot inside him as his mother beamed at the check in girl. The check-in girl examined the passports, checking the dates of birth.

"I beg your pardon," she said, "my mistake."

As Calvin moved further into middle-age, more and more strangers assumed they were man and wife. Even Calvin had to admit his mother did not look her age, while he looked much older than his. It was as if time addressed the imbalance of their years, bridging the gap by taking the years from her and giving them to him.

"No problem." Calvin felt his stomach tighten as the check-in clerk attached labels to the suitcases.

"Please be sure your hand luggage fits the guide frames provided," she said, handing back the passports.

Calvin nodded and watched the suitcases move along the conveyor and disappear behind the fringes of plastic strip into the baggage area, half-expecting alarms to go off and security to abseil from the ceiling. Nothing happened and he laughed quietly to himself.

"If you could move along, sir. We are busier than usual, what with the *Pangaean* fiasco."

Calvin looked around and mouthed a weak apology to those behind him, handed the passports and tickets back to his mother and wheeled the trolley out of the queue.

Wheeling the trolley back to the stand, a repeat of the check-in clerk's mistake played over in his head, revulsion and self-pity buckling his stomach. He thought of his case, now somewhere in the bowels of the airport, being x-rayed and scanned, possibly sniffed by dogs trained to find contraband. The tightness grew.

Calvin shoved the trolley into the row, the movement and the smack of metal on metal jolting something loose inside him.

"I have to go," he blurted to his mother and scrambled to the gents.

"Is everything alright, Calvinsweetheart?" Mother called after him but he did not look back.

He slammed open the men's room door and dived into the nearest cubicle, just managing to sit with his trousers and pants round his ankles before a stream of hot, loose shit spattered the toilet bowl. His backside bubbled, firing dribs and drabs for a few seconds before something inside him flipped and the torrent resumed. He groaned, feeling his innards slopped into the water beneath him. Calvin sucked in a deep breath through his mouth and placed his palms on the toilet walls either side of him to steady himself. The flow slowed to a dribble and stayed there. He sat and waited for it to stop, unravelling his anxieties in his head.

The whole misunderstanding with the check-in clerk had been the final straw, but what was really bothering him was inside his suitcase. He wished he hadn't packed the bloody thing, but there was nothing to be done now the suitcase was on its way to the plane. At least he had dismantled it, packing the components separately, in the hope it would seems less conspicuous to anyone checking his baggage.

He ordered the penis pump from a website specialising in that sort of thing. The pump, if you believed the testimonials, guaranteed to increase the male member size. The men in the videos he downloaded from the internet while Mother slept, had driven him to such measures. They all seemed so much more endowed than him. He could hardly hope to satisfy Cilla with his pathetic, natural size.

His bowels settled, Calvin remained seated and flushed, allowing the cold water to splash up and cool his rectum. As he stood to begin cleaning himself he heard the outside door to the toilets open.

"Calvinsweetheart, are you okay in there?"

Calvin winced.

"I'm fine. Please wait outside," he said, wiping his backside with the shiny airport toilet paper.

"They'll be calling our flight soon."

"I'll be right there, Mother. Please. Wait outside."

He heard her footsteps moving towards him.

"It smells like someone has a tummy upset."

From the sound of her voice she stood just the other side of his cubicle door.

"Mother, please…"

"Don't you 'Mother please' me. You know how you get with your irritable bowel. Now open this door and let me help you."

Calvin wiped his arse one final time, before flushing the toilet and hoisting his trousers up.

"See, I'm fine," he said, opening the cubicle and traipsing to the sinks.

"Be sure and wash your hands properly."

Calvin watched his mother leave the gents through the mirror over the sinks. He washed his hands and splashed cold water on his face, stepping back to look himself up and down. A smile crawled across his face but vanished as a wave of self-pity threatened to send him running back to the toilet.

"You'd still be helping me wipe my arse if I'd let you, wouldn't you, Mother?" he snapped at his reflection.

A toilet flushed and Calvin turned to see a pair of white pants and tan shoes visible beneath the door three up from his cubicle. He turned back to the mirror and watched his face fill with red. In the reflection the door opened and a man in a white linen suit stepped out, an overcoat draped over his arm.

"Mothers, eh?" said the man, stepping up to the sink beside Calvin's and washing his hands.

"I'm sorry. I didn't realise there was anyone else in here."

"Don't apologise, lad. I learnt long ago there's little we men can do to control the women in our lives. Trying to get a grip on a woman's mindset is like trying to ride a wild horse. You're going to be thrown more often than not."

The man in the linen suit dipped his fingers one last time under the running tap and smoothed his moustache with the water.

"Have we met before?" Calvin said, eyeing the man in the mirror, looking away as the man turned to face him.

"No, I shouldn't think so."

"You look familiar somehow."

The man looked from his reflection to Calvin's and back again.

"That's remarkable," he said. "Quite remarkable. The resemblance I mean. They do say everyone has a *doppelganger*." The man extended his hand. "Claude."

"Calvin."

"Indeed," Claude said.

He turned back to the mirror, smoothed back his long, straw-coloured hair and for just a moment Calvin almost saw it.

"Well, must be off, time and tide and all that."

He picked up his overcoat from beside the sink and marched to the door. In the mirror Calvin watched him turn back.

"Don't let her organise your whole life," Claude said and disappeared from view.

Calvin adjusted the collar of his shirt, shook his head. About to turn away from the mirror he stopped, raised a finger to his face and held it under his nose curving it a little to make a moustache. His eyes widened and he scurried for the door.

Angry travellers filled the airport concourse, spreading out from the *Pangaean* check-in desk. Calvin looked back and forth for the man in the linen suit.

"Did you see him," Calvin said to Mother. "The man in the suit?"

"Indeed I did."

"Which way did he go?"

"Across there, toward the *Ganda* desk. Disgraceful behaviour."

"Wait here, Mo—"

"I don't think some *Pangaean* employee going through a bin is any-

57

thing you need to worry about, Calvinsweetheart. We have a plane to catch."

"*Pangaean?*"

"The man in the cobalt blue suit, looking like something out of the eighties. Going through bins."

"Blue? He wasn't wearing blue? You must have seen him. He came out of the toilet just ahead of me. Where did he go?"

Calvin stopped himself, aware his voice was rising to a shout.

"Calvinsweetheart, have I done something to upset you?"

Mother reached up and pushed his fringe across his face, sorting out the parting in his hair. He felt himself bristle.

"No, Mother."

"Now, what's this about a man in the toilets?"

Calvin looked about him once more.

"Nothing... nothing, Mother. We'd best go."

They joined the security check-in queue and Calvin removed his belt and jacket, ready to place in the grey plastic trays.

"Where shall we go tonight?"

Calvin stood silent for a moment.

"I have plans," he said, straining to keep his voice level.

Mother looked up at him, her eyebrow arched once again. Calvin watched her raise her hands, putting one to either side of his face, the edges of her long red nails pressing into the skin of his cheeks.

"Calvinsweetheart," she said, pulling his face down toward hers, "you couldn't possibly leave me alone on the first night in a strange city."

Calvin felt her grip tighten a fraction as she said this. He mumbled an answer.

"What's that, dear?"

"I said, I have a date." Calvin felt himself flinch as he said this.

"A date! With whom? You don't know anybody at home, so you certainly can't know anybody in Amsterdam."

Calvin squirmed in her grip looking, left and right. The people in front and behind in the queue stared nervously at the pair. At the security terminals ahead, Calvin saw a burly female security guard take a step towards them.

"Mother, you're causing a scene. Let go."

"Calvin, your inconsiderate behaviour is wholly unbecoming of a good son," said Mother, the shrillness of her voice increasing with the steady metronome of each syllable. "How you can think of seeing some trollop, when–"

"Her name is Cilla." Calvin looked Mother in the eye and spoke slowly. "I met her on the internet."

"I knew it. The hours you spend on that vile machine had to be more than just work." Mother released Calvin's face and made a grab for the laptop bag. "How can you think of meeting some foul stranger from the internet?"

They had reached the head of the queue and Calvin pulled free, stepping forward to place his jacket, wallet, keys and belt in one of the trays and his laptop directly on the conveyor behind it, careful to keep himself between Mother and the bag.

"My goodness Calvin, can't you see you're being groomed? Cilla won't be her real name."

Mother made to step around him but Calvin shuffled with her, keeping himself between her and the conveyor.

"I know it's not her real name. She told me her real name. I know everything about her."

"Calvinsweetheart, how could you?" Mother's voice became a snarl.

Calvin felt his stomach twist further.

"I knew you wouldn't understand, Mother."

"Is everything okay, sir? Madam?" asked a tall male security officer, with a severe crew cut.

His female counterpart eyed Calvin and his mother. Calvin felt the knot in his stomach squeeze again as Mother glared back at the guard.

"Yes, thank you, young man, simply a private matter between a mother and her son."

Calvin felt his face fill with heat.

"Shoes, please sir."

Calvin bent, unlaced his shoes, placed them on the conveyor and stepped forward. Calvin realised, as the man's large hands patted him down, it was the first physical contact he'd had with someone other than his mother in too many years. He felt his stomach tighten again and groaned as the security guard checked his legs.

"Are you alright, sir?" The security guard stopped, crouched down with his hands either side of Calvin's left leg. He looked up at Calvin and waited for an answer.

"Fine. I'm fine," managed Calvin.

The frisking finished, Calvin stepped through the metal detector. The barrier remained silent. He stood on the departure gate side looking back at his mother as the female security officer performed her physical check. Calvin felt the urge to run taunting him. Surrounded by security barriers and trained security personnel he was even more trapped than usual. He pushed the feeling down as his tray of belongings trundled up the conveyor to him, and concentrated on putting his belt back on.

"Is this bag yours, sir?"

A female security officer from behind the conveyor's x-ray scanner stood up holding Calvin's laptop bag in the air before him. Calvin stared at the bag and a feeling of falling rushed through him.

"Is this yours, sir?"

"Yes, it is."

"Did you pack this bag yourself?"

Calvin nodded.

"Could you speak up, sir?" the officer said.

"Yes, I packed the bag myself."

"According to the x-ray there appears to be a suspicious item inside. Follow me, please."

Calvin followed her around the end of the conveyor to the rear of the security station.

"Calvinsweetheart? Is everything okay?"

Calvin looked over. His mother stood holding her shoes.

"Fine, Mother, they just want to check my bag."

"Could you tell me if there is anything requiring declaration in this piece of luggage?" The security officer said this loudly. Calvin understood the rise in volume was intended as a full stop to his conversation with Mother.

"No. Just a laptop and few personal items."

The security officer placed the laptop bag onto the tabletop between them and slowly unzipped the main compartment. Calvin watched the woman's thick masculine fingers pull the zip around the case, enjoying their contrast with the deep pink polish on her nails. The tightness in his stomach moved towards his groin. She flipped the lid and Calvin gasped involuntarily. He felt sweat forming on his brow.

"Sir, are you okay?"

"Fine. I'm fine." Calvin dabbed at his forehead with his handkerchief, smiling weakly.

She tapped a finger on the laptop case.

"There is nothing here that you want to explain?"

Calvin stared at the case. He knew what she was getting at. It was right there, nestled into the case in the pocket designed for a computer mouse. He thought he had been so clever.

"Sir?" Calvin felt himself freeze, ice sweeping down his spine, locking him in place.

She snapped on a latex glove and reached her manicured hand inside, plucking the item from the mouse bay. Sickening exhilaration flooded Calvin's limbs as he watched her hold the item up between her sheathed fingers.

It looked something like a hand grenade crafted from black rubber. A valve stuck out of the top where it could be connected to something. The security guard gave it a slight squeeze, a squeak of air escaping.

"Calvinsweetheart, what's happening?"

Calvin looked across to where a male security officer was attempting to shepherd her along. "Young man, I will move along as soon as you return my son." Her voice was becoming shrill.

"Sir?" Calvin turned back to the female security officer. "Could you explain exactly what this is?" She pushed the hand grenade-shaped piece of rubber toward his face. "Sir?"

Calvin felt his voice catch in his throat, coughed to clear it and tried again. "It's part of a pump," he said in a whisper.

"I beg your pardon." The security officer's eyes tightened and she took a step forward. "Please speak up, sir?"

Calvin tried to raise his voice. "It's part of a penis pump," he said again, his eyes moving nervously to where his mother was standing, still fighting security's attempts to move her on.

"I said, speak up, sir." The female security guard waved a hand as she said this and Calvin watched as two more security officers, men, moved around the station toward him.

Calvin laughed nervously and tried again.

"It's a pump," he mumbled to the woman holding the pump portion of the penis enlarger.

He had just time to watch her eyes widen before the two men were on him, pushing him to the floor

"It's just a pump," he tried to say, but somewhere between the air being hammered from his lungs and the anxious speed of his words they were hearing something else.

Calvin felt a knee push into his spine and squealed. One of the officers smacked his face hard to the floor. Straining his eyes in his sockets, Calvin could just see Mother, held in place by two more security officers.

"Calvinsweetheart!" she bellowed. Then to the men holding her, "You leave my boy alone. Leave him be."

Calvin heard the female officer bark a code into her radio: "Suspect is restrained and device appears to be dismantled at present."

"Don't fuckin' move."

This voice was close to Calvin's ear, one of the men restraining him. Calvin thought about jail, about prison. He wondered if Cilla would write to him. Cold floor against his cheek, Calvin watched Mother's pudgy-ankled foot stomp in time with her squeals of protest and smiled.

Providence

Dale Challener Roe

"I can get your bag back." The voice came from behind.

"Excuse me." The words spat out of my mouth, my body whipping around.

"I said, 'I can get your bag back'."

I glared at him. Scruffy, in a faded and cracked leather jacket. A backpack, emblazoned with a Canadian flag, thrown over one shoulder. Trust a Canadian who hadn't lost his luggage to think he had the solution to my problem.

"I'm sorry." He raised both hands, took a step back. "I wasn't trying to eavesdrop. It's just…"

"Just what?" Just thought he'd step in, unasked, and be of some help? Like I needed a hero to sort my crap out.

I snapped the phone shut and shoved it in my pocket.

"It was pretty hard not to hear. You were practically yelling."

"If you haven't noticed, it's a bit noisy around here. Though I would have thought it hindered one's ability to listen in on a conversation."

"You know what? Don't worry about it." He shrugged his shoulders and opened his hands up. He started backing away from me the way you would from one of those end of the world street barkers. "You seem to have everything under control."

He turned his back and walked away, shaking his head. Good riddance. But I couldn't stop watching him, striding out onto the concourse. In a few seconds he'd be swallowed.

Damn.

I raced after him, grabbing hold of the worn leather to stop him when I caught up.

"I'm sorry. I'm just… It's been a bad day and it's not even ten and I haven't had my caffeine injection for the day." I rubbed at my temple where the start of a headache niggled. "Can we start over? I'm Lily." I held out my hand. "Well, Lilith. Lilith Thomas. But I never liked Lilith. Seemed like I should be wearing black, have too many piercings and–"

"Smite me with the fury of the Old Testament?"

"I'm sorry. I'm not usually so–"

"Stubborn? Angry? Frustrat–"

"Lost."

He put his backpack down and took my hand. "I'm Mat. Although, if you're 'fessing up to Lilith… I guess I can tell you, I'm actually Math."

"Math? Like mathematics?"

He nodded, squeezing my hand just firm enough to send shivers through me.

"Family name?" I asked, trying hard to ignore the way my hand in his made me feel.

"Lazy name. I was supposed be to named Mathew, just one 't', but the clerk got distracted filling out the birth certificate and my parents were supposed to get it changed, but they never followed through with anything."

"You can follow through?" I raised an eyebrow, allowing my hand to linger a little longer than I should have in his.

He let go of my hand and shrugged again. "I suppose, if I couldn't I'd have never left home."

His words hung between us, until I realised I was staring at him and blushed. "You coming or going?"

"I'm heading back to where I grew up."

Reflex almost led me to crack a mathematics joke about his answer not really adding up—just to see his smile come out again—but I held back. Instead I searched for something meaningful to say, and "I guess home means different things to different folk" slipped out.

"It's more like home might still be where I used to hang my hat. I've been gone for a while."

"How long?"

"Three years this time. All up though, almost a decade."

"What part of Canada are you from?"

He looked confused, until I pointed to the flag on the backpack.

"I'm not Canadian. It was a joke from my friends before I left the first time. They said with me being the typical ugly American, the world should think I was from somewhere else."

"So you're a backpacker?"

"Travel writer."

A spark of excitement ran though me at the prospect of getting a straight answer for the first time all morning. "In your professional opinion then, how long will this," I waved my arm to indicate the chaos around us, "last?"

"That depends. If you're like me, and can't just hand over the price of a new ticket, it may take a couple of days. A week tops."

"A week!"

"The upside? The government, or other airlines, will do what they can to get everyone to their destinations. At least here they're forced to put you up and feed you in the interim. But if you can buy a new ticket, you can leave whenever you want, assuming there is a seat to buy."

"But what about the luggage?"

"In a few days they'll realise they can seize anything *Pangaean* owns, but they can't hold the passengers' luggage as assets of the company. How it finds its way to you is another thing. I have this mate in London who drives lost luggage between Heathrow and Manchester in his taxi, he reckons…" His voice trailed off and my shoulders slumped. "You need your bag that badly?"

"I'm a bridesmaid on Wednesday just outside D.C."

"Who gets married on a Wednesday?"

I bit my lip, keeping the phrases 'pretentious pricks' and 'folks who believe the world revolves around them' firmly under lock and key.

"Ah… I get it. Inclusion-by-default and you'd rather be somewhere else?"

He'd known me two minutes and read me better than anyone else I knew—including my family who hadn't even noticed my apathetic response to the invitation.

"Yes and no. It's a family thing."

"Why not just go without the bag? Once this is all straightened out they'll send your bag to you."

I was already shaking my head. "My bridesmaid's dress is in there. I insisted I buy it on the way home. I stopped off in Paris. It was my–"

"Your own small act of rebellion?"

I nodded my head.

"Ouch."

"There are plenty of flights to D.C.—but I can't get a new dress on such short notice. Oh God…" I buried my face in my hands. "I wish it wasn't all about the damn dress."

"You live in D.C.?"

"Providence."

He laughed.

"Yeah I know." I peeled my hands from my face. "Not exactly the haute couture capital of the USA."

"Providence." He smiled that small smile again, and I wondered what I was missing—caught up in my own life dramas again.

"Yeah? Providence. Is there a problem with that?"

"Problem? No. It's just that… I'm heading there, too."

I love watching people drink coffee—or whatever their comfort beverage is. You learn a lot about people from what they order and how they drink it. When Math suggested coffee to avoid my question, I knew I could kill two birds with one stone.

Alone, I'd have ordered something frozen, whipped, and drizzled with any of a list of diabetes-inducing syrups. I'd never let anyone else order that for me, though. I wouldn't make them try to remember—or pay for—all that silliness. And in the back of my mind it's like stamping 'high maintenance' on my forehead... and I'm not.

Math offered to buy, so I ordered a large mocha. He got the coffee of the day, tasted it before he started adding anything. I wondered if he learnt that travelling or had always done it.

"So you don't believe in fate?"

He chugged about a third of the coffee before answering, "No I don't," then added an obscene amount of sugar and milk. It turned the colour of caramel and was probably as sweet.

"So what do you call the two of us meeting here, thousands of miles from home? Coincidence?"

"I don't believe in coincidence either."

Pardon? What sort of answer was that?

It was an either-or proposition and waiting in line, I'd organised my responses in line with all the anticipated answers. There was no opt-out clause. I was always ahead of the conversation, ready with an intelligent answer. But he'd caught me off guard.

Fate or coincidence—was there anything in between?

"Why are you going home? You don't exactly seem enthusiastic about it."

"A bit like your wedding, huh?"

"You don't like answering a straight question do you?"

"I could say the same about you."

"It's my cousin's wedding and I have no choice. If I didn't work in the family business I'd have faked an extra week away for work to avoid it."

"I got fired. And I did."

"Did what?"

"Have a choice. I was trying to get fired."

"Do people do that?"

"I did."

"Why?"

"I was tired of it."

"What did you write about?"

"One of those travel-on-a-budget columns. They'd send me places, presumably on a shoestring budget, and I'd write about cheap places to stay, and free sights to see. Then at the end of the day I'd check into my three-star hotel."

"Sounds like a fun job."

"It was for a while. Then… something changed." He stirred his coffee, watching the tiny muddy whirlpool. "I got tired of writing columns that weren't true. Weren't me. I got fed up leaving out hidden treasures I'd found because it didn't fit within the pretend budget."

"Why didn't you just quit?"

"Mostly for the fun of aggravating the magazine. And the best bit… they had to buy my return ticket because they let me go."

"Savvy bit of contract negotiation."

"Never leave home without a 'get home free' clause."

"How did you get fired? Write an article on how to see the red light district on ten euros?"

"I stopped using apostrophes."

If I hadn't been between sips, hot coffee would have sprayed all over him, possibly via my nose.

"I didn't stop using them entirely." He was smiling, and trying not to laugh. "Mostly I stopped using them in contractions. I mean, really, if I spelled won't without an apostrophe would you misunderstand me? I still used them for possessives."

I adored his rationalisation—as if using no apostrophes at all would cross some moral line in the sand.

"And that was enough to get fired?"

"My editor was a little bit… OCD. After three articles, he asked them to let me go."

"And now they're paying for you to go home?"

He nodded.

"So, if someone else is picking up the tab, why don't you just go buy another ticket? It's not like they've got your backpack."

"The magazine gave me an advance for the ticket, and now it's spent."

"So you're stuck because you can't pay for a ticket, and I'm stuck because they have my bag?"

He raised his eyebrows.

"And you don't believe in fate?"

He shook his head.

"Or coincidence?"

And smiled. "Nope."

"So what do you believe in?"

"Things simply are. People see what they want to see. Those who want a higher power, see the work of a higher power. People who want to believe good things happen to good people choose to see that. People who believe in a random universe see coincidence."

"So you think I want to see fate in our situation?"

"Not necessarily. Do you really think I spoke to you because it was fated?"

I let the silence sit there for a while, sipping my mocha and wishing I'd asked for a serving of marshmallows.

"What changed?"

"Pardon?"

I was practically giddy that I'd finally caught him off guard instead of the reverse. I ploughed on. "You said something changed, and all of a sudden you didn't want to write your column any longer. What changed?"

This time he held the silence, stirring his coffee again. I started to think I'd overstepped my bounds. Did it really matter to me why? He was a random stranger who bought me a mocha in an airport on the worst day of my life and focusing on his life meant I didn't have to think of my own.

"I'm sorry. It's none of my business. I shouldn't ha–"

He held up his hand to stop me. "It's okay." He quickly downed the rest of his coffee. "I found out I have cancer."

❧ ❧ ❧

69

Being stuck indefinitely in an airport at any other time would have been hell on earth, but two hours wandering with Math was like a half-way-house heaven. I kept the questions to a minimum and just enjoyed his company. When we tired of the shops, we settled into a small group of seats tucked away in a corner, apart from the hubbub.

"So you really think there's a reason we met?" He eased back in the uncomfortable plastic seat, feet propped up on the edging around the windows.

"No, not necessarily. But I do think it's possible."

He raised his eyebrows... just a little bit mocking. He'd already developed a habit of playfully baiting me without saying a word.

"Don't you think it's odd we're travelling from different parts of the world, both headed to the same hometown? We're both at a crossroads, and we're each in a position to help the other?"

"I just offered to get your bag back. It's not like it's a life altering thing."

"Don't mock me."

"I'm not mocking you."

"I'm being serious."

"So, what's your crossroad?"

"Huh?"

"You said we're both at a crossroads. You already know mine. But you haven't mentioned yours."

I bit my lower lip and wondered how I allowed such a thing to slip.

"The wedding?"

A snort of a laugh shot out of my nose. "In the grand scheme, the wedding, the damn dress... are chicken feed."

He raised his eyebrows.

"I just won my family's advertising agency the biggest account they'll never have."

"You're in advertising?"

"You say it like I have two heads and eat babies."

"It's just—"

"Just what?"

"You don't seem the baby eating type."

"I'm not."

"So, what account did you lose?"

"I didn't lose anything. This time Friday I was sitting in the *Pangaean* boardroom sealing the deal. Then this happens."

"So… you win some you lose some. It wasn't like it was your fault."

"You don't get it. This new account was my ticket out. Away from my family."

"Why don't you just go somewhere else? You'd have little trouble making your own way."

"I wouldn't. I'm good at what I do."

"So what's the problem?"

"Loyalty. I'm not in advertising because I love it. It's what my family does. It was always a given that I'd do it, too. But…" Could I really say it? Truly be honest? Not just with Math but with myself? "What if there'd been no family company? Where would I be if I'd been allowed to find out what I wanted?"

"You can't spend your whole life twisted in 'what ifs', Lilith."

"You don't get it."

"Oh, I think I get it Lilith. Better than you. You're in a wedding you don't want to be part of, you work in a job you hate, belong to a family with members who don't get you and have a life that really belongs to someone else."

"You make it sound ridiculous."

"No more ridiculous than someone who quits their job through guerrilla punctuation."

I looked away, smothering a giggle and that's when I caught sight of him. Immaculately turned out in a tailored suit, matching fedora pulled down tight over his forehead, desperately trying to control an impromptu press conference. I almost didn't recognize the head of *Pangaean* without the blonde ice-queen shadowing him. A shudder ran through me when I remembered the way she glared at me as her boss flirted with me.

Watching him squirm before the hungry reporters, something inside me snapped. I knew he'd be desperate to convince the media today represented nothing more than a little unforeseen turbulence for *Pangaean*. He'd do anything to save his father's company, the company he would one day inherit. Lie, cheat, bribe, steal—anything required for the sake of the company. And I'd be put in charge to help him do it.

I wasn't like that. And didn't ever want to be.

I turned back at Math.

"I'm tired of jumping through hoops, being loyal."

"You don't have to. You can be your own person," Math said, as I watched the fedora bob above the heads of the reporters and disappear through an 'employee only' door. "Explain something to me?"

"I'll try?"

"The way you were giving me the third degree about fate and coincidence… You believe in destiny, don't you?"

"I suppose. Why?"

"If you believe in fate, why do you ignore it?"

"I don't. I'm talking to you aren't I?"

"I'm not talking about us. If you really believe in destiny, then why ignore the signs?"

"What signs?"

"If I was the type to see the tinkering of a higher power, I'd have to wonder at the purpose of being trapped in this airport, my life put on hold, with nothing to do except examine the direction of that life. Might it be a sign to do something about it? Go in a new direction?"

I wanted to bury my face in him and cry. And I did. Silently. Resting my forehead against his chest, and then my cheek. Comfortable and safe. I stayed there listening to the quiet, steady thump of his heart.

I knew he was going to say something by the way he breathed in and my cheek moved with his expanding chest.

"What do you really want, Lilith?"

I lost track of time. It seemed to be both super-condensed and never-ending. As I made my way back from the *Freedom* counter, I spied Math sitting with…what I assumed was a belated lunch. He handed me an iced coffee and a sandwich wrapped so tight it could have survived a spacewalk.

"Did you get your ticket?"

I wasn't sure how to answer, looking around at all the other *Pangaean* refugees. I nodded and took a sip of the iced coffee.

A frown flickered across his face. Or was it my imagination?

"Time to repatriate your bag then?"

"How?"

Instead of looking me in the eye, he wrestled open his own hermetically-sealed sandwich.

"We're going to—"

"We? What the heck am I going to do? If I knew how to get my bag back, I wouldn't need the gentleman in the torn leather armour."

"It'll only work if we do this together."

"Are you crazy?"

"You need to ask me that?" He smirked, examining the inside of his sandwich.

I bit my bottom lip. "I'm not sure, Math."

"Lilith…" he stared at me, all trace of humour gone.

"Fine. What do you want me to do?"

"I want you to put your drink and sandwich down, that's right, now lean forward and rest your elbows on your knees."

"What?"

"Shhh." He placed his hand on my back. "Don't cause a scene. Not yet."

"What am I doing?"

"Having an asthma attack."

"But I—"

"Where's your ticket and baggage claim check? Don't look up, keep your head down."

"In my purse."

"OK. Keep your head down."

"I'm confused."

"It'll work better if you're confused. Now start breathing heavy."

"But we haven't even kissed yet."

"Quiet, smart-arse."

He stood up.

"Where are you going?"

"To get your bag," and he was gone.

"Are you okay, miss?"

Not knowing what to say, I shook my head. More people joined, with more inane questions and observations. They'd be calling me out for an Oscar next year.

"Excuse me… please…"

Finally I saw Math's shoes appear underneath me along with my suitcase. "She'll be all right now," he announced and the people began to drift away. Drama over.

"Now to keep it authentic, let's play this out," he whispered to me. "Do you mind if I unzip this outer pocket and fish around for nothing in particular?"

"Go right ahead." It was taking all my willpower to keep from laughing. I'd like to say I couldn't believe a ruse so simple could work, but all I could think was why were we the only ones trying it?

Finally he put a plastic inhaler in my hand.

"Where did that come from?"

"It's mine. Pretend to take a couple of breaths of that."

I did. He moved closer so only I could hear him.

"Now sit up, slowly, look relieved. Take a couple of minutes to catch your breath."

I sat up as slowly as I could bear. "Sneaky," I whispered. "What did you say to make them give it up?"

"I mentioned the possibility of a wrongful death suit."

He laughed and I hid mine behind a raised hand, just in case someone was watching. Then, as the laughter ended, an awkward silence replaced it. I could tell he was trying to figure out how to say goodbye.

"Will you make it in time for the wedding?" he finally asked.

"I will. Barely."

"I thought you–"

"I have. But you don't ruin someone's wedding."

"And then? Home? Back to the agency?"

"Yes." Disappointment clouded his face. "There's two things I need to take care of."

"Like what?"

"I think it's time I had a talk with my uncle. Someone else can pick up the pieces of… this."

"Is that what you want to do?"

"I don't know."

"Why leave?"

"Because I need to find out what I want and I can't do it if I'm still at the agency."

"What's the other thing?"

"The other?"

"You said there were two things."

"Oh… oh that… that other thing."

"Well?"

"I have this friend, who's sick. And he might need some help for a while. Until he's better."

Neither of us said anything for a long time.

"Lily, I–"

I pulled the tickets out of my purse before he could finish the sentence. "Going my way?"

"Lilith, I can't accept it. Just because I got your bag… It's not a fair trade."

"You think it's about the bag?"

"There's no such thing as destiny, Lilith."

"Then don't think of it as destiny."

"So what should I call it? Coincidence? Fate? Kismet? I don't believe in any of that."

I took his hand. "Just call it Providence. We both know that's real."

No Passengers Allowed

J.M. Strother

As airports go, this one was pretty screwed up. An ongoing strike at the entrance to the international terminal left a mess of irate picketers and confused travellers in its wake—chaos defined. Sam Harris cut through the angry bodies, ignoring their shouted grievances, and headed inside. He found little relief from the bedlam. Everywhere he looked, nothing but festering lines and swirling eddies of people. Typical airport.

He glanced at his watch and set off to locate the check-in. His first task was always to get the lay of the land. Assess the situation. Mitigate the unexpected.

He found the *Pangaean* counter soon enough. *Pangaean* and *Royale Atisari Airlines*, to its left, functioned as two islands of calm efficiency in an otherwise tempestuous sea. Further down, *Ganda Airways'* frustrated passengers snaked interminably through retractable-tape cattle corrals; two harried clerks doing the work of four. *Freedom Air's* malfunctioning electronic check-in machines left passengers arguing among themselves and staff trying to mollify the situation.

Sam nodded. He'd made a good choice with *Pangaean*; counters fully staffed, lines nice and short, and everything moving quickly.

It was a lovely day to fly.

He glanced again at his watch. Time for a little caffeine to jump-start his workday.

Sam scouted for the best perch to observe the world. Café Délicieux looked good. While crowded, a few empty tables remained near the faux windows—a suitable vantage point to monitor the check-in lines. And, if he squinted, he'd be able to make out the arrival and departure times from the overheads in the middle of the terminal.

The café line failed the efficiency test, snaking slower than *Ganda's*, through the same damned crowd corrals. It took Sam forever to come face-to-face with a barista.

"Coffee, tall and black," he said.

She raised her eyebrows. "Just coffee? Black coffee, straight up?"

Sam knew folks didn't go to places like *Café Délicieux* for plain coffee, but he wasn't most folks.

"Yes, please. Black coffee, straight up."

He paid a small fortune for the luxury—they saw you coming at the airport. He hated to think what those flavoured double latté s with extra shots cost the customers around him. At least they didn't charge extra for a napkin.

By the time he had his coffee in hand, only one table remained empty near the windows. He moved in on it quickly, lest someone else nab it. With a satisfied sigh, Sam sat and checked his watch—an entire half-hour lost on a lousy cup of coffee. He took a sip and smiled. Scratch lousy. The coffee was excellent.

The *Pangaean* lines had lengthened during his wait, while the *Atisari* lines remained short, their entire counter fully staffed. Even with two of eight stations closed at *Pangaean*, Sam didn't worry about the schedule. Plenty of time.

He sipped his coffee, watching the ebb and flow of passengers. A haphazard collection of humanity crammed into close proximity under stressful conditions, each obsessed with their own sets of worries. Simple percentages told him loose cannons roamed out there, just waiting to go off. It amazed him more people didn't go postal in airports. Over the coffee cup rim he searched for potential trouble. In his line of work, one could never be too careful.

Trouble hit his radar as he placed the empty coffee cup on the table. A man stood poised halfway between the *Atisari* and *Pangaean* counters, scrutinising the crowd with professional intensity; tall, wide shouldered, sporting a buzz cut, and not an inch of flab. Sam pegged him for ex-military, probably special forces. The man appeared tightly wound, working the crowd… searching for someone.

Interesting.

"Excuse me, mate, can I borrow your pen?"

Sam looked up, to see a young man, early twenties, hovering over him.

"I beg your pardon?"

"Your pen? I need to write down a phone number before I forget it." The young man pointed to Sam's breast pocket and the gold-plated pen.

"Sorry. No."

The man glanced over to a pretty girl sitting alone. When Sam's answer penetrated he looked back with a scowl. "What? I just need it for a sec."

"Sorry. It's out of ink."

"Yeah, right." Sam heard him mutter 'jerk' as he moved on to accost the woman at the next table. "Excuse me, miss, can I borrow a pen?"

Sam tugged on his jacket breast to cover his shirt pocket and looked back over the main terminal. He was dismayed to find the special forces guy gone. He scanned the crowd but saw no sign of him. An irrational worry lingered. He flipped open his cell phone and called Mitch.

It rang three times.

"Hello?"

"Hi, Mitch. Sam here. I'm about to catch my flight out. Been a heck of a week. Anyway, I was thinking of having a barbeque this weekend and was wondering if you could make it?"

"This weekend? Sure. Sounds wonderful. Wouldn't miss it for the world."

"Great. See you then. Gotta go. Can't miss my flight."

He hung up, and felt the tension in his muscles melt away. According to Mitch, no problems existed. Sam need not concern himself about the military guy or anything else at this stage. He noticed the *Pangaean* line lengthening rapidly and decided to at last join the fray. He disposed of his cup and napkin on the way out.

All efficiency had evaporated with the morning dew. More than a hundred people now waited and it seemed every other passenger required special handling—oversized luggage, mothers with children, a guy in a wheelchair.

At this rate he'd never make his flight. Just perfect.

☯ ☯ ☯

The line snaked forward ever so slowly.

The kid in front of him knocked over mommy's oversized suitcase for the third time. This time it clipped Sam smack on the shin.

"I'm sorry." The frazzled woman with a baby on hip, yanked her little cretin, one of two running around, away from the fallen case and fumbled to right it once again. "Josh. Henry. Please stand still."

Some people just should not be allowed to fly.

Sam stepped aside and let a party of three behind him go ahead, to put some distance between himself and the tiny menace.

What would three more places matter? He had expected to lose his spot in line at least once, if nothing else, to buy a pack of cigarettes he would never smoke. The slow progress negated this.

He looked over at the lines for *Royale Atisari Airlines*, the one place where check in progressed smoothly. Rumour had it the Crown Prince of Atisar was flying home today. He wondered if he'd find the same efficiency tomorrow.

He glanced at his watch, and made a mental note to never fly *Pangaean* again, filing it alongside *Ganda* and *Freedom*.

A sudden flurry of movement at the far end of the terminal, accompanied by a surge in noise level, diverted Sam's attention from *Atisari* to the entrance. He strained to see if said Crown Prince was arriving earlier than expected. But it soon became obvious the commotion belonged to a group of young men swaggering through the crowd with an air of self-importance, dragging an adoring crowd and detachment of paparazzi with them.

He heard shouts of, "Marco! Marco!"

Oh yeah, the Argentine soccer team played here yesterday, and were heading home.

"Are you a football fan?" The man behind him followed his gaze. He spoke with a heavy German accent.

"Uh, yeah. I like the Vikings."

"Ah! An American."

Sam really did not want to talk. He tried ignoring the German to cut off the conversation.

"I've been to America," the man said, extending a big beefy hand. "I am Christian Stein."

He pretty well had to shake the guy's hand. "Sam. Sam Harris." At least to you.

"So, you are from Green Bay?"

Sam looked at the guy like he was nuts. "That would be *The Packers*. *The Vikings* are from Minnesota."

Christian looked chagrined. "It's such a big country. So many places to keep straight. I never went to Minnesota."

Me neither, Sam thought. God, how he wished his cell phone would ring and end this conversation.

"I spent most of my time in Detroit," Stein informed him. Oh great, a regular windbag. "I'm an engineer. I helped bring the new GM plant on line a few years ago. What a shame, how things worked out for them."

"Yeah."

"Now I work here, retooling a heavy manufacturing plant. You have to go where the work is, ja?"

That's why I'm here, Sam mused. "I suppose so."

"But all work and no play... I don't want to be a dull boy. I'm going to Dar es Salaam, in Tanzania. We play there every other year, for the Friendship Cup. They are our Sister City. It's a long flight, but worth it."

"I'm sure it is. Would you excuse me?" Sam pulled out his cell phone.

"I have to check my final connections."

He turned his back to the big German and called the *Pangaean* number. It rang three times and then went into hold hell, just as he hoped it would. Since the German had no idea who was on the other end, he faked a conversation, made disappointed noises, and hung up in a huff. Apparently the ruse was enough—the German made no move to reengage.

An interminable ten minutes passed and the line shuffled forward slowly. Sam was considering what to do to slow things down even more when his cell phone rang.

"Hi, Jeff. How you doing?"

"I'm sorry?"

"Is this Jeff Marks?"

"You must have the wrong number."

"Terribly sorry."

Click.

That was the signal. The Crown Prince had just left the hotel.

Sam waited. One minute later, the PA announcement came.

"Sam Harris, please pick up a red courtesy phone for a message. Sam Harris, please pick up a red courtesy phone for a message."

His cue to get the hell out of line.

"I'll save your spot," the German assured him.

"Thanks." Like hell.

He took the message at a courtesy phone near the restrooms. It was the same voice that had asked for Jeff Marks. "Hi Sam, it's Mitch. Hope I catch you before you board. Our client says everything is go. Have a great flight."

Sam hung up and went into the men's room.

He sat in the far stall, not so much to pretend to shit, as to use his thighs as stabilizers. Even though scanners did not look for bamboo, and detectors wouldn't find curare, it was too dangerous to carry the pen loaded. An over-zealous security agent might ask to inspect it. Or someone might simply ask to borrow it, like that idiot in the café . God knows what might happen.

When Sam emerged, the pen sat in his shirt pocket, loaded with three tiny darts. He needed only one but professionals always have backup.

Now to linger, near the back of the line. Wait for the good prince to walk by.

He hoped to God the annoying German wouldn't look for his return.

There seemed to be some kind of disturbance at the *Pangaean* counter. Two men hidden behind shades and squeezed into tan blazers stood on either side of the line's head. Sam recalled the special forces guy and brief panic fluttered in his gut. It only took a moment for him to realise they were not looking for him. These men were muscle, hired for crowd control.

Something was going down.

A weasel of a man moved behind the counter, accompanied by more tan blazers, going from agent to agent. The women all looked stricken. Sam moseyed over to the end of the line.

"What's going on?" he asked.

A black fellow in a business suit turned toward him, anger clouding his face. "They are closing down!"

Sam assumed he meant the closure of more check-in counters, despite the long wait. But as he watched the weasel work, things began to become clear—he collected employee IDs, one after another.

"All of them?"

"The whole fucking airline!"

"Jesus Christ."

The crowd at the front of the line grew rowdy. Sam's gears turned. On top of the strike at the other end of the terminal, *Pangaean's* demise assured mass pandemonium. He could not ask for better cover. Savvy travellers broke from the line and raced toward other carriers. Sam realised he needed to reposition himself, fast. The Arrivals/Departures display in the centre of the terminal hung in the path to *Royale Atisari Airlines*. He hurried to grab the best possible position beneath it.

A short line started to form at the *Atisari* counter, to the horror of its agents. Options were fading fast, and people were desperate for a flight out, any flight.

"Do you think *Royale Atisari* flies to Dar es Salaam?"

Shit. The big German again.

Sam looked up at the boards. One by one the *Pangaean* flights changed from ON TIME to CANCELLED. Other airlines changed from ON TIME to DELAYED.

"I don't know. I've never flown them," he answered as civilly as could be. "It wouldn't hurt to ask."

"Where are you going?" the German asked. "I can inquire if they go there too."

"Thanks. I'm heading back to the States—New York, Chicago. Anyplace, really."

The German nodded, and trotted off toward the counter. Sam stole glances down the long main hall, looking for any sign of the prince.

A woman at the *Pangaean* counter descended into hysterics, screaming at the weasel, demanding to see the manager. He could not hear what Weasel said, but she exploded, launching herself halfway over the counter, grabbing for his throat. The tan blazers intercepted, and none-too-gently wrestled her away.

"Everyone, please remain calm!" Weasel shouted at the simmering crowd. "We will get things sorted out in due order. Your luggage will find you… eventually."

The crowd surged forward, overwhelming the two henchmen posted to the line. Fists pounded on the counter top. Angry travellers yelled for satisfaction. Sam began to worry—maybe things would get too far out of control. A riot might break out. The Crown Prince might be whisked away to safer environs.

But someone at *Pangaean* was thinking. Food service carts appeared, pushed by grim-faced stewards no longer wearing badges. They passed out soft drinks and sandwiches to appease the masses. No alcohol. Sam had to give it to Weasel; he was mollifying the crowd and disposing of spoilage all at the same time. Very smart move.

"I am sorry, they do not fly to America."

Damn. The German was back again.

"But they fly to Tanzania!"

"That's terrific. So you'll get to see your Friendship match after all."

"Yes!" The German was grinning ear to ear. Sam strained to look around him, toward the entrance.

A small knot of people came through the doors at the far end.

Godammit, the German was going to screw up everything.

"They have a special flight leaving soon, no passengers allowed, but I will be on the flight after. They said they would track down my luggage for me. Wonderful people, the *Atisari*. So… hospitable."

"Maybe you should book your next vacation there," Sam suggested, moving laterally to try and clear some space.

He needed to get rid of the German, like pronto. As inconspicuous as his pen was, he couldn't very well pull it out and point it at the Prince while engaged in one-on-one conversation. The knot of people approaching had all the earmarks of a security detail—four stone-faced burly men wearing dark glasses, arranged in a loose perimeter around a central figure.

Please, dear God, just get rid of the German.

"That is a wonderful idea!" The German clapped him on the back. "I'll go see if they have any brochures."

Sam stared after him in disbelief. He took out his pen and adjusted his stance.

The security detail swung wide, to avoid the commotion at *Pangaean Airlines*. He should have anticipated that. He looked down, as if thinking of flight options, and took a few steps to get realigned. He frowned up at the display screens, but kept the security detail in sight.

Shit.

From the corner of his eye he saw the German break away from the *Atisari* counter and head back his way, all smiles. "Look!"

He held up a set of fanned brochures for Sam's perusal. Small white villages nestled on seaside hillocks. Pristine beaches sported bikini-clad women scampering in the surf.

Sam turned his head. The security detail was close enough for him to finally see the prince, dwarfed by the men surrounding him.

Opportunity was slipping away.

From the corner of his eye Sam caught sight of a redhead skirting the angry mob, sprinting towards them. As the distance closed between, them Sam saw her eyes, cold and determined, staring straight at him, or through him. Sam stiffened. Just then, a child skipped out into the space between them. The redhead deftly side-stepped the little girl, ploughing into the German, sending his pamphlets flying.

"Ach!" The German bent to scoop them up. The woman stumbled, found her feet and kept running, still focused on some point well beyond them. Sam breathed, then steadied himself, took aim and clicked his pen as the Royal party swept by.

The prince brushed at his neck in annoyance.

"I need to get moving, Christian," Sam said, as the German stood. "I think I'll just punt, maybe try the train."

"If you are ever in Germany, please come to Bamberg and look me up." He fished out a business card. "We're a very hospitable people too."

"Thanks, Christian. I'll be sure to do that. If you ever make it to St. Paul, I'm in the book." Sam took the card. "I'd best check on the status of my bags."

Christian looked over to the *Pangaean* counter, doubtful of success on that front. "Good luck, my friend."

Sam threw a final look in the direction of *Royale Atisari*, suppressing a smile. The security detail knelt in a tight knot around the prostrate prince, hovering like mother ducks. Behind the counter, a ticket agent frantically spoke into her phone, as the others stood in stunned silence, routine duties now forgotten. The line of passengers building at *Atisari* surged to the right, pushing against the barriers to see what was happening. Noticing the commotion, some of the sports paparazzi dashed over, drawing more of their own like flies.

What a shame.

Who could have anticipated a heart attack at eleven-years of age?

As Sam lingered, a new altercation at the *Pangaean* counter caught his attention. Weasel traded verbal blows with a belligerent male passenger, his face remaining impassive as the exchange heated up. The heavyset man grew red-faced and then launched himself through the luggage check cut-in, fists flying. The hired muscle, joined by airport security, fought the man to the ground and cuffed him as he lay face down on the filthy floor. They hauled him to his feet, still struggling and shouting as they led him away.

A rather attractive, though mousey, woman in her early fifties, looked on in dismay. One of the officers spoke to her then left her standing there, dazed. She'd have more than luggage to retrieve.

Sam looked back to Weasel, a smug, self-satisfied look spreading across the man's face. Weasel straightened his glasses and collar, swept his gaze over the yammering hoard. He was in charge and damn well loved it.

What a bastard.

Sam fingered his pen and headed for the counter.

He cut in from the left, bypassing the angry mob. A few noticed him and jeered, as if crashing this line mattered one iota. He waved his hand, still holding the pen, to get Weasel's attention. The man finally looked over at him.

"Can you tell me how long it will take to get my luggage forwarded to London?" Never mind he had no luggage, nor was he going to London. He just wanted the man to come closer.

The man looked down his glasses at him. "It will take as long as it takes."

"What the hell kind of answer is that? I want to talk to the manager."

Weasel stepped closer, confident in the muscle backing him up. "The manager is… unavailable. I,"—he put a heavy emphasis on I—"am in charge here, and I am telling you, you will get your luggage in due time."

Weasel turned away to direct the activities of his crew, locking down operations.

"Thanks for nothing," Sam said, clicking the pen. Weasel brushed at the back of his head, and went on barking orders.

That one, Sam figured walking away, was a public service.

Thirteen Feathers

Rob Diaz II

I despised travelling.

This wasn't a simple, everyday dislike of traffic or airport delays, but a real, deep-seated hatred within me; the kind of feeling usually reserved for racists, car alarms at 2.30 in the morning and genetically-modified vegetables. It was a loathing only made worse by someone insisting you had to travel.

"Why do you have to be so damn difficult, Larissa?"

Thomas, my brother-in-law, was the one telling me I had to go. He punched the breakfast table and my latté jumped, splashing over the lip of its cup. Rosandra, my best friend and most trusted psychic, jumped from the seat to my right and went to fetch a towel, an act I'm sure was more about having an excuse to leave than needing to clean up a small dribble of coffee.

"I'm not being difficult. I simply don't want to go to Paris."

"We're going, and that's final!"

I stabbed a knife at my bagel, a little harder than intended, and it slid across the table. Lowering my voice as a counterpunch to his verbal bullying, I said, "If Paris is where we are destined to be... it is where we will go. The signs aren't—"

"Shut up with that nonsense! Martin must be grateful to be free of this crap."

"Thomas Warren! Never bring up my husband when you're angry at—"

"He had enough of your lunacy when he was alive and I bet he's glad to be rid of you in death. No wonder he never 'shows his presence' or whatever these... freaks you hang out with call it." He gestured at Rosandra returning with a dishcloth. "Open your damned eyes, Larissa—they're just trying to get their hands on your money."

He pushed away from the table. More coffee spilled. He stormed to the door, pausing only to instruct me to be ready to leave whenever he returned. The door slammed so hard the dishes on the table rattled. Luckily no more coffee was lost to his tirade.

"You shouldn't let him talk to you like that," Rosandra scolded.

"*Let* him? How can I *stop* him?" I paused and took a deep breath, dabbing at the tears which had started to crowd in the corner of my eye. "They're just words, they have no power." I sniffed and reached for the bagel. "He's telling people he's my boyfriend."

"Oh he is, is he?" Rosandra looked at me with a suspicious squint. "If you were to date him I'd have you com—"

"I'd never date him! Besides... Martin... he's only been gone a few months..." My voice faded as I held back the tears.

"It's been almost a year," Rosandra started, but stopped as she saw my eyes. "How can you go on vacation with Thomas?"

"I have to go! Fate demands it. If—"

"Fate? Are you talking about your recent... indiscretion? Larissa, I'm not sure you're thinking clearly."

"I had a vision."

"The practice of self-reading is anything but accurate and is strongly discouraged in most societies. You can't be objective. There are anecdotes about—"

"—it causing blindness? Old wives tales told to children to scare them and keep them from getting to know their minds." I waved my hand dismissively and tore off a chunk of bagel. "I didn't intend to self-read, it just… happened."

"So tell me about this vision again."

"There was crying. There were feathers. Look, the details don't matter, the tarot cards I pulled right after it confirmed what I had seen: I have to take a trip, whether I want to or not."

"I've told you, Larissa, you can't trust a Tarot set you bought for yourself; it has to be gifted to you."

"Martin was planning to give me one, but then he… well… then he died."

Silence filled the room for a few moments before I continued. "Look, it's fine. My travel agent put together a dozen random trip itineraries for me and I'll stick the ticket to Paris that Thomas forced on me in with them. I'll randomly choose one at the airport. Fate will guide my hand. I just know I have to go, even if it means going with Thomas."

"Before you rush off, humour me."

"I don't want a reading."

"This one's free. Come," Rosandra motioned, moving into my sitting room. I sighed and followed her.

"Let your energy flow to me…" Rosandra's words were like tendrils of incense smoke, snaking upwards through me. Her eyes alternately rolled back into her head or stared somewhere not-quite-in-the-general-vicinity of my left earlobe. "I see… flying. Birds flying past your head. Your soul will soar when you follow where the eagle leads. You seek answers… answers will be found, though you may not like them. Your root chakra is out of balance—you're restless. I sense you must go on a journey, and there are many paths. There is only one True Path for you—choose it wisely. The consequences are great for those around you."

Rosandra's wheezing breath returned to normal as her eyes settled into their usual positions. She stretched. "Well?"

I laughed. "I'm glad I didn't pay for that one. After days of trying to talk me into staying, you just told me to go."

"Who am I to argue with myself?" Her smile was forced and thin over the top of her coffee cup. "Are you ready?"

"I have my thirteen tickets and my passport. My bag is packed. You're here to drive us to the airport."

"My car's a mess!"

"You can drive mine," I said, tossing her the keys. "Oh, I forgot perfume." I hurried to the bedroom and grabbed my favourite Sunflower scent, spraying it on. "Thomas hates this one," I said aloud, adding an extra spritz.

"Be careful with Thomas." I jumped and turned to find Rosandra in the doorway.

"I can handle him," I said, not fully believing myself.

I didn't tell her his aura had shifted. The one time I'd mentioned his lemon-green hues she'd told me it confirmed her suspicions he was a liar and cheat. Now it was black. I knew he was hiding something.

The front door clattered open. Thomas's voice cut through the house: "Hurry up. I'm putting the bags in the car!"

The door slammed. I put on my sky-blue raincoat and looked in the mirror one last time. I was really going. I grabbed the small dreamcatcher Martin and I made together on our honeymoon. Twelve feathers dangled from the round, webbed frame. It was broken and missing its green feather, but I never travelled without it so I hooked it onto my purse as we got into the car.

❂   ❂   ❂

"You stink," Thomas said when we stopped at the first set of lights, putting the window down despite it being bitterly cold.

"I don't care. I hate travelling and I find this scent calming."

The ride was spent mostly in silence, with Rosandra and Thomas ignoring each other in the front seat while I watched the feather dangling from the rear-view mirror and drifted in and out of sleep in the back. As I slept, the dream I had every night consumed me.

I'm standing in the rain, beside Martin's closed casket, searching for any remaining aura, any shred of his presence. Nothing; he isn't there.

The explosion was so complete—virtually nothing remained; the house, our home, reduced to rubble.

At least he didn't feel any pain.

I walk to the birdcage near the casket and release thirteen white doves, just as we did at our wedding. All but one flies away, disappearing into the overcast sky; the last lands on the casket.

A faceless man and woman stand in the distance, watching me. Overhead, twelve jets fly simultaneously, each turning to go a separate direction. The rumble of their engines startles the thirteenth dove and it flies away, a single feather falling onto the casket as the masked couple leave in my car… talking about account numbers.

"What numbers?" I asked, suddenly awake.

Rosandra slammed her foot on the accelerator and I thought I heard something in the trunk.

"Nothing. You were dreaming."

"What was that sound?"

"The luggage must have shifted in the trunk," Thomas said.

When we arrived at the airport, Rosandra stopped at the first available drop-off point. "I'll park and then come wait with you," Rosandra said.

"Oh, that's not necessary," I said.

"Go get in line and be useful," Thomas interrupted. "I'll go with Rosandra and we'll meet you inside."

I got out and took my suitcase from the trunk, leaving Thomas's case and a lumpy duffel bag behind. Inside the door, I closed my eyes and reached into my purse. I grabbed a ticket randomly, hoping Fate would send me to Brussels or even Antarctica. Opening my eyes, I looked at Fate's selection and sighed.

Paris.

France.

The loveliest place I've never wanted to go.

Dutifully, I joined the *Pangaean Airlines* queue and waited for Thomas. He eventually joined me, his presence announced by passengers shouting as he pushed through the line to catch up to me. I stood as far from him as I could while the line crawled forward, limited in my distancing efforts by the retractable ropes. Thomas kept cursing about the woman in front of us dropping pink feathers from her boa; I imagined them swirling around me like little, pink birds.

"Next!"

I hurried to the counter, leaving Thomas behind as he scolded a young boy for bumping into him.

"Flying to Paris today?" Allison, the lady behind the counter, asked me. Her name badge was decorated with the watermarked outline of the *Pangaean Airlines* logo: seven feathers, one for each continent.

"Yes, Fate has me heading that way."

"Are you alone?"

"Very," I sighed.

"She's with me," Thomas said, elbowing me aside, dropping his bag on the belt and slapping his ticket on the counter.

"Packed your own bag? Did you at any time leave the bag unattended?"

"Yes," I answered. "I mean no. I mean… Yes, I packed my own bag; no I didn't leave it unattended."

Thomas gave a curt no. She processed our tickets, handing back our boarding passes as our luggage disappeared.

"Next!"

Thomas struck out for security, moving easily through the crowd. I was struggling to keep up and gave up entirely when my phone signalled the arrival of the Celtic cross I had ordered earlier. I flicked through the images of the Tarot cards, feeling more uncomfortable as each card passed.

"Knight of Cups in the situation position," I mumbled. "Someone is lost and will be found. Justice in the challenges/opportunities position… something will be set right." I flipped through the last few cards and felt my stomach sink.

I ran back to the ticket counter, passing an auburn-haired woman leaving the area. "You need to give me my bag back!"

Allison looked at me with a scowl. "That isn't possible, I'm sorry."

"But—you don't understand," I said, shaking. "Look!" I shoved the phone in front of her face. "The Chariot, reversed!"

She pushed my hand away. "Ma'am, I have people waiting to–"

"But the Chariot reversed means we're not going anywhere! It's entirely my fault. I chose the wrong ticket! Give back my bag and–"

"What are you doing?" Thomas grabbed my arm to pull me away from the counter.

I showed him the shimmering image of the upside-down chariot on my phone.

"Look!"

"Get that away from me! You need to stop wasting your time and money with this New Age nonsense—it's meaningless drivel. Go back to the shrink and let him fix you."

I wrenched my arm free and was knocked away from Thomas by a thick-set man escorting a suited man to the counter. I watched the suit climb onto the baggage scale.

He cleared his throat and announced, "Ladies and gentlemen, your attention please. As the representative of *Rourke International Administrators and Liquidators*, I regret to inform you that as of 6.30am *Pangaean Airlines* was put into involuntary administration. All operations are now suspended. All *Pangaean Airline* flights, including this one, are cancelled. Anyone still wishing to travel today will need to find an alternate airline."

"See?" I said to Thomas and Allison. Turning to the dazed crowd still waiting in line, I shouted, "I'm sorry. It's my fault! I chose the wrong ticket!"

I walked away as the would-be passengers found their voice. Thomas caught up to me, continuing his lecture into the coffee shop. I ignored him. "I'm going to the restroom," I said and walked away.

The ladies room line crawled slower than the check-in line, but I got inside eventually. I saw Rosandra come out of a stall marked with an Out of Order sign. She seemed out of breath. Sweat glistened on her forehead.

"Rosandra? What were you doing in there?"

"I had to pee, what do you think?" She always told me I couldn't trust the aura of another psychic because it was too complex and varied, but her aura, normally the brightest blue, was the darkest black I'd ever seen.

She was lying.

After she left, I leaned against the broken stall until the door pushed open and I quickly went inside. The toilet seat had a plywood cover on it on which the duffel from the trunk sat. A note, in Rosandra's handwriting, was pinned to the bag with a blue feather.

> *I saw a woman in a blue raincoat carry this bag in here. She*
> *had a dreamcatcher on her purse and dropped this feather*
> *from it. Someone called her Larissa.*

I opened the top of the duffel, revealing a young boy. I quickly untied him. He appeared unharmed, but sedated. I looked at the boy, sleeping innocently, and started to cry. Why was Fate doing this? Why was it making me go to Paris with Thomas? Why did it take Martin away? Why was Rosandra hiding children in restroom stalls? Why did things like this happen whenever I travelled? I sobbed like I hadn't in a year, as my loneliness and confusion consumed me.

"Are you alright in there?" Someone rapped on the door.

"Yes, sorry," I said, composing myself. I decided the boy was safer here than he would be if I tried to sneak him out. I removed the note and slipped through the stall door.

I stared at myself in the mirror.

"You okay?" the auburn haired lady from the check-in asked.

I nodded and smiled weakly, glad when she turned and left without asking anything else.

"Have you been crying?" Thomas hissed at me when I found him. I shook my head. "For Christ's sake keep it together!"

"Where's Rosandra? Who is the boy?"

"This is bigger than some stupid boy, Larissa! Don't go screwing it up like you screwed up my brother's life." He grabbed my arm and pulled me away from the crowd as he put his phone to his ear.

"Hello Mackenzie," he said into the phone in a deep voice. "He's safe."

A bored child threw a paper airplane past my head.

"There's a bird!" I shouted.

"Shut up!" Thomas held the phone against his chest as people around us looked for the bird. In the confusion, I pulled my arm from Thomas's grip and ran toward the throng of angry people near the *Pangaean* counter.

I got the attention of a security guard watching the crowd. "The man you're looking for is Thomas Warren. He will be near the coffee shop in ten minutes. The boy is unharmed."

"How do you–" the guard stuttered.

"I'm a psychic," I said, backing away. I spotted the paper airplane and picked it up. The word 'eagle' was handwritten on it inside the outline of a feather. I tossed it back into the air, toward a crowd gathering near the *Royale Atisari* counter and then headed toward the potted palms outside the coffee shop.

Thomas caught up to me quickly, anger burning in his eyes like the end of the filthy cigarettes he usually had clamped between his lips.

"What the hell do you think you're doing? Once we're in Paris you can disappear, but we're all stuck here until the damn airline starts flying again so sit on your fat arse and stop crying. Don't you have a horoscope to check?"

I stared at him, angry words wanting to come out, but I held them as we sat in fuming silence.

Eventually, I saw a man flashing a badge and shoving people aside. As he reached for Thomas, I jumped back, pushing myself as far away as I could. "Mr Warren, I'm arresting you–"

And I turned, relief washing through me as I walked away.

I found an oasis of quiet by a closed check-in counter and took off my raincoat. My phone rang—Miss Rita, my medium.

"You're travelling?" Her voice soft and soothing.

"I… might be. It's become complicated. I want to know if… my family—my dear husband—approves of me travelling."

"Larissa, I'm merely a tool for those who wish to communicate with you. I cannot specifically summon someone who has crossed over. Your husband doesn't show his presence, I know not why. But… your mother is here… showing me… doves."

"My mother isn't dead."

"Another female relative—an aunt, perhaps? She's definitely coming across as motherly. She's showing me… feathers… and a reunion. There's barbecue. She's indicating you like barbecue?"

"I… umm… do like barbecue but what does that–" and my phone died.

Barbecue? I paid her to tell me about a barbecue? Maybe Thomas was right.

I shook my head to clear my thoughts. I hadn't wanted to go to Paris and it was clear Fate shared my disinclination. There was no one for me to be reunited with there. I opened my purse and pulled out another ticket without looking at it.

I left my raincoat behind and waited in line at the first check-in counter I came to. When it was my turn, the clerk looked confused—the ticket I handed her was not for her airline. I apologised and hurried in the direction she indicated.

Arriving at the correct counter, I checked in, giving automatic answers to the clerk's questions as I stared at his badge: twelve feathers arranged in a semicircle, one hanging straight down.

"We'll see if we can redirect your luggage from *Pangaean* for you… once things settle," he said. "Though I can't guarantee anything."

I thanked him, stuffing the boarding pass into my purse and finding my way to the nearest security line. Passengers ahead were buzzing with news of a bomb scare. The chatter only increased when the line stalled and guards shifted places as another passenger was selected for further screening. I reached into my purse and pulled out my paperwork, finding the boarding pass and passport wedged between two Tarot cards. Everything went silent and my heart raced as I stared at the cards. I traced my finger around the image on the first—the eagle at the top right-hand side, the wreath and the ribbon forming a yin-yang symbol—the World Card, the end of a long and difficult journey. I flipped to the second—the Death Card—and stared at the sun glowing behind the skull.

An end and a beginning.

I set my shoes and purse on the belt and walked to the scanner, watching my bare feet take each step and wishing I had gone with purple nail polish instead of red, to better balance my aura. I looked up at the security guard as I stepped through the machine because that's what you're supposed to do and stopped as my eyes met his.

"Martin?"

"Larissa?"

Several timeless seconds passed as I stared at him. Then, together, we said, "Thomas told me you were dead!"

I stood, frozen. "I buried you," I whispered.

"I buried you, too," he replied, just as quietly. "The house was... the explosion was so big. I—"

"I know," I said, not knowing what else to say. For the third time today, tears rolled down my cheeks; this time I didn't try to stop them. We stood in silence as I tried to think of the right thing to say or do.

"Hey, lady," yelled the man behind me. "This ain't some kinda family reunion. Get moving!"

Martin pulled me to the side, breaking our silence as he did. "I'll try to get someone to cover for me. If you've got time before your flight... maybe we can–"

"–talk." I finished his sentence, just like I used to. "I don't have to go anywhere... you know how I–"

"–hate to travel. I'm not meant to be working today. I'm flying to Texas on the 3.13 flight this afternoon. Momma died. The funeral is Wednesday. She always loved when I'd run the grill, so I've got to be there early–"

"–to honour her." I took hold of his hands. "It must have been your mother Miss Rita heard."

"Miss Rita? She still reads for you?"

I laughed and squeezed Martin's hands. "Some things never change.

I'll wait. Right over there."

I sat on the little bench on the secure side of the scanners and put my shoes on, questions racing through my mind. Watching Martin, I noticed a single green feather—the one missing from our dreamcatcher—hanging right next to his ID badge. It was the only answer I needed.

I pulled out my itinerary and looked at it for the first time to see where I was headed. Nonstop to Dallas, departing at 3.13pm, with bus tickets through to Paris, Texas.

Fate was taking me to Paris after all.

One Behind the Eye

Richard Jay Parker

Kathleen ran her finger lightly around the edge of her eye socket as if it would absorb some of the ache inside her head. The pounding was a dependable travelling companion, her journey's soundtrack. A symptom of her past that had become as real a part of her as flesh and bone. Her heart fed the pain with a pump action. Adrenaline was always in plentiful supply before she got on a flight. Now the whole experience had been extended indefinitely.

She needed a painkiller, but when she rummaged in her handbag for the third time no stray pills dutifully materialised from the crevices of leather within. From her uncomfortable seat she looked across the airport concourse to the shops at the other side. Not even the promise of a pharmacy could get Kathleen to budge. She also desperately needed to go to the bathroom to fix her face and pee, but she wasn't going anywhere. *Pangaean Airlines* had cancelled all outgoing flights and while their stock plummeted, the value of their foam and metal benches rocketed briefly.

She tried to distract herself from the familiar spasm by playing the Frankenstein game with the steadily thickening soup of human vexation surrounding her. What gruesome parts were these people made up of?

She scanned the row of people seated opposite her. The faces were united in spleen for the airline but they all looked like respectable, every-day people.

But what traumas had they experienced in their lives? What made them the people they were even if outwardly there was no indication?

When they looked at her sitting quietly—thirty-four years old, red, naturally crimped hair hanging over her face—did they suspect the ugly experiences she was composed of? If they looked closer would they see the real evidence?

She supposed not many people played the game. Yet she felt reassured somebody among the teeming crowd in the airport lounge had probably lived through what she had.

Her gaze returned to the young mother, at the end of the row, as she knew it would. She was curled up on the bench with her two-year-old, both asleep, daughter tucked into the crevice of her neck. They shared the same flushed cheeks and seemed oblivious to the pandemonium around them. Sleep ironed away life's blemishes. For most people anyway.

There was a lot to be said for exhaustion.

Fatigue should be devouring her slowly. Her pounding circulation and the need to take Don's call kept her awake. Spine straight. Overly alert. The phone hot and sweaty in her palm.

How long had it been since he'd returned her call?

There was a flight to DC with Balder Airlines. He said he'd get her on it—sit tight. He said, leave everything to me. She was relieved to have him. Thankful for Don making time for her, going out of his way to get her home.

She looked away from the mother and her child, further along the row. A man in a white linen suit hid behind a newspaper. Next to him an elderly couple sat beatifically among the glum faces. What had they both been through together to make this episode merely an amusing in-convenience? Their years meant haste had become a luxury they couldn't afford. But it also meant their experiences had probably encompassed things all the people bitching around them couldn't begin to conceive of.

People accepted ugliness as an inevitability at different stages of their lives. Who knew how old they'd been when they'd recognised that? Kathleen already implicitly knew it. She had lived less than four decades and already the parts bolted to her weighed her down. Had she shouldered any kind of burden before Sophie?

She fought to keep her thoughts from turning to those endless days spent in the poky waiting room, with the broken television, where hope excised and fear attached. Praying each dialysis would prolong the time she had with Sophie—hoping it could extend their togetherness beyond Sophie's fourth birthday.

Like now, she'd sat in that crowded waiting room and watched the activity of other people. Mothers visiting children, children's impatience at having to visit their parents or brothers and sisters—young minds not understanding their presence in that room or not wanting to think about it.

She'd sat with them but apart. Nobody had room in themselves for more than they were facing. Doctor details and coffee runs were occasionally shared but nobody wanted to be in that hushed society they hadn't chosen to join.

Silent company but familiar faces mirrored her own apprehension. All of them waiting for but dreading their moment with the doctors. Counting the minutes down but not wanting to step out of the security of the waiting room to be told what they didn't want to hear.

Doctor Blythe, Doctor Nese and Doctor Tilly—names her mind had worn threadbare. Sophie's entire future had hinged on the snatched minutes they could spend with her. Their quiet compassion had been overwhelming. Had it been because they'd always suspected the outcome?

It was from through spending time with these doctors who delivered Sophie's progress reports that Kathleen learned to read and anticipate the future from faces.

Composed diplomacy.

Contained optimism when there was a scrap of something positive to offer.

The fatigue of hope draining through an hourglass.

She'd known deep down once all those faces passed her by, she would be all alone.

Sophie and Kathleen never talked about the treatment. Sophie knew she was very ill but never asked what would happen if she didn't get better. Kathleen wondered if Sophie just assumed the treatment would make her well again—like medicine for a cough.

When it happened it was too late for Kathleen to give Sophie the talk she'd rehearsed but hoped never to repeat. She'd assumed they had still more shuttling to do between home and the hospital.

Returning home alone that first, numb evening, was nearly too much for Kathleen to take. Sophie's lilac sneakers lay at the bottom of the stairs where she'd kicked them off to put on her slippers. Her cereal bowl on the kitchen counter sat with dregs of milk and cornflakes. Her indentation left in the cushion of the couch. The house still smelled of her.

Kathleen realised how much of her life was saturated with love for her daughter and watched the house become the dried out husk of their brief life together. She put it up for sale. Watched family after family become brief visitors to her grief. She waited for one of them to make an offer. She'd take anything. She no longer cared.

The waiting ate away at her. She felt like a trespasser in her own home. Estranged from a family that had adopted an 'out of sight, out of mind' attitude when she'd emigrated from the UK, she'd been totally alone. In her sleep she spoke to the doctors, waking and expecting to be back in the cramped room with the broken TV. She would have given anything to be back there and still have the prospect of seeing Sophie connected to the machine.

When her own illness was diagnosed she'd been relieved. Relieved she wouldn't have to face all those years that wound ahead of her. But she'd beaten the cancer without trying, discharged three days after surgery, returning home in bewilderment. Her new family of doctors assured her she would lead a normal life again.

Nightmares bled from night into day and everything should have ended there. Single mother becoming single again. Experiences soldered to her, leaving her feeling like the Bride of Frankenstein. And then Don came into her life.

Don understood. He touched her and made her realise she hadn't been touched for so long. He made her remember herself. He made her feel unique—needed again. And when she let his life fill the emptiness of hers, she wanted what he wanted.

❧   ❧   ❧

The bench area directly behind the slumbering mother and daughter yanked Kathleen from the past. A woman was having a fit. A group of would-be passengers stood around her looking concerned, but Kathleen could see they just welcomed some excitement during the long wait. Then a man appeared with a bag. Moments later the incident was over and people dispersed. But the panic lingered with Kathleen.

It's over, she told herself but she kept looking at the woman as if it would happen again.

The couple were chatting normally now. The woman stifled a laugh with her palm. Kathleen felt like the joke was on her more than anyone else.

This was beyond how uptight she normally felt before a flight. A desperate need to go to the bathroom seized her. Fix her face. Empty her aching bladder. And the people opposite had been staring at her too long.

But now she couldn't rise.

A panic attack soaked through her back.

And her head...

She had to get painkillers—her blood felt like iron filings forcing through her temples.

The world dipped away as Kathleen stood up, as though she'd downed several bottles of wine. Kathleen had emptied plenty in her time but the dry sickness accompanying this was unlike any nausea she'd experienced before.

The palm of her hand prickled. She turned it over and saw something that looked like a baby rodent cradled there—hairless and translucent, the blue veins of its bloated body visible through paper-thin skin. It panted. The tiny body pulsating against her clammy skin. Kathleen flicked it away, the body landing with a clatter on the dirty floor. A hundred heads

105

turned in its direction.

When she looked down, her phone lay several feet away, spinning in small vibrating circles where it had landed.

Kathleen scooped it up.

It was still ringing.

"I've got you on the next flight to Washington. Everything OK?" But there wasn't a hint of concern for her in Don's voice.

"No. Everything's not OK." She looked at the people eyeing her and suddenly had no sense of how loud she was talking. She tried whispering. "I've got to leave."

"What are you talking about? Is someone watching you?"

"No." She realised she'd shouted it because of the sensation in her eardrums distorting her own sense of volume control.

"Kath, what the fuck? Have you been drinking?"

"I… must… leave." She made a concerted effort to dangle each word directly into the phone. "Now."

"And go where?"

He was right. Where could she go? She'd booked out of the hotel. Her luggage had been checked in.

"I don't feel so good."

She reached out to hold onto the top edge of the seat she'd been sitting on.

"Take a Valium and keep your eye on the screens. They're adding another flight to DC and as soon as they do you're booked on it. I'm going to wait for you this end."

She didn't hear him ring off but knew he had. She squinted at the pharmacy in the shopping courtyard and strode towards it, tensing the muscles in her legs and trying to walk decisively through the crowd. The neon got closer and as shoulder bones slammed hers, she wasn't oblivious to the objections, just unsure of which direction they were coming from, the sounds swirling around her like a palpable fug. She felt disorientated, not by trying to focus on her trajectory but by trying to remember why she was making the journey. The reason kept sliding off the back of her brain even though her bladder felt like it was about to rupture.

By the time she reached the edge of the concourse and leant against the wall, she couldn't remember why she had left her seat. She focused on the ladies bathroom door and the long line of passengers waiting to use it. For a moment her bladder forced itself into her consciousness and she thought maybe she could sneak into a staff toilet to relieve the pain. As she stepped away from the wall she was lost in confusion again.

Her body yearned for some sort of release but different signals cancelled each other out. Her head throbbed and she felt giddy. Was she forgetting to breathe or had the syrupy atmosphere started to drown her? She gulped in air as if it would taste of the answer and felt her tongue grazing the side of her mouth. She was parched. Liquid in before liquid out.

She headed into the sports bar but the crowd between her and the bar was too daunting. She saw a seat nearby and felt the need to sit. Somebody objected. There had been a coat on the back of it. It was OK. It was her coat. She would send Don to the bar to get her a glass of water. She would just sit and wait for him.

"Excuse me." It was a woman's voice, patience barely in check. "Can I help you?"

Kathleen squinted about the room and locked on the source. She was sure the voice had come from the news reporter staring down at her from the plasma screen mounted on the wall. He was a male reporter standing in front of an airport terminal. Her terminal? Male reporter with a woman's voice. That convinced Kathleen she had to be on her guard.

She challenged the presenter. "Have you seen Don?"

"Excuse me. Sorry. We've already taken this table." It was a male voice now, more polite than the female's.

She'd been right to challenge the presenter. Now he'd dispensed with his female subterfuge.

A movement at the corner of her eye, she shifted her attention.

She looked at the small, frosted square window set into the wall beside her. Something skittered behind it—something trying to fly against it. It looked like a moth, eyes glinting silver. But its body seemed to be covered in thick, dark fur. It started banging against the window.

Harder, so she could hear each impact.

Harder, until it started leaving fragments of itself with each strike, white and liver-red rivulets running down the pane.

Soon its broken body could barely lift its own weight, one wing hanging limply while the other tried to frantically compensate. She could hear it—an almost imperceptible squeal. She couldn't allow it to harm itself further. She pushed on the window and it hinged open. Sophie was looking at her from the other side, features motionless, smiling with her mouth but not her eyes.

"They're hurting me." Her white lips remained tightened by the grin.

She quickly closed the window again.

Sophie was dead.

Sophie couldn't feel pain anymore.

Something repulsive was happening to her and being in this bar was a bad idea. She had to get back to where she had been. Where things had been normal. Back to the bench.

She got off the chair and apologised. She wasn't sure for what but when she looked back at the table she saw it wasn't near a wall. There was no small window and those sitting round it were looking at her through a spectrum of confusion.

"Bitch is stoned," she thought the news presenter said.

She strode back towards the bench, people looming in and out of view, a carnival of alarmed faces floating by her.

Where had she put the phone?

Had she just left it at the table?

It was too late.

She couldn't go back.

Not even to see her daughter.

When she got back to the bench she looked for her seat but the row was full and nobody was familiar. No sleeping mother and child, no elderly couple, no couple playing a joke on her. She was in the wrong place. She looked around frantically and noticed the fire extinguisher on the support pillar crawling up the wall. All thoughts of finding her seat were momentarily forgotten as she watched its canister bending slowly inwards like a caterpillar and straightening as it slid slowly upwards. Its motion washed her with waves of nausea but she walked to it and put her hand against the space above it. Moments later the plastic nozzle was pressing against her wrist as it tried to continue on its course.

She stepped back from it slowly, not wanting to take her eyes from its movement lest it do something erratic when she turned her back. One step at a time until eventually she was absorbed by the crowd. The extinguisher disappeared from view. She turned and searched for her waiting area. Squinting hard at the faces on the other benches, she saw the legs of the child on a mother's lap. She strode toward them but her heels kept her from moving fast enough. She removed them and left them behind. When she reached them, Kathleen expected to see her empty chair. But somebody was sitting in it—a goth-girl with face jewellery. Molten indignation erupted inside Kathleen.

She didn't know what she said to the girl, the only audible sound the hum of her own voice boiling inside her skull. The girl got up and moved away, stumbling on the bag she wasn't fast enough to pick up. Kathleen sat down, expecting to feel safe again but didn't. Her accelerated circulation made the tips of her fingers throb. She looked at the sleeping mother and child and tried to use them as an anchor to stabilise her surroundings.

The mother woke up and looked at her. Kathleen didn't know how long she stared at her but it eventually seemed to anger the young woman. She couldn't understand what the mother was saying but it was clear she didn't like being looked at.

Kathleen didn't want to look away.

Couldn't.

An ugliness animated the mother's features in a way Kathleen hadn't suspected when she'd studied her peaceful face earlier. The malignant scowl was suddenly shared by a procession of different faces inhabiting the middle of her shoulders—Doctor Tilly's, Doctor Blythe's... Sophie. They were all repulsed by Kathleen, but she couldn't look away from the fierce reproach in their eyes. Then it was the mother's again, her mouth chewing words like meat.

Her daughter was awake now.

Crying.

The mother stood up.

Kathleen wanted to explain she would lose her grip if she looked away, but the words froze inside her. The mother moved, stepping closer.

Can't look away.

Don't look away.

Alcohol, hot and bitter on the mother's breath assaulted Kathleen as the woman shouted at her, so close spittle lashed at her burning cheeks. She kept staring, unable to tear her eyes away. Then the mother exploded, her hand smashing into Kathleen's face.

The strike was hard and momentarily the whole scene righted itself as pain kicked in and she listened to the impact fizz in her right ear. She found herself on her feet and saw the look of horror in the mother's face. The little girl screamed and, looking down, Kathleen knew why.

Half of Kathleen's face lay on the floor.

It was no hallucination.

The glass eye stared up at her from the piece of plastic moulded to reconstruct her face after cancer had eaten into her cheek and eye socket. She used make-up on the insert and the magnets clipped it so snugly into place it was scarcely visible. The overhang of hair helped to mask it—the only give away, the unblinking fake eye. The face piece covered the hole in her face, the hollow Don used for smuggling.

A small plastic bag fell from the recess of her eye socket onto the floor. The white powder scattered around her stockinged feet.

The bag had been leaking inside her skull.

The canvas of her reality folded inward again and she sank to her knees, clinging to the rock-face of the floor as people made high-pitched noises and their shoes moved the sound around her in circles.

Don would have some time to wait.

Chase the Day

Jason Coggins

From the sliding doors to the baggage claim belt, to the taxi drop-off point and the check-in zone, the floor of Terminal One was littered with the debris of travel interrupted. Stranded passengers erected suitcase forts and sleeping bag moats around tiny patches of floor claimed as their own. A young, pale-skinned woman picked her way through the rubble. A leather satchel swung low around her black army boots. Around her neck a Polaroid camera leapt and recoiled with each step. It was testament to her single-mindedness that these two disparate bouncing objects did not entangle—or strangle—her.

Quiche had a plan and no one said anything about it being practical.

Nearly two hundred souls, smelling of armpits, were marooned across the concourse. It helped to pretend these strangers were camping out in her backyard. But that game had brought her no closer to achieving her quest. This time, as she crossed the terminal floor she decided a more intimate tactic was needed. Quiche looked at the clutter of people's lives as though washed up with the tide, and in excruciating slow motion renewed her journey. Her first footfall brought the toe of her boot in contact with the corner of a sleeping bag. The next step cheekily pushed an upturned novel a whole centimetre toward its owner. It took her triple the time to cross the concourse playing this game of transparent stranger. By the time she reached the other side she was trembling. Her sneaky footsteps had brought her into contact with more people than she had talked to in her entire life. She collapsed against a wall and clutched her chest, breathless and guilty. She would not be playing transparent strangers again.

"Are you okay?"

Quiche turned to find herself confronted by the knowing eyes of child—large, dark and receptive like radar dishes.

She had meticulously avoided any conversation since arriving at the airport. Her first instinct was to pretend she had not heard the dusty skinned boy. Her fingers darted to her satchel, the weight a reassuring alibi. She would feign being busy. Yes, there was something very important deep within her satchel demanding her full attention. When she looked up next the boy would be all gone away.

"You're funny," he said, after a minute or so.

This was not good. A fat finger of words jabbing her in the face. Quiche peeled her fringe from her eyes, looking around for an escape route. Off to her right a refugee camp formed around a row of vending machines. She would make a dash for it. If the boy followed, she would either lose him in the crowd, or the vending machines would transfix his boyish nature with their chocolatey promise.

She buckled shut the satchel's flap. It was now or never. She shot one furtive, gazelle-like glance over her shoulder. In that fleeting instance the boy's knowing eyes pierced deep into her awareness and she believed those rich, wide eyes were capable of taking in everything up to and including radio waves.

She thrust her hand into her cardigan and produced a Polaroid picture. It was faded and creased. Cracks ran across its surface.

"Him?" she said, proffering the photograph to the boy. He took the photograph and studied it. Within its yellowing frame, a moustached gentleman stared back from an airport in the 1970s. He wore a white linen suit, trousers flared in the style of day. He also wore a long trench coat in the same colour. His moustache was neatly groomed and long hair fell gracefully behind his ears. At his side a small child was thumbing her nose at the camera.

"Who is he?" the boy asked.

Quiche shrugged, assuming the photo said all that needed to be said about her quest.

"Ahmed!"

The boy had little time to respond before mother came into view. A shimmering cobalt burqha enveloped her from top to toe, her eyes obscured by a rectangle of black mesh. Quiche was immediately mesmerised by the shimmying fabric and the way it hid all trace of the person inside. Before this woman and her veil there could be no cross talk, no facial tics or arbitrary nuances of behaviour to confound her brain. At last, someone she could turn to for help. The woman said something in her language to the boy. He replied and gestured towards Quiche, who grabbed a smile from the ether and painted it onto her face.

The woman in the veil took the photo from her son's hand and studied it. When she spoke next he translated: "She says an airport is a place somewhere between heaven and earth. A place where answers wait for questions and their asking."

With that the woman pointed out across the concourse. On a bench next to a napping mother and child a pair of neat, white linen trousers crossed and uncrossed. The small child shifted in its mother's lap so its face nestled in the nook of the mother's arm. They were as oblivious of Quiche as to the woman with the cold expressionless face glaring with lunatic intent toward them.

Quiche had eyes only for the newspaper suspended before the trouser owner's face.

The photo was pressed back into Quiche's hand and the boy was led away.

"Bye bye," he chirruped.

Quiche did not reply. The trousers jutting out from beneath that newspaper had her a-tremble. Quiche weighed up the number of people in the world sanguine enough to wear white linen from top to toe. Surely outside a Mark Twain look-a-like jamboree, very few indeed. Another page turned and the newspaper briefly sank, giving a tantalising glimpse of straw-coloured hair. She looked at the crinkled photo in her hand and another tick was placed against the checklist in her head. The trembling grew. Her spare hand grabbed the wrist of the hand holding the photo, but all that did was send the tremors down her legs into her feet. She began to dance an excited little jig.

The next ten minutes passed as she willed her target to lower the newspaper and reveal his identity to her. The booming loudspeaker announcements faded into white noise, the clamour of hundreds of stranded passengers forgotten. The obstructive rectangle of the broadsheet collapsed in on itself. It was as if Quiche's senses plummeted, screeching down a tunnel, at the end of which was a face.

The man from the 1970's! Still immaculate in a white linen suit and trench coat. With that, Quiche turned and rushed off to the toilets.

Suspicious glances and desperate lunges for the hand drier moved Quiche around the lavatory like a chess piece. When at last the cubicle she had been waiting for vacated, she sprang into it without a backward glance and slammed the door shut. The quest—her plan—all depended on the stashed bag she had secreted behind the cistern yesterday.

Five minutes later her cubicle door flew open. The eyes of a woman shaving her legs in the sink fell in baffled appraisal on Quiche—a pale young woman lost deep within the bowels of a dark blue overcoat, army boots unseen beneath the hem. The words *Pangaean Airline Security* emblazoned on the broad lapel. She waddled out to catch a glimpse of herself in a mirror. The reflection staring back at her was of a head several sizes too small to be wearing a man's coat. Regardless, she thrust her arms forward so they popped magically out from inside the dark tunnels of the sleeves.

She retrieved a gold tube from the satchel, uncapped it and theatrically twisted the lipstick upwards, drawing it back and forth over her lips with all the care of an infant wielding a wax crayon. When done, she looked into the mirror, pleased with the indiscreet red pout that blew a kiss back at her.

Now Quiche was ready to put this plan to bed.

Back on the concourse the seat was empty and all manner of shouty chaos was going on. But more important for Quiche, the man from the photograph was gone! The panic inside her head was almost musical; a discordant crescendo which did not relent. The orchestra spluttered out when she glimpsed the familiar white linen of her target. He was inside *The Leg Room* perched on a stool rolling a long glass absently between his fingers.

Quiche took two long, deep breaths, licked her lips and pressed onward. Inside the bar, the staff looked as empty as the bottles racked up behind them. Both stock and good will were running short in the face of the *Pangaean* crisis—service was reduced to minimal robotic interactions— the snatching of cash transmuting into the slapping down of liquor.

"May I take this seat?" Quiche said to the white shoulders at the bar. The long trench coat trailed down his back and over the legs of the stool. This gave the impression the man was suspended mid-air, propped up on the bar by nothing more than his elbows. He continued rolling the gin and tonic between his fingers. There was a distance to his stare Quiche was reluctant to interrupt. She took the seat. The bar man looked at her with blood shot eyes.

"One of those," she said gesturing at the man's drink. "But hold the gin."

"A tonic?" the bar man replied.

"And keep 'em coming," she said in her most worldly voice.

The man from the photograph was noting her from the corner of his eyes.

"Askance," she said.

"Pardon me?"

"You were looking at me askance."

"So I was," the man chuckled. "Please, forgive me. I did not mean to be rude." He leaned back on his stool to appraise her. "But when I worked for *Pangaean*, the staff was a tad better tailored than you."

Quiche reached for the top button of the overcoat. Self-conscious-ly—but with the best haughty air she could muster—she did it up. Any more comments like that one and her resolve would dissolve completely. She needed him to be nice like she remembered. Before returning to his drink, the man from the photograph checked his watch and glanced up at the departure board. Quiche was now sweating and regretting doing up the button. The coarse material of the coat's collar rubbed against her neck and ears. She had to jut her chin forward just to prevent her head being swallowed by the cavernous garment. Fighting the urge to make like a tortoise and retract her head into its shell, she pushed the faded photograph across the bar top.

The man gave her the askance look again before picking it up. Quiche studied his face as he took another drink. He was a cool customer all right.

Please be nice. Please be nice, she thought.

"You were a precocious little girl," he said. "Your friend though, he should have known better." He returned the photograph to the bar, care-fully avoiding the wet circle marks left by his drink.

It was the opening she needed. She dove into her satchel, not failing to notice the next swig he took from his drink was a big one. Her fingers found the *National Geographic* magazine within and produced it like a magician pulling a rabbit from a hat. The man downed his drink. The ice cubes clinking loudly as he placed the empty glass down on the bar. She whipped open the magazine to a page book marked with a magpie's feather. It was a large, glossy image marked 1984: three men posed on an orange ziggurat in a South American jungle. Two of them wore the obligatory khaki of explorers, the other conspicuous in white linen shirt and shorts.

Her companion stood up. "Well good luck with your journey," he said. "Time nor tide and all that."

Quiche's hands darted in and out of the satchel again, pressing a 1963 copy of Time magazine to her chest as she began to recite from memory:

"After the Second World War, Eagle Ridgeline emerged as one of the United Kingdom's most important aviation concerns. Claude Mason, aviation engineer turned business mogul, steered the company into civil aviation and soon with a fleet of British-built short and medium-haul airliners, Eagle Ridgeline operated flights ranging across continental Europe."

Quiche intoned the words of "King of the Eagles. Claude Mason: a profile" like a small child presenting a science project to class. "In 1954, Eagle Ridgeline merged with Emerald Sky and formed the new long-haul carrier christened *Pangaean Airlines*. The clarity of Mason's aviation and business acuity will be sorely missed when he retires at the end of the month."

With that she thrust the copy of Time forward, the profile and portrait opening at a well dog-eared page, impossible for the man to escape.

"Remind you of anyone?" she added with a brave squeak.

The sepia photograph on the page depicted a pensive looking Mason, pipe in hand and a patrician's kindly smile flashing for the camera. Fifty years lay between the photo and the man standing in *The Leg Room*. Barely a hair or wrinkle changed between the two.

"I never liked that pipe. Damnable social convention," he muttered. He sat back on the stool and gestured to the barman to bring two more gin and tonics. Quiche collected the *National Geographic* and Polaroid from the counter and returned them along with the other magazine to her satchel. She looked up, with an expression that took pleased and cranked it up to ridiculous.

The two drinks arrived and Mason slid one to Quiche. "Blue blazes! All these decades avoiding journalists and it's a slip of a girl who sniffs me out."

She knew now was the time to find the voice that had deserted her for most of her life, but when she spoke it came out thin as a mouse's whisker: "I was seven when they took that Polaroid of us. Mum flew me off to my grandparents at any chance she could." Quiche took a sip from the G&T in the hope it would give her more courage. "I always flew with *Pangaean* as a 'U.M.'"

"An unaccompanied minor," the ageless aviator said into his drink. "If memory serves me correctly, they scolded us for building suitcase igloos."

Quiche hiccupped on the drink. All her life he had been a face in a gallery of kind faces kept in her head. It was such a small gallery. She hiccupped again. She felt the colour rising in her cheeks clashing with her deliberately indiscreet lipstick. She felt such a fool; sat lost in the gargantuan, misappropriated overcoat. She wanted to tell him how much the suitcase igloos had meant to her. How she had revisited the gallery in her head often... until one day in her uneventful late twenties she chanced upon a certain *National Geographic* magazine lying open in a dentist's waiting room.

But the hiccups and the embarrassment prevented her. Her brain tried to unknot her tongue—ordering it to give words to the euphoria that had gripped her when she tracked down *Pangaean's* first advertisements. His features as fresh and kindly in those 1950's ads as they were that day in the 1970s when he befriended a lonely, little girl who often found herself envying orphans.

"I suppose you are wondering how I do it?" he said. She flushed, and succeeded in nodding and shaking her head at the same time. "Call it the pioneer spirit. Back when I started, no one took air travel for granted. Least of all us aviators. We pushed our jets and ourselves to the limits, but in doing so we shrunk the globe and squeezed all the adventure out of it."

He grimaced at the memory and pinned a folded dollar bill between his glass and place mat. "The pioneer spirit was never going to let me play at tycoon much longer than I did. It told me there was one last adventure waiting for me up above the clouds. 'Fly west', it said. 'Fly west'. So I did and have been doing so ever since."

This time he was up from his stool faster than Quiche's eyes could follow. "So remember, miss. Chase the day and you will never grow old." He went to doff a hat that was not there. "Old habits," he chuckled, turned and left the bar.

No, this was not how it was meant to play out!

Quiche fought back the buzzing building in her ears. She gulped back the hiccups and with the taste of acid in her mouth rushed out of the bar. Back in the chaos of the terminal it was all unravelling… but she had one outside bet left.

Stick to the plan, she told herself. Trust in the plan.

Mason stood off to one side studying the departures board. The clang of public address announcements and the bustle of the crowd jostled the words she had prepared. Her feet lost beneath the overcoat as she waddled up to his side. To speak she had to poke her neck upright so her mouth emerged from the collar.

"Is it lonely?" she said tugging on the sleeve of his trench coat.

He turned and with relief she noted his features were still full of warmth for her.

He hesitated before he replied. "It would probably be the most damnably lonely thing in the world if I didn't fly *Pangaean*. Before my 'disappearance' I set up the Legacy Ticket so I could fly business class in perpetuity. The air crews change but there is always a familiar face or two to keep me sane."

Suddenly a weight bore down on her shoulder. A hand spun her around and she was staring face-to-face with an airport security man. He wore the scowl of security personnel the world over—angry little Lego man eyes drilling into her with a fury that drove all possibility of saying something into her boots.

"Impersonating an airport security officer is a statutory offence," he prodded the *Pangaean* insignia on the over coat's lapel. "I'm going to have to ask you to come with me."

"I wouldn't do that if I were you, my good fellow," Mason interjected. "If it is *Pangaean* identification you require then you should feast your eyes on this." He flipped open his wallet and inside a gold ID card shone out. The writing and details on the Legacy Ticket blurred beneath the bright golden glow it gave off, but from the photo and emblem there was no denying it was *Pangaean* in origin… and also belonged to someone much more connected than a security grunt.

"It's all right," Quiche's small voice came from within the overcoat. "He can have his coat back." Before Mason or the security guy could protest she slithered out of it, standing before them—and the whole terminal—in nothing more than her skin, bra and French knickers.

"Stars and garters!" Mason exclaimed, as he whipped off his own trench coat and covered up the girl's modesty.

"Bloody hell, I'm out of here." The security guard had wits enough to appreciate the situation had spiralled out of control. He slipped through the gathering, gawping crowd.

"Thank you," Quiche said, considering how far she had travelled since daring transparent strangers.

"Think nothing of it." It was Mason's turn to be embarrassed. He glanced up at the departures board. "Look, please keep the coat until you reclaim your baggage. I've got to catch my flight and for the first time in forever I'm flying with someone other than *Pangaean*."

"Oh, I am so sorry." She consciously tried to paint 'mortified' on the white board of her face and set about emptying the pockets of the trench coat. A note book, a spare tie, a set of playing cards: she handed them to him one by one. As he glanced up again at the departures board she found the item she had been hoping for all along. A single ticket.

"Thank you," he said absently as he received the ticket from her grasp. "And sorry, I simply must dash." With that he was clipping off across the concourse.

She waited for his white suit to clear customs and disappear into the departure lounge before she turned and hurtled off towards the check-in counter for *Balder Airways*.

Yes, I understand this is first class check-in.

Yes, you accept cash?

No, I only have my satchel and passport.

No, I do not have any special dietary requirements.

Yes, I must have a window seat.

No, that seat right there.

West, thank you very much.

No, just west.

Quiche boarded Flight Q566, breathless, with five minutes to spare.

Somewhere to Pray (Kurush)

Benjamin Solah

It's 7.15am. My heart's racing. I'm not sure how I've made it this far.

I clutch my *Pangaean* boarding pass. The Dubai flight boards at 7.45 and I'm pretty sure I checked in with my eyes closed. Focus Kurush, I tell myself. Half an hour. Escape is so close, just one last hurdle.

Head down, I avoid looking at anyone. Breathe in. Breathe out. One foot in front of the other. This is my mantra. I thought I'd be safe on an early morning flight. Fewer bodies crowding in, pushing. There's more people here than I expected.

Kurush, I tell myself, this is a means to an end. It will be okay. All these people… you don't have to remember. It is different. You don't need to be swallowed by fear.

I walk at my own pace, taking my time. People don't understand. I can hear what they're saying about me, bumping and jostling past. I have different things to consider when flying. It isn't easy for me. Not like them. And the more people, the less it helps.

This is the last time I will feel like this. No more fear. No more running. This is what it means to turn my back on the country I have called home all my life.

I hesitate as the sliding glass door nears. The crowd slows; the line grows, each waiting their turn to enter. On the other side sits security and customs. Suits and uniforms. Scrutiny. Things beeping constantly. A human supermarket checkout.

I stop. My legs paralyse, ignoring my mind forcing them onwards. I think of my brother Mihr and I'm terrified of the price check they'll call on me. I look down at my boarding pass.

Kurush al-Zaidi.

"Our names might as well be highlighted red on boarding passes," my brother Mihr said once. "That's how they look at it."

But our father disagreed.

"Your tongue is like a horse—if you take care of it, it takes care of you; if you treat it badly, it treats you badly."

Our father, proud of the European Union, assured us our rights were protected. After all, Mihr and I were born here.

"It's like a bad lottery for Muslims," Mihr told me down the crackling line after they arrested him. "It doesn't matter what country's passport you travel on."

I didn't believe Mihr brought it on himself. His outspoken nature winning him the 'no-fly jackpot'?

Mihr was flying to the US, I tell myself. You're not. They'll allow you to leave.

But I don't know...

My legs turn anyway, steering me from the glass door to safety.

Time is ticking.

My window of escape narrows.

Don't blow this, Kurush. There is no money for another ticket. This is what I tell myself over and over, shuffling up and down, crisscrossing no man's land in slow-motion.

Time drains away.

Whenever someone meets my eyes, I stop and stare out the window, check my watch or boarding pass. Eventually I rest against a wall, try to look casual, but one knee jerks and dances on its own, allowing the rest of my body some normality.

My eyes pan across the concourse. The place is filling with people.

I look beyond them, study the plants, the vending machines, the walls. I catch dark eyes mirroring mine. They stare through a gap in text on a glossy poster.

IF YOU SEE SOMETHING, SAY SOMETHING.

An older woman, walking by, spots the same poster. She looks to me, smiling, as if to say she's not scared. Her crinkled brow a contradiction. I want to tell her I'm just as scared. I'm not guilty of anything except trusting this was my home.

I want the wall to absorb me, to disappear.

I clutch my beard. Wish I'd shaved it off and in the next moment I'm staring up at the sky apologising.

My brief prayer startles the woman and she scuttles past in her walking frame. I try to smile, reassure her, but she's gone and doesn't dare turn back.

I look at my watch. 7.35.

I have no idea how long it takes to move through security and customs.

Pull yourself together, Kurush, I tell myself. Be brave. Close your mind, not your eyes, and just walk through. It's like ripping off a Band-Aid. Do it quickly.

The hand on my watch jerks to 7.37 and I go.

My body feels detached, in the control of someone else. I look at the ground and focus on my feet. Worn shoes on polished tiles. It occurs to me again how weird walking is; signals from your brain moving your legs. I'm awed by things like this.

It takes me a few seconds to realise I should be looking up. Listening. All around passengers stare up into nothing, listening hard. There's a collective gasp. What have I missed?

En masse they turn and look at the departures screens. My eyes follow.

Los Angeles (Etruscan)—BOARDING NOW.
Buenos Aires (Freedom)—DELAYED
Paris (Pangaean)—CANCELLED.
Belgium (Ganda)—DELAYED.

123

I feel sick as the board updates in real time. Little bubbles popping in my gut.

Toronto (Pangaean)—CANCELLED.

Another pop.

I see cobalt-blue clad Pangaean staff bolt past me. My jaw hangs open. The cancellations continue down the length of the screen.

Finally…

Dubai (Pangaean)—CANCELLED.

The damp slip of paper in my hand is worthless. I'm back to square one; I don't have time to save again. The same mute expression is reflected in every face I look to. Jaws clench. Fists ball. Boarding passes fall to the ground in pieces.

People break from the line at the sliding glass door. Within minutes others emerge in the wrong direction escorted by security.

I pulled the Band-Aid but had to stop. Now the hairs sting, half pulled. I can't keep pulling and there's no way to press it back down. I'm caught… just when I thought I'd finally escaped.

❧ ❧ ❧

Time festers. My only friend is the vending machine; the vibrations against my arm almost soothing in this hidden corner of no man's land where I huddle.

I struggle to swallow the saliva accumulating in my mouth. It is worse than peak hour. All these people have nowhere to go. The thought of thousands more passengers backing up from cancellations makes me sweat. My chest heaves.

Why the cancellations?

I can't get a grip on what's going on. The droning announcements don't reach into this little crevice. Out on the concourse they sound too much like disembodied voices booming through megaphones. The mass of angry people keeps me from the airline desk.

So I wait; watch people who don't see me. Better to imagine their lives than remember my own.

Across the gorge of luggage, a three-year-old pulls out of her father's grasp and tries to climb onto his shoulders, her legs kicking furiously to get a hold. He pulls her down onto the empty chair between him and a boy playing a hand-held computer game and returns to his newspaper, ignoring her cries for attention.

But she's persistent and soon atop his shoulders. I watch her eager eyes take in everything the world offers—the scores of passengers piled on top of each other—reading, sobbing, sleeping, talking into phones, arguing among themselves, staring off into space. I think she wonders who each person is, wanting to ask them what they're doing here, happy to breach that barrier between strangers she hasn't learnt yet.

I'm staring at her and I force myself to glance away, fighting my fascination. People don't take kindly to men's interest in children.

When I look back, her overactive legs, swinging back and forth, freeze. Her eyes lock with mine.

I chance a smile, giving her the attention she craves, in a crowded place where everyone is turning inwards. The fluttering in my stomach reminds me I should look away, eyes always find me.

I try to look calm, but she notices my erratic eyes skipping between hers and those around me. Her lip trembles. Can she sense what I'm feeling? She reaches her hand out, ignoring the distance. It's too much. I look away.

"Case, whattaya doing?" her brother asks. "Dad, that weird man's looking at us." I push myself into the carpet and clutch my backpack as the father looks up and over to me, the man with the beard cowering by the snack machine.

"Shhh, Tom," he scolds, but I see his eyebrows pinch. He plucks his daughter from his shoulders and straps her into his lap with one arm, turned away from me, despite her protests demanding she see the world as she wants.

"Sit still, Casey."

She refuses, squirming and twisting. Her arms stretch to me one last time. I look away, staring at the stray strands of hair on the ground beneath my feet.

Everyone is looking now, eyes darting away as soon as I catch them. Unseen stares burn invisible holes in me.

Voices amplify and surround me, many voices merging into one.

"Come on Muhammed, have a drink."

I shake my head.

"You wanna be like us, don't you? Have a fucking drink."

I duck. The beer bottle cuts the air above.

"My name's not Muhammed!"

The airport is silent. My hands protecting my head. I look up. There is no beer bottle.

My legs are on autopilot, propelling me through the maze of luggage without conscious thought. I am running from bad memories... out into the mêlée of people rushing this way and that, single-minded in their need to get somewhere. Perhaps they hold a ticket out of this place. They navigate with more freedom than I could. I hold my backpack to my chest, too afraid of what might happen if I let it fall behind me. I turn slowly in circles, disorientated. Wanting somewhere quiet. Away from the eyes.

My shoulder flies back.

"Watch it, mate!"

I chance a glance behind me. My chest constricts. A bald white man glares at me over his shoulder. I hold my backpack even tighter. I step back. Get knocked. Turn. A suitcase hits me in the shin.

"Sorry," I whisper, turning and turning again.

I duck and shielded by my backpack stumble my way to the edge. Hug the walls with advertisements full of fake smiles more welcoming than the real people around me.

I'm alone. The eyes on me don't actually see me. They only recognise a stereotype. I try to step away from eyes that never blink, only narrow or widen, either scared or angry. They don't know me. They don't know what I've been through.

My heart pounds. My throat tightens. I freeze against the wall.

I'm desperate to shout at them to stop staring, to leave me alone. Go away. I've suffered. I'm the victim, but I put my hands over my mouth to stop myself.

A man in a suit near a café argues with a woman. She cowers like I do but no one notices because eyes are on me, the foreign man. They cannot see the same red blood underneath my dark skin. I want to scream, "I am just like you!" I am a human, too.

☯   ☯   ☯

My nose twitches at the smell of disinfectant as I enter the men's room... looking for quiet. Men shave in the basin, bringing their homes into the airport. Another combs his hair. Two others chat at the urinal. No one thinks they're dangerous.

The first cubicle is out of order. I step into the next, pushed out by the stench. In the third cubicle, I shut the door and feel the tension in my chest ease. I sit and allow the semi-quiet, the freedom from scrutiny to wash over me. I get down on my knees, wince at the cold tiles and bring my forehead down. My eyes close and time loses meaning. The trembling in my body stills. I'm both in and apart from the airport. I'm not sure how long this lasts.

Please God, let me leave this place soon.

"What the fuck. Is that humming?" someone says on the other side of the door.

"What?"

"You can't hear that?"

I open my eyes and come face to face with two polished loafers sticking under the door. My body goes rigid, steel shooting from my heart to become a brace. The smell of leather and wax overcomes me. Nausea swells and sweat trickles down my face.

They're the same shoes that...

"Either some fucking towel head is praying or someone's trying really hard to take a shit."

I can hear him sniff at my door. I bite my lip to stop it twitching.

"What the fuck are you looking at old man?" I can hear items clatter into a basin, the squealing door cueing departure, followed by laughing.

The loafers twist back in my direction and a gasp escapes. The loafers come through the door, stabbing red-hot pokers—in… in… in. I push against the toilet bowl. Only two feet, feeling like a million in such a small space.

"Fucking terrorist!" His feet come at me again, joined by others. My skull shudders and rattles with each kick. Bottles smash around me.

I grab my head with my hands, curling into myself. My body burns and I smell blood on the hot concrete below.

After all we've done for you. The words of a dozen angry voices echo in my ears.

My head sears like a sunspot exploding. Beer pours over me. My body encased in a blanket of icy needles. Bitterness crawls in the corners of my mouth, onto my tongue. My body jolts to avoid the poison. I lurch forward, shoving fingers in my throat. Liquid explodes from my mouth and nose.

Fucking terrorist. Fucking, terrorist. The chant moves between memory and reality.

The door shakes. He slaps at the other side and shakes it again. The lock groans under pressure.

He kicks the door one last time. "Fucking terrorist."

I'm bent over on the tiled floor, vomit dripping from my nose. My early morning breakfast seeps along the cracks in the tiles. I can run, but I cannot escape my memories.

       ☯   ☯   ☯

I don't know how long I hid in the cubicle or spent cleaning up. My watch is now in the backpack. At the door, I glance both ways before slipping out. The stares and side-glances come to me like fireflies go to light.

I'm tired. All this running. All this hiding. My energy is spent. I want somewhere to stay and pray. Somewhere quiet to work out what to do next. Praying in the toilet filled me with peace. Took me, if briefly, away from this place.

I sit in the first empty seat, too exhausted to keep walking. Unsure of what else to do, I turn inwards. Seconds become minutes, minutes become hours. Sections of the airport fill and empty like tides rushing back and forth. *Pangaean* passengers like me are left behind, the rubbish on the high-tide line.

Across the sea of people, a young woman tiptoes between the strewn bodies, searching. Her wide eyes innocent and serious. What could you find in this place? There's nothing. Perhaps she's not looking for anything in particular, just something. Anything.

She reminds me of my own search and I stand. I need to pray. My walking becomes crawling standing up, momentum the only thing making me put one foot in front of the other. I ignore the voice inside telling me there's nowhere to go. I fight the urge to sink into the floor.

And I freeze. I'm at the glass door to security and customs—back to where I almost escaped.

I've come full circle. Back to the mayhem of check-in.

Agents and *Pangaean* customers argue desperate to fly out. The shouts bounce off the high ceiling. I feel the press of bodies all around. My body begins to shut down, abandon me.

"You goin' through, or you just gonna stand there?"

My legs won't move. Glares sear me from all sides.

"Sorry, sorry," I mutter.

Slowly I back away from the sliding glass door, the backpack between me and them until my back hits something.

I turn and see trolleys lined up like a tethered conga line. I crawl behind, into the unseen space between the trolleys and the wall. Enough room to fold myself safely away from the eyes and memories chasing me.

My legs hurt from the metal poles but I shift my weight so it's less painful. I'm a kid again, crawling under the legs of my aunties, chasing Mihr who is always faster and better at hiding. Only then it was fun.

"Who are you?" a small voice asks beside me. I turn and find a young boy. His skin is olive and his eyes are dark; he's like me. I wonder if he's real.

"Kurush. What's your name?"

"Ahmed. Why are you hiding?"

His serious young eyes stare at me without looking away; he's not learnt to be ashamed yet.

I don't know how to answer. I want to protect him from the knowledge we're not welcome—even if we're born here. He hasn't learnt that yet. I wish he didn't have to. I wish he could grow up and just be Ahmed.

"I'm looking for somewhere to pray."

"You can pray here." Like the girl atop her father's shoulders, Ahmed has a clear view. Behind the baggage trolleys is the most unseen place in the whole airport. I wiggle away from the end where the carts jerk from their carrel into service.

I close my eyes. The soundtrack of Ahmed pretending the whole thing is a spaceship calms me. The whooshing sound he makes could be waves.

Please God, get me out of here.

My chest releases. I forget the stares, the chaos. The memories subside. I forget I even want to leave. Running would leave Ahmed with one less friend in a place divided by us and them.

I open my eyes. I'll stay.

"What the fuck's going on here?"

The trolleys shake. My heart thunders in my ears. A pair of shiny white loafers appears at the end, where I crawled in. Cold sweat lathers me.

"I'm scared," Ahmed says and holds onto my twitching legs.

"Security! Security!"

The ground vibrates with the thunder of thousands of curious feet. My vision goes a blurry. My mouth pasty.

"Who's in there?"

"It's a man and child."

"Oh, dear God!"

I can hear the hiss of rumours spreading, though I can't see who's saying what.

"Get out of there, mate."

I can't and don't want to move. Ahmed squirms further down the tunnel away from the yelling. A white arm reaches into the dark crevice, clawing at me.

"Fucking terrorist abusing our kids, wait till I get my hands on you."

He grabs my leg and pulls at me, the line of metal stabbing me. I will myself to resist, to not give in. But I feel fainter… and fainter.I throw up a hand to shield my eyes; the fluorescent light blinds me as I'm dragged out. A bald man stands over me, his fist balled, arm pulled back ready to punch.

"What the fuck are you doing?"

The paste in my mouth is glue. I can't say a thing.

"Ahmed?" a woman's scream rises above all the general chatter. "Ahmed!"

I'm pushed aside as he goes for Ahmed.

"Come on there, little mate, I'm not gonna hurt ya. We've got the scary man now. Come on."

Ahmed blinks like a strobe light as he's brought out in the open. The bald man screws his face up.

"It's one of them," he says, giving Ahmed a push. "Don't worry about it." He turns away. "We thought you were fiddling with one of our kids. They do it all the time. It's part of their culture."

Something rises in the back of my throat, acidic, turning the glue to sour bile.

"He's got a bag."

"A bag?"

"What's in the bag?"

"Where's security?"

"What's your name?"

"It's Muhammed, I bet."

"They're all called Muhammed."

A maelstrom of voices fall upon me. I push back against the trolleys. They tower over me. I recognise the father from earlier step forward, side by side with the bald man, their fingers in sync jabbing the air in front of me.

"Someone get security."

131

"What the hell's in his bag?"

"He could have a bomb."

"He's got a bomb."

"SOMEONE GET SECURITY!"

Ahmed crawls away unseen and sits next to the little girl who climbs human mountains. She smiles and waves.

The yelling crashes over me, wave after a wave. Someone spits in my face. They push and jostle to get closer. Anger froths over. A fist swings and there's a rush. Bodies topple. Hands claw and tear for position. I clutch my backpack, bury my head in it, whispered prayers slipping between my trembling lips.

"Move! MOVE!"

I hear something like pins falling as people yell. The air tastes thick. I choke on the heat.

Capsicum spray.

"Sir, put your hands in the air." My eyes burn and I can't stop rubbing them. "Sir... sir... you have three seconds."

"I can't open my eyes," I scream. "Please, don't hurt me. Please, not again."

"What's he saying?"

"What's in the bag, sir?"

"My family." Blinded, I feel the bag snatched from me. "Photos of my family..."

"Your hands in the air, sir."

"I was praying. I WAS just praying!"

The pressure in my chest is too much; my heart has no room to beat. I raise my hands. My eyes are on fire. I try to open them. Through swollen slits I see a pistol in my face.

"Please," I plead, sensing movement. "Take the bag. Just let me go. You don't want me here? Let me leave."

THE YIN BOOK

The Guilty One

Emma Newman

Medae breathed out slowly as order unravelled around her. If there was one rule in her line of work, it was to stay calm. And if there was a second, it was to know which rules to break, and which to respect. She never broke her first rule and she wasn't about to now.

Confused travellers pressed in on the desk as the clerk, now wide awake, was ushered away. Time to move, take stock, plan.

She extricated herself from the crowd, which was one ill-word away from a mob, and walked to the far side of the concourse. She was aware of tightness in her shoulders, in her stomach, and turned her mind to the fear lurking in her body. She breathed in through her nose, out slowly through her mouth, monitoring her pounding heart and the surging adrenaline. She knew these physiological markers well, but they were not her master.

Once her body calmed, she considered her immediate options. She could try to retrieve the case now, or simply flee. Moving now was tempting, but she knew fear made it attractive. Fear told her to get it back at all costs, then run. Before the sedative wore off. Before Manfred suspected something amiss and woke JJ. Before JJ realised she'd stolen from him and sent his people after her.

She twitched at each glance in her direction.

Was her dilemma on display? No. She remembered the third rule: Don't assume it's all about you.

She learnt that rule on her first-ever assignment: she'd thought a man who approached her for a light was looking for an opportunity to apprehend her. When she handed him the lighter and he asked if she'd been in the city for long, she assumed he was checking her movements against the timeframe of the crime. It wasn't until he thanked her and walked back to his wife she realised he'd only seen a cold woman alone on a street corner who might help him get his nicotine fix, not a thief with a prize hidden under her coat.

She reminded herself everyone here was thinking of themselves, and everyone related to her journey out of the airport was worrying about their job. Nobody would suspect there was a stolen painting in her suitcase. With that framed clearly in her mind, she decided to find a place to wait it out and make her decision. She had invested too much to run before a solution had a chance to reveal itself.

❧　❧　❧

She managed to buy coffee and bottled water and find a seat in the café before the herds arrived; they were still confused about what was happening. Now she'd made her first choice, she had to identify the risks involved in waiting along with everyone else.

The most pressing risk being JJ raising the alarm. He may not involve the police, but she didn't doubt for a moment he'd send his security people, if not come himself.

She checked that thought. Why would he come here? He could assume having stolen the masterpiece she would leave the country straight away, by any means at her disposal. It didn't have to be the airport, but she had to plan for the eventuality his people would come here.

She reminded herself he would be looking for Keely. Medae had different clothes, hair colour and passport. He would be able to pick her out, but only with close scrutiny. His people would have trouble if they were working from just a description or an old photo. She checked her watch. In three hours she would contact her employer—no need to wake them now—and advise them of the unavoidable delay. They might even send help.

Once that had been tidied away, she remembered the diary in her backpack and pulled it out. She was glad she had taken that too; it saved her from buying the chick-lit schlock at the airport shop.

What did she expect? A list of business contacts, or private details of his father's shady operations? She opened the first page and found a handwritten journal entry dated a month after she had started to work for him.

> *Christ. Gone and got a therapist. Not only that, bought a journal and I'm writing in it. What next? Listening to emo and relating, fifteen years late?*
>
> *Got to do something though. L had to see a doctor. Got too rough. Doc's on the payroll so there's no worries there, but couldn't sleep afterwards. Don't care about her, just don't understand what happened.*
>
> *Why do I do this? Do I even want to know?*

Medae choked on the coffee. A therapist? John Hildebrand Junior, cast from the same ruthless, prize arsehole mould as his father, in therapy? No wonder it was in the safe. He wouldn't want anyone to know he was human and just as screwed up as everyone else. She gave herself permission to read ten pages more, then move on.

Ten pages covered six months. He wrote sporadically, mostly after sex. Sometimes he talked about the women involved, identified only by their initials, which fascinated her. At first she wondered if it was to protect their identity, but he had written it assuming no-one else would ever read it. No, an initial was the ultimate in narcissistic detachment; enough to remind him of all the different conquests, not enough to assign any humanity to them. Like bank robbers not asking hostages for their names. Names make it personal.

The borderline addiction to rough sex was the reason he was in therapy. It was clear he was scared—of taking it too far in the future, but more of the cause. His scrawled words painted a picture of a frightened man, not the mogul-in-training she had teased for two years with high heels and pencil skirts. But the coffee cup was empty. The ten pages consumed.

JJ was right to be worried; he was brutal. She wondered about the other bruised and battered women. What had kept them in the bedroom without a goal like hers? Perhaps they endured for their own reasons, a thought that stirred something unpleasant in her stomach.

She picked up her bag and stood, stretching again in an effort to stave off the stiffening brought on by exhaustion and bruising. The coffee shop was separated from the rest of the concourse by waist-high plastic screens, giving her a view as she put her coat on, considering where to go next. The crowd was building as the chaos from *Pangaean's* collapse spread outwards. A sweep picked out an individual in a dark jacket, moving differently to everyone else. She knew by the way he moved he wasn't there to travel or pick anyone up.

He was a hunter.

He watched the people around him with the emotional detachment of a man paid to do so. Looking for someone—someone who didn't want to be found.

Medae wanted to be as far away from him as possible. Reciting the third rule in her head to counter the urge to run, she left the coffee shop with a relaxed gait. She headed for the perfume counter, intending to blend in with the other bored women there, and watch this man.

She positioned herself to look like she was shopping for a pair of sunglasses, but still had a good view of the area the hunter stalked. He was broad in the shoulder and moved with the confidence of a physically capable man. With his casual jacket and his hands in his pockets he would blend in. To Medae's eyes, however, he was as obvious as a virgin at a frat party, and, to make it worse, his face seemed familiar.

She struggled to maintain her cool as she recalled the faces of JJ's men. Was he one of them? There were so many, and while she had done her best to remember them all, she had other things on her mind too. The hunter's face was nondescript enough to make her doubt her recollection. JJ was surely still unconscious, unaware of any need to look for her here.

Don't assume it's all about you!

There were thousands of people in the airport he could be looking for.

❧   ❧   ❧

Medae drifted for another half an hour, looking for a seat to perch on and read the next part of the diary, but the place was filling up, not only with the people stranded from the original flights, but all the others scheduled for the morning. Places to rest and wait were becoming scarce.

She found a nook between a seating area and a palm. The fatigue was swamping her and she needed to sit until it passed.

She spent the next hour with another six months of the diary. JJ was getting used to writing about his thoughts, and each entry was longer than the one before it. Reading each page took her a step further into his inner world. He talked about the small American town he spent his teenage years in, living with his mother who seemed to shut down after a bitter divorce. Medae found herself relating to his frustration with small-town life, a childhood spent fantasising about escape into a wider and more interesting world. The empathy ended when she read about how he was plucked from it by his wealthy father when he came of age, whereas she clawed her way out all by herself.

Reading it became compulsive, reducing the clamour of the airport's frustrated masses into a background hum. This man, whom she had spent two years studying, plotting against, was writing as if he were another person. She searched for signs of the boorish machismo she had been so comfortable hating, but as the months passed in the diary, there was less and less of it.

When she came across an entry about a car crash in his early twenties, she wondered whether that was the root of it; nothing like a near-death experience to make someone stop messing around and get on with the serious business of making money. He mentioned reconstructive surgery, and she wondered if a new face allowed him to create a new identity. She could relate to that.

> *The therapist is right. It's something to do with Keely. This all began when she started to work for me. What is it about her? She drives me mad. Last night I put my hands around B's throat as she came, but I was thinking about Keely. I want to see her under me.*

Medae's breath caught in her throat. He was writing about her—at least the version of her he'd known. And she wasn't just a letter; her's the first full name in over sixty pages.

"You stuck here too?" An elderly woman leant down, invading Medae's personal space. "

"What?"

"Are you stuck here too?" the woman repeated and Medae nodded, regretting the engagement. She was one of the elderly Medae most hated to look at: skin hung over bones like old-fashioned curtains with too much drape, liver spots and hollow cheekbones. What was she doing flying at her age anyway?

"Terrible business. First time we decide to fly and this happens. It's our grandson's wedding. Couldn't miss it now could we? He's marrying a girl from Paris. I hope they get this sorted out soon."

Medae nodded a couple of times then realised the woman didn't actually intend to have a conversation; she just wanted a face to speak to. As the old woman burbled, Medae glanced around, spotting a ladies bathroom nearby—an easy way to extricate herself from the old woman's attention.

Medae joined the queue for the facilities and read as she shuffled along, but nothing more appeared about her—just musings on his overbearing father and pathetic mother, which didn't surprise her. The only surprise, the man glimpsed on these pages was the same man responsible for the trauma burning across her back. For the briefest of moments, she stopped seeing JJ as a bastard who deserved to be ripped…

No place for that kind of thinking.

Someone knocked on the door of a cubicle. She looked up to find she was one person away from the start of the queue, and the woman at its head was knocking on the door of a cubicle marked 'Out of Order'.

"Are you alright in there?"

"Yes, sorry," came a muffled reply.

"There's a big queue out here…" The woman shrugged at her audience and dove into a stall as one became free.

Soon Medae was locking her own cubicle door. She listened to the snivelling next door and, when she emerged, the woman in the sky-blue coat came out of the out-of-order cubicle, bleary-eyed and puffy-faced. They moved to the sinks in synchrony. As Medae washed her hands, she confirmed it was the woman from the check-in queue. She glanced at her hands, noted the lack of wedding ring, and wondered who her companion was. A lover? A brother?

"You okay?" Medae asked, out of curiosity rather than concern.

The woman smiled weakly, nodded unconvincingly, and followed Medae out.

A few paces back into the huge space, Medae paused to consider her next move. She looked straight at the hunter, lurking in the seating area she'd crammed herself into previously.

The moments stretched like a rubber band as they took each other in, both studying the other's faces. She still couldn't place him, and she couldn't hurry away without seeming guilty, so she brazened it out until that awful stretching snapped when a child's screaming tantrum erupted behind him.

He turned, distracted by the noise long enough for her to hurry away, moving around a corner and out of his immediate line of sight. She saw the weeping woman walking ahead, and decided to follow. Her companion waited, leaning against a partition wall separating a duty free shop from the concourse. He didn't smile at the sight of the woman approaching. He looked tense, but then everyone here did.

"Have you been crying?" he asked, and the woman denied it. "For Christ's sake, keep it together," he hissed at her, taking her arm into the crook of his own.

Medae slipped into the shop, moving out of their sight but close enough to hear. The man strode off though, the woman forced into step alongside him. Something odd was going on there, but she let it go. She had herself to think of.

❦   ❦   ❦

It was easy to evade the hunter in the chaotic Brownian motion of the stranded travellers, but harder to find a good place to hole up and form the next part of the plan. She wanted somewhere easy to leave, with a good view, so she opted for a mezzanine-level coffee shop packed with strained faces and whimpering children. She pushed her way through to its edge, the staff too busy to notice she hadn't bought anything, and leant on the rail overlooking the concourse. This would do, she thought, ducking down to sit on her coat and read some more.

> *Closed a deal today. Felt nothing. Time was when I'd feel like the Don, but now... don't give a shit. Another half a million gets wired into my account, so what? It's just numbers now, doesn't mean anything. Shit, maybe I should stop seeing this bloody shrink, I'm questioning everything. Feels like I've been using a cheat code in the game of my life. Now I have unlimited money and unlimited ammo, the game's no fun. Sick of pretending to be the big man. Who the hell am I anyway? Enough of this shit. Time for a whisky and a whore, that'll sort me out.*

The hairs on the back of her neck stood on end.

Who the hell am I anyway? The words lingered, making her nauseous. She shut the book. Why keep reading? But in the next moment she was flicking back to the last page read, unable to stop herself. She looked at the date, realised it was written a week ago and remembered the deal she'd helped to administrate. It was huge. JJ seemed thrilled. That night he took the staff out to a swanky restaurant, champagne all around and played the part of the conquering king.

Then it hit her. He played the part. Just as she had. All that time she'd written him off, he was doing the same as her. Suddenly he wasn't just a fool she'd out-manoeuvred.

Another bout of nausea bubbled up from her stomach.

"Excuse me madam, you can't sit there." A red-faced man in his fifties wearing the uniform of the coffee shop was standing over her.

"There aren't any seats."

"I'm afraid it's fire regulations; you can't sit on the floor blocking an escape route, I'm sorry."

He stood his ground and she shrugged. Her backside was numb anyway. She needed to walk, leave these uncomfortable feelings behind in the coffee shop and regain her composure. But there was only one entry left in the diary. She was desperate to read it. She perched on the edge of a concrete planter, palm fronds scraping her back as she flicked to the final entry. The date was last night.

> *Keely's fixing me a drink. Told her I was having a shower. I just fucked her to within an inch of her life and she was everything I knew she'd be. Slut. Got to call the psych tomorrow. I know why I'm doing this; I have to write it before I forget. She was over the desk and it came to me, this thing that's been bugging me all this time, the thing the shrink was pressing me about; the type I like. Small blondes in heels.*

A memory flashed up: her employer checking she was a natural blonde. He explained the target preferred a particular type of woman, and she fit the profile. That's how she made the short-list. It had been humiliating to be asked, but with so much money on the table she simply nodded and reassured him she was. Now she was a redhead. Her long blonde locks disposed of.

I remembered that bitch from my final year at school. Carrie, the one I'd been mad about for two years and when I finally got it together with her in the cabin at the beach I thought it was special. Monday everyone was sniggering behind my back. She told a girlfriend I couldn't get it up and that nothing happened. Went through the whole bloody school. And it was a lie. A LIE. BITCH. It came to me like it happened yesterday, just as I took Keely from behind. I hurt her, but now I think I know why. I'm so angry at her, godammit. Hurting these women, wishing they were Carrie.

Medae shivered, recalling a weekend at the beach hut in her final year at school. In fact it was only the hut she could remember clearly—the one who had taken her there had been sweet, but so bland she struggled to remember him. But she could remember how her friends had bitched about him as he approached her at school the following Monday, and making the decision to trash their time together so he wouldn't tarnish her halo of popularity. He was one of the losers. She couldn't even remember his name, hadn't recognised his face, but then if he'd had surgery too…

She dropped the diary, head spinning. She was the one who'd made JJ. The reason she fit the profile was because she set the profile—one moment of cruel teenage selfishness had set the type in JJ's mind. Now he needed to conquer and deliver his own form of payback. Over and over. All these years later, he hadn't recognised her consciously—she looked different enough from past surgery—but similar enough for an old part of his mind to be niggled by her.

She wanted to vomit. The man she'd just ripped off, whose one true prized possession she'd stolen with joyful abandon the night before, had been ruined by her years before. The noise of the airport surged in her ears and she wanted to run, leave the painting to its fate and go someplace where no one would ever find her again.

"Excuse me."

She snapped her head up to look straight into the eyes of the hunter. All she could do was stare back. This was it. She'd lost.

When she didn't move, he put a hand on her arm, flashing a badge under her nose as he did so. But instead of cuffing her, he pushed her to one side, reaching past her to clamp down a hand on someone seated on the other side of the planter.

"Mr. Warren, I'm arresting you on suspicion of fraud, embezzlement and kidnapping," he said, as Medae stumbled aside, seeing the woman who'd been weeping in the toilet come into view, moving away as her companion was taken into custody. Medae staggered back, taking it in; the relief on the woman's face, the fury of the apprehended.

Medae laughed; it emerged, shrill and brittle from her tight throat. She wasn't being hunted at all. It wasn't about her and it never was. She saw the diary on the floor and picked it up. She was guilty, but of a crime worse than she was running from now. For the first time in her life, the third rule had been broken. JJ was all about her, and living with that was going to be harder than anything else about this job. It was time for a fourth rule, one that would hold her together and protect her from this surging guilt.

Regret nothing.

Excess Baggage
Carrie Clevenger

The baggage proceeded down the belt like a line of squared coffins in out-landish colours and fake crocodile hide, interspersed with a few lumps of ecru and charcoal. Leon and Bullwick, graveyard shift workers, yawned in unison over the beige hulk. They had to shout to hear one another over the gigantic belt feeding the baggage into the x-ray machine.

"What you up to tonight?" Bullwick fixed beady eyes on Leon. He mopped at the sheen of sweat on his brow and shifted his portly frame on the comparatively tiny stool.

"It's Mindy's birthday. I'm going to take her out with what's left after rent."

Leon had been with Mindy for six months, while Bullwick couldn't keep a girl beyond the drunken haze of the occasional Saturday night.

"Where do you plan on taking her out? The Crown? We could meet for a pint or two?"

"No, not a pub. No. Marco's maybe, or that new place—Kiri-some-thing or other... I don't know." Leon shrugged his thin shoulders. "I still need to get her a present. I spent too much on video games last week. I'm hoping this overtime is enough to get her something nice."

"I know girls," Bullwick said with a wink and leaned in closer. "You buy her flowers, right, and then she's all yours for the night."

"She's allergic to flowers, Bull," Leon said, rolling his eyes. "Besides, I was thinking of getting her something a bit nicer."

"Nicer than flowers?" Bullwick slid off his stool with a grunt and shuffled to the belt to straighten a piece of luggage that had turned sideways. "Whisky?"

"This is why you're still single, Bull," Leon snorted, glancing up at the conveyor belt. "You're bloody hopeless."

The procession of baggage was fairly abbreviated this morning. Perhaps he'd go on an early break, smoke and grab a cuppa. He needed the lift. His sleep was sporadic at best.

"Maybe a necklace. Scottsky's has a sale on emeralds."

"Does this look like a full flight's worth of luggage to you, Leon?"

Leon opened his mouth to say something but his jaw clamped shut when he saw Bullwick's eyes widen at something behind them.

"Gentlemen."

It was the super, flanked by two men he'd never seen before. Bullwick stopped the belt and jumped to attention. With the din from the machinery halted, they could hear a murmuring commotion rising from the terminal side.

"What's going on?" Leon asked, and eyed the silent men.

They wore suits. Suits were never good news.

"I'm afraid you'll need to get your belongings and take the rest of the day off," the super said, his face even redder than usual. Mr Pinkerton, Leon remembered. He didn't come down to the x-ray area often. His job was the paper-pushing sort, angry fliers with lost luggage and complaints about invasive body checks.

"Why?" Bullwick asked, before Leon could open his mouth.

"The airline has… ceased operations. Temporarily," he said, cutting his eyes at the men at either side of him. "You'll be paid for the rest of today but tomorrow we'll need to see if you can be reassigned to another airline. You have fifteen minutes. Please leave your stations and exit by the employee entrance. I mean it—it's a madhouse in the terminal."

Without staying for questions, he turned on his heel and led the men back up the metal stairs and disappeared through the door.

"Well, that's a load of shite," Bullwick growled, scowling and sweating again. "Who does he bloody think he is, shutting us down like that?"

"Relax Bull, he said he'll have us reassigned–"

"No, he said he *might* have us reassigned. You know what that really means?"

Leon started to pull down the black vinyl cover over the control panel of the machine and then dropped it.

"What does it mean Bull?" He asked the question flatly, mostly to humour the brute. He wasn't in the mood for another of Bullwick's union speeches.

"We've lost our bloody jobs over this shite!"

Leon raised an eyebrow. "Right, well in that case I'm off to get my bag. You coming?"

"In a minute," Bullwick said, pulling a case off the belt.

"What are you doing? That's a passenger's case!"

"Right, and a nice sturdy one. Might have some valuables in it."

Bullwick was the perverted sort who carried out baggage checks unnecessarily, just to sniff through a woman's knickers or to touch her private devices for kicks. Leon didn't like his 'hobby' much, but they had been friends since high school, so he turned a blind-eye. Leon intended to be a pilot, but a propensity for high blood-pressure blackouts ended that dream. The baggage check job worked perfectly for him: not stressful enough to trigger a blackout, and since there were always two people working he had someone watching out for him, just in case. Bullwick arranged to be scheduled with Leon to keep an eye on him, and also to score a ride to and from work.

"How can you steal from someone like that?" Leon said in a harsh whisper and tugged on his friend's arm. He may as well have tried to uproot a tree.

Bullwick having popped the locks on the case knelt sifting through the contents. He selected a pink silky garment and held it up. Thong underwear. "That's the ticket," he said with a smile and stuffed them into his pocket.

Leon pulled the case away from him and began to close it, when something caught his eye. Under the neatly folded garmentry, a long leather tube, at least a foot and a half long and a few inches in diameter, split in the middle, clasps keeping the two halves together. He frowned.

"I bet that's worth something," Bullwick chuckled and snatched it out of the case under Leon's arm. Without ceremony, he undid the clasps and pulled the tube apart to reveal a roll of canvas. As it unfurled, his face fell.

"Just stupid art," he said and threw it back on top of the pile. Leon picked it up and turned the canvas over.

"It's a nice painting," he said, holding it under the light to examine it closer.

"Take it then," Bullwick whispered. His eyes locked with Leon's, daring him.

"I couldn't–"

"You said you haven't got Mindy a birthday present, right? How are you going to afford your rent and her present if you're unemployed? This is your redundancy pay. It's just a daft painting—no one will miss it, and she'll love it."

Leon sighed through his nose, thinking. For once, Bullwick seemed to be right.

"All right," he said finally, and rolled up the painting carefully, before replacing it in the container. "But this is it. You've got your... knickers and I'll take this painting. Let's get our stuff and get out of here."

🌀   🌀   🌀

The painting fit in Leon's knapsack with a little rearranging and Pinkerton never returned.

"Let's go through the terminal," Bullwick said with a nudge that felt more like a shove forward.

"Are you bloody daft? There's picketers and pissed off fliers up there!"

"I know," Bullwick said with a grin. "I want to see what's going on for myself. Solidarity and all that. Besides, your Bug is closer this way. Less chance of someone asking what's in your bag."

Airport employees parked in the overflow lot because it rarely filled, and the airport didn't lose potential revenue from closer spots taken. If they left by the employee exit, they'd have to walk past security, then around the building out close to the tarmac, with all the noise and that horrid jet-fuel smell that turned his stomach.

"Alright, alright," Leon said and slid his backpack on. "I suppose a quick jaunt through the terminal won't hurt."

"That's the spirit of adventure," Bullwick said, giving his trademark grin of approval.

As Pinkerton warned, the terminal was in absolute disarray, with passengers milling about, some shouting into phones and others crying. One gentleman was on the phone with an unlit cigarette between his fingers, muttering an apology to either his wife or his mum, which Leon had to admit, wasn't much difference when he thought about it.

"Do either of you handsome gents have a phone I could borrow? Mine's out of credits."

Leon recognised the woman vaguely, but she looked different, upset. Pissed off, too. He raised an eyebrow. No way was he going to surrender his phone to someone who appeared that unstable. Bullwick however blushed a bit and fished out his brick of a phone. It was an older model because he believed phones were for making phone calls, not 'taking bloody photos and sending poxy emails'.

"Sure, as long as it's local," he said and Leon cringed at the sight of pink silk and lace peeking from Bull's pocket.

"Put those somewhere else!" Leon hissed before catching the look on his friend's face. He gave out a short laugh. "You can't be serious Bull!"

"What?"

"You're blushing like a schoolboy. You fancy her, don't you?"

Bullwick's blush faded, ushering in a deep frown. "No, I don't!"

"I've seen you talking to her before–"

"Ta for that," the woman interrupted, tossing the phone back to Bullwick, who fumbled before securing it once again in his pocket. Leon sighed and tugged on his friend's arm.

"We are definitely getting out of here before anyone else stops us."

Once they cleared the building and the Volkswagen was in sight, Leon breathed a sigh of relief. They'd gotten away with it.

"Am I dropping you off?" Leon asked. Bullwick was trying to light a cigarette; the breeze coming in kept extinguishing the little flame. Leon rolled his eyes.

"Put the bloody window up then!" He wrinkled his nose at the acrid smell as the cigarette lit. "Jesus! Roll it back down."

"Make up your bleedin' mind." Bullwick rolled the window down again and draped an arm over the sill.

"I'll just come home with you," he said and coughed, a thick cloud of smoke whipping out his window. The Beetle echoed his sentiment. It wouldn't be long before Leon would have to tinker with the tiny motor again to squeeze another few months out of her.

"Fine with me but you need to be gone by at least five."

"You kicking me out?" Bullwick grunted and adjusted his seatbelt over his gut.

"Mindy's birthday?" Leon prompted him.

"Ah. Pub right?"

"No," Leon said through clenched teeth, "And you're not invited. I'll just drop you off on my way out."

"No pub?" Bullwick looked disappointed.

"No. No pub, Bull. We hang out all the time. Stop looking hurt like that."

Bullwick stared out the window, rows of houses, neat and nearly identical, whizzed past as Leon drove through the streets surrounding his home. Bullwick lived on the other side of town in a rat-trap flat with a window unit, above a couple that always bickered. It was no surprise he always tagged along to Leon's flat though it wasn't really a flat, more a partition of a house he rented from an elderly woman always off visiting grandchildren.

Leon pulled in to the curb. A dark car pulled in behind him. He frowned at the rear- view mirror. "That's odd."

"What is it?" Bullwick mumbled as he dug behind his seat for his bag. Leon slipped his backpack over one shoulder, gripping the strap until his knuckles turned white, eyeing the car behind. He hadn't seen it on this street before.

Had it followed them?

It wasn't too close, certainly not enough to see the driver's face in the dawning sunlight. The paint, oily and slick, blacker-than-black reflected the blaze of colour erupting in the eastern sky.

"Just go to the door," Leon hissed.

     ❧   ❧   ❧

Once inside, Leon loosened his grip on the knapsack, letting it slide down his arm to the floor. Bullwick went straight to the kitchenette and emerged shortly after with a thick ham and cheese sandwich in one hand and a frosty bottle of beer in the other.

"Left one in the freezer for you," he said around a mouthful of his snack and grinned, holding up his own prize. Leon sighed.

Come in, Bullwick. Something to eat, Bullwick? Help yourself, Bullwick.

Leon peered through the window. The car was still there, emerging from the fleeting shadows of daybreak. No light emanated from inside. He released a shuddery breath and locked the deadbolt.

"Let's see if they're showing last night's fight on the sports channel," Bullwick said and disappeared into the den without waiting for Leon.

"I may as well get a quick shower in," Leon said, heading upstairs. He flipped the lever to start the water, drowning out the drone of the telly below. Bullwick always made himself at home. If the phone rang, he'd answer it. It could be Mindy. On that thought, it was best to hurry. He stripped quickly before ducking under the hot spray.

Upstairs the phone rang twice and stopped. Bullwick hefted himself out of the davenport and ambled to the foot of the stairs. He stumbled over Leon's backpack lying on the linoleum, misshapen and straining from the special acquisition. Leon's bird better appreciate it, thought Bullwick. She was always chewing Leon out about something. He unzipped the bag, and unrolled the painting.

It looked old, with cresting waves of air-hardened oil. Signature and everything. He shrugged and carried it back into the den, sipping his beer thoughtfully, looking it over. Then he tucked it under the sofa, much like anything else he lost interest in.

❦   ❦   ❦

Leon ran his fingers through his hair and reached for his towel before hurrying downstairs.

"What was that fancy place for dinner we were talking about–" His eyes widened. "Bull? Bull!"

The front door gaped open to the morning. Bullwick stared up at the ceiling, a neat blackened hole in his forehead. A puddle pooled under him, spreading slowly, shining deep garnet in the light. Leon's eyes snapped to the curb. The black car was gone.

Instinct kicked in and he dragged Bull's body away from the door and slammed it shut, bracing himself against it before turning the lock. Then he fell to his knees and pulled Bull's head in his lap, bloodying his hands and towel.

What did they want? Why Bull? He'd never harm a fly.

The remains of his ham sandwich lay scattered over the hallway.

The backpack?

It was open. The painting gone.

"They wanted the bloody painting, didn't they?" he sobbed, leaning over his friend's silent body. "Oh shit, I knew I shouldn't have taken it."

Leon sat up and took stock of his situation. The painting was gone. His friend was dead. Mindy would be waiting for him to call her about her birthday dinner.

He could hear Mindy now: "I always told you he was a dead weight Leo. You never would listen and now look at you. Wanted for murder are you then? You are pathetic."

He could see her throw all his perceived faults back in his face. It was too much to digest.

Digest. Sandwich.

Oh, Bull. You stupid fuck.

"Why did you answer the bloody door?" he spat the words at the prone figure lying in the congealing blood. The silence overwhelmed him, even over the low drone of the television in the den. He pulled himself to his feet and managed to make it upstairs, where he discarded the bloody towel and washed his hands. He slipped into trousers and a thin t-shirt, even though he was shivering.

They killed him for a stupid piece of art.

It had to be that.

Bull owed nothing.

Hell, he had nothing. Bull always came to him to borrow money, when he was broke, which more often than not. He wasn't in trouble or he would have said something.

A faint tinny ringing drifted up from downstairs. Bull's phone. Leon crept down the stairs and stood over the body. The ringing stopped and immediately began again. Leon whimpered and felt in his friend's pocket to fish out the device.

"Hello?" he said in a half-whisper.

"You have something of mine," said the voice. A man's. He sounded very angry and somewhat drunk.

"I don't know what you're talking about." The lie tumbled out of Leon's mouth.

"You will give it back, or you'll end up like your friend." The call disconnected.

Leon let out a strange, inhuman mew before dropping the phone on Bull's chest. The phone on the kitchen wall rang and he recoiled from it as if were a live snake.

"Fuck you!" He shrieked and slapped the phone off the wall.

"Hello? Hello?" A woman's voice. "Leo? Hello?"

He picked up the receiver and crushed it against his ear, wiping his face in an attempt to sound calmer than he felt.

"I've been trying to get through to you for ages! I saw on the news *Pangaean* folded. Did you lose your job?"

A pounding began in his head and he slid to the floor. She kept talking at him as he clutched the phone, shivered and said nothing. Her incessant questions, asking if he was alright, over and over. He couldn't answer.

"Leo? I'm coming over now, do you hear? I'm calling a cabbie right now unless you tell me what's going on."

"It's… it's Bull," he said finally, between violent shakes.

"What about him? You didn't invite him to our dinner did you? Tell me you didn't."

"He's… he's… dead."

For the first time Mindy fell silent. Leon could hear his heart thundering in his ears.

"Leon McLadd, if this is your bloody idea of a fucking *joke*, I–"

"No joke," he whispered. "He's dead. He's dead." Leon kept repeating those same unbelievable words, over and over, as the receiver slid from his hand and his sight went black.

☯ ☯ ☯

The pounding at the door woke him with a gasp. He rubbed his head, hopes soaring. A dream. He had somehow knocked himself out cold and dreamt the whole thing. The microwave clock proclaimed in serene blue numbers that it was shortly after ten. He pulled himself onto his feet and kicked the phone out of his path in haste to answer the door.

The pounding persisted. He faintly heard the word 'police' and paused as the reality of the situation washed back over him. Bull still lay there, arms splayed over his head, the puddle beneath him not much bigger than before, except now the distinct sharp tang of both urine and faeces filled the air.

You probably meant to go after you finished your sandwich.

Leon slid the bolt back and opened the door a notch. Identification was shoved under his nose and his body afterwards into the nearest wall.

"Don't move a bloody muscle, lad," a thick voice growled in his ear. Two paramedics rushed in and pounced on Bull's body, checking for signs of life. Leon snorted into the plaster.

"He's bloody dead, you idiots." He even laughed a little.

"Leo?" It was Mindy's voice.

That fucking bitch, she called the cops.

Leon struggled under the cop's weight, but where he was lithe and light, the cop was built like an ox and just as heavy.

"You know him?" He heard the officer ask, and the sound of heels clicking up the steps through the door. "

"Oh, *Leo.*"

Leon was handcuffed and flipped over in one practised motion. Mindy stared at Bull's body. The paramedics stripped off their gloves and one radioed in speaking code for what he could only assume was a dead-man pick up call.

"Don't even look at him, you bitch," Leon snarled and suffered a smart blow to the head for it. "You hated him. *You hated him!*"

"Easy now, lad," the cop said.

"Get her away from me!"

Leon was ushered out his front door, as an officer began to recite: "I am arresting you on suspicion of murder, you do not have to say anything–"

"Oh God, Bull, I'm sorry. This is my fault. I did this." Leon shook as he sobbed. "I killed you."

"Save the confession for the station," the ox-like officer said and crammed him into a waiting paddy wagon.

Where the Heart Is

Tina Hunter

The airport parking lot was overflowing but flashing my badge secured me a spot near Neets' green Toyota. I parked and sat there. I shouldn't have come back to work yet.

"Tori?"

I looked out my window and saw Neets staring at me. I waved half-heartedly before stepping out of the car.

"You took your merry time," Neets called out. "Did he tell you anything else about the luggage?"

"Leon?"

She nodded. We had one dead baggage handler, another who looked good for it, but swore an anonymous caller shot his friend for a painting. This whole thing was a mess.

"Just that it looked old-fashioned and had women's clothes inside. His dead friend swiped a pink thong from inside."

Neets led me inside the terminal. It was a zoo. Five hours since the airline shut down and you were lucky if you had a spot to stand without brushing up against someone else.

"Rex, this is Detective Tori Young," Neets said to a young man, standing in front of us, sweating bullets. "Detective Young, this is *Pangaean's*

Operations Manager."

"Detective Patel said we'd be expecting you," he said, holding out his hand. I ignored it and stared at him. Rex swallowed hard. Normally that would have given me a boost, but not today. I couldn't get Eddy out of my head.

Rex led Neets and me away from the crowds, behind the counter and downstairs to the baggage area. It was a mess, luggage all over the place. Some of it appeared to be opened and rifled through already.

"You already started to search the luggage, Anita?" Neets shook her head.

"Found them that way. Funny thing though, they're all old-fashioned."

I looked around the room. Someone else also had an interested in our suitcase. But was it because of the painting, or something else?

"Is this just the luggage for the *Pangaean* flight to Paris?" I asked Rex.

"Sort of," he said with a shiver. "It wasn't the only flight cancelled but most of the other luggage has been removed."

"Most? Then you should get someone in here to remove ALL of the other luggage."

"Y-yes, of course," he stammered and then stood there, as if unsure what to do next.

"Rex? Did someone tell you to keep an eye on me?"

"No. Of course not, Detective, it's just… we're all very busy."

I walked up to him, getting inside his comfort zone.

"Then you really better hustle."

He tripped over himself trying to leave. Again, I felt nothing. Why couldn't I get any joy out of intimidating people?

"You're moody today," Neets said, following me over to the opened suitcases. "He's not that horrid."

"I'm always moody." I tried to sound nonchalant. I didn't want Neets to worry about me. She was my partner and I liked her.

"You know what I mean. You've been acting funny—like you'd rather be somewhere else." Neets stepped in front of me and looked me in the eye. "Where were you last week?"

I stepped around her and grabbed the first opened case.

"What? I'm not allowed a vacation?"

Just because I liked Neets didn't mean I wanted to tell her about Eddy. I didn't want to become her next charity case. Neets would find a way to help; there was no stopping the woman. She bent down and started going through another case.

"I was just asking if you'd rather be wherever you were last week."

"Who wouldn't rather be on vacation?" I tossed aside the suitcase when I found a man's suit.

"You're the only person I know who would rather be working than be anywhere else." She sighed and put the suitcase aside. "But I can tell you don't want to talk about it, so I won't push."

I was blessed with silence for four more suitcases.

"By Jove," Neets said, "Found it!"

"You're sure?"

She pushed the suitcase in front of me and I saw a pink camisole, crushed up against a running shoe; a perfect match for the thong we had in evidence.

My Blackberry went off, a special marching band tune I had programmed in this morning.

The hospital.

"I need to take this," I said, quickly glancing at the name on the luggage tag. "Put a call out over the PA system for Medae Newman. Say it's something to do with her luggage."

I've always hated hospitals. The smells. The sounds. Eddy wasn't my responsibility. I didn't have to be here. Did that mean I wanted to be here?

"Nurse." I flagged over the girl closest to the triage desk. "Is Edward Melendez out of surgery yet?"

The girl looked me up and down and must have decided I was important enough to stop and help. I wanted to slap her. I took a deep breath instead.

"Not yet, but you can wait. Waiting room four, about halfway down the hallway."

"Thank you." I hated the sound of relief in my voice. I was risking my job being here. I shouldn't have abandoned Neets. We should have been looking together for the Newman woman. Yet here I was, rushing to a hospital waiting room to sit on my arse and do nothing.

Damn it. They told me he was stable.

A nurse I recognised was talking to a doctor and another man when I entered the waiting room. She recognised me too.

"Detective Young," she called me over, "Doctor Gibbons, this is the woman who has taken an interest in the boy."

I shook hands with the doctor, meaning it, wanting to make a good impression on the man.

"Detective Young. I'm afraid the stitching holding his intestines together is tearing. Now, because Eddy is a ward of the state, Mr Waldor is here to listen to my suggestions about other methods."

Waldor held out his hand with a bureaucratic smile that made my skin crawl. "I'm here acting in the best interest of the child," he said.

Like hell you are.

I left his hand hanging.

"Wonderful. So what's been decided then?" I asked the doctor.

He looked at the nurse in a way I did not like.

"Mr Waldor here believes we should try the conventional stitches again."

"After they didn't work?" I looked at Waldor hard, the same way I looked at a criminal in the interrogation room. Waldor cleared his throat but otherwise didn't flinch. That bothered me more than what he said.

"It's the most cost-effective solution. Now I know what you're thinking—"

"You have no idea what I'm thinking."

"—but I'm not a heartless man. If the conventional treatment fails a second time we will move on to something else."

"And what is this something else?" I asked Doctor Gibbons.

"It's more like a plastic staple which—"

"And what are the consequences if the conventional stitches fail again?"

"Nothing life-threatening. However, there may be long-term digestive complications."

"May," Waldor stressed, "It's an acceptable risk."

This was it. If I continued on there was no turning back. I had to know for sure this was what I wanted, that it was more important than everything else in my world.

There was a window on the side of the waiting room. I walked to it and looked into the theatre. Nurses and doctors were milling about doing things I didn't understand, or care to. All I saw was three-year-old Eddy, his dark skin contrasting with the green sheet over his tiny body.

He had no one. His parents were dead; there was nothing anyone could have done. I couldn't bring them back, make his life whole again. But I couldn't do that for any of the victims I met.

Why him? Why, whenever I saw him, did I want to gather him up in my arms and carry him away?

Protect him. Save him.

Was that all this was? Wanting to save him?

One of the nurses moved out of the way and I could see Eddy's small face, nearly obscured by nose tubes. He looked so peaceful. Not the scared little boy I'd spoken to every day since the murder—the little boy who couldn't find the voice to respond.

It didn't really matter why; I just had to do something.

"Mr Waldor," I called over my shoulder, "If I were to pay, would you agree to the plastic staples?"

"Now, Detective Young, we all want what is best for—"

I spun around and shouted.

"I said, if I pay will you agree? Yes or no?"

Finally he reacted, stepping backwards as if I had hit him, stuttering his response.

"I... uh... I believe so."

"Good. Doctor Gibbons you have your answer."

The doctor nodded and entered the theatre. I turned back to look through the window at my Eddy.

My Eddy?

Where the hell did that come from?

I was so lost in thought I didn't notice Waldor had left until I needed to take a seat. The nurse was still there, reading a magazine. I sat next to her.

"You better be sure about what you're doing," she said quietly.

I slumped further into my chair. She laughed, and put the magazine down.

"That's good. If you aren't sure, it means you're actually thinking. Children are not puppies, Detective."

"I am aware of that, thank you." I said, "Aren't you supposed to be working or something?" I pointed harshly at the magazine. She just smiled.

"Until Eddy's guardianship issues are worked out, a member of the staff has to be with him at all times. I knew you had taken a personal interest in Eddy so I figured I should phone you when his vitals started to crash."

"Thank you." I rubbed the heels of my palms into my eyes. It was just past 1.00pm but I felt like I'd been up for days.

Why didn't anything make sense anymore?

"You know your Blackberry is blinking."

Sure enough it was.

I took my phone out of the hip case. Five missed calls, two emails. One of them was from my boss. I shouldn't be doing this. I could lose my job.

"I can phone you when he's out of surgery if you like?"

"Yeah. I'll just take a few of these calls out in the lobby." I stood up to leave but turned back to her. "Could you phone me if Child Services shows up again?"

No-one could find Medae Newman. Passenger calls went unanswered and the check-in clerk couldn't remember a thing about her. And then there was the email I received from an anonymous curator at the Louvre.

"There's something else," Neets said over the phone, "There have been rumours going around about the 'missing luggage' we have in custody as evidence. They're saying a disgruntled employee stole thousands from *Pangaean* and the company is really just confiscating luggage that might belong to this employee."

"Maybe our Ms Newman is the former employee with a grudge and that's why she stole the painting?"

"I don't think so," Neets said.

"Why?"

It sounded like Neets was moving, then she spoke in a whisper. "I was looking through her luggage. All the clothes are brand new and there isn't a single personal item in the entire case. Nothing. I also ran a search on Medae Newman. There's nobody by that name living here, or in Paris."

"An alias?"

"Yes. I think she's a pro and would go out of her way to make sure she isn't caught. Why tempt fate by going through the luggage to try and find the painting?"

"So someone else went through the luggage?"

"That's what I'm thinking," Neets said. "And what if they were looking for Newman's suitcase?"

I picked up her train of thought. "And when they found out two baggage handlers had beat them to it, they followed them and shot one in the head. But they didn't search the house to recover the painting for some reason." I sighed, "It's got flaws but it's a theory."

A messed up one, but it kind of worked. And if I knew Anita Patel, she'd leave no stone unturned until she found all the pieces that made up this puzzle. It's why I loved working with her.

Obsessive? Yes.

Genius? Always.

"The painting's the only plausible motive. Did you hear anything else about it? Auctions? Collectors?"

"Actually a stolen property report came in from a John Hildebrand

Junior."

"*Pangaean's* owner? S'truth!"

I laughed. "What are the chances his airline crashes and a prized possession gets stolen on the same day?"

"You know I don't like coincidences," she laughed. "Is there anything else I should know?"

I hesitated. The email about the painting and its rightful owners could just be a hoax. "No, nothing else."

Neets laughed. "Liar! But I won't include that in my check-in. Have you phoned the boss yet?"

"That's my next call."

Not that I wanted to make it. George was not a man who understood personal time, and up until now, I had never needed him to.

I found a comfortable seat in the far corner of the lobby and made the call.

"You want to explain where the hell you've been? Your first day back and already you're taking time away from the case?"

"I had a personal mat—"

"Personal my arse. I don't care who you've been fucking on your own time, but that crap has no place on my time. You. My office. One hour." Click.

That went well.

"Sit." George's red face was a sure sign he was ready to explode. I shut the door behind me and sat across from him, ready to update him on the case.

"Detective Patel has probably filled you in on most of the details—"

"I want your impression of the case, Young."

"Right." I clasped my hands together tightly. I hadn't felt so nervous in a long time. "I think this Newman woman is a pro, likely hired by someone in the art world."

"Oh?" He actually looked interested.

"Yes. This isn't a theft born of opportunity. She used an alias, had an escape route worked out. A premeditated crime. And it's possible when the airline went under, Newman contacted her employer–"

"Who sent someone after our victim?" George leaned back in his chair. "Makes sense."

"Actually sir, I don't think Newman and whoever she works for are responsible for our murder."

"They have motive."

"Yeah, but," I struggled to find the right words, "Why kill someone when you're on the right side? I got an email from someone claiming to work at the Louvre, identifying our painting as one looted during the war. Newman was retrieving it, not stealing it. It's still wrong but... it doesn't add up to murder."

"All right," George said and put his feet up on the desk between us. "Let's say for a moment you're right. So who did kill our baggage handler?"

I couldn't help but smirk. "I'd look hard at the owners of *Pangaean*, particularly John Hildebrand Junior seeing as he reported the painting stolen."

"Now that was stupid. He should have known we would do our research on the painting. What did he have to say for himself?"

"I haven't questioned him yet."

George's feet hit the ground.

"Why not?"

"Well... you know... I was away for a bit this afternoon..."

"Damn it, Young" George got up and shut the blinds on his office door.

I was going to get fired. Fuck!

"Even though Patel is your senior, you were put in charge of this case. I was giving you a chance. You can't just take off in the middle of the day because your boyfriend calls."

"Boyfriend? Sir, I–"

"Shut up, Detective. You and I had this discussion at the beginning of your term here. You don't have family, for those who do I make a few exceptions, but you have no right to put your sex life ahead of this department."

"Sir, I don't know where you are getting this from but—"

"Christ, everyone in the office is talking about it! Constantly checking your phone before and after interrogation this morning? You couldn't even walk into the station right now without checking in with 'Eddy'. I don't care if he can make you sing the fucking opera and tap dance at the same time—"

"That's enough," I said, slamming my hands down into the arms of the chair and forcing myself up. "If you'd spent two seconds thinking about it—"

"You watch your tone, Young!"

"—you might have realised there was a sole survivor from the Melendez murder-suicide named Eddy—"

"I don't care where you two met—"

"—who is a three-year-old boy!"

The silence of those few moments was louder than anything I have ever heard.

"What?"

I slumped into my seat again.

I'd just had a yelling match with my boss, who had been about to fire me anyway. There was officially nothing I could do to save my job now.

"Eddy is Edward Melendez, the little boy from the case I took two weeks ago, the one who survived the bullet his father put in his gut. He's been in and out of surgery since. Yesterday was the first day the doctors told me he was stable, which is why I came back to work today."

George sat down in his chair like it might break underneath him.

"So what happened this afternoon?"

"He was rushed in for emergency surgery, and Child Services was going to fuck it up so the nurse called me."

I actually got a smile out of George.

"So let me get this straight," he said quietly. "You took your first vacation time in over a year to watch over a three-year-old in the hospital, who you have no personal connection to?"

"You make me sound like I've gone nuts."

"Have you?" George said seriously. "I mean, why?"

"I don't know," I said quickly.

Why did I go to the hospital when I knew I could lose my job?

Why did I take vacation time to look after him?

He had the hospital staff and Child Services, what did he need me for?

It didn't matter what I asked myself, all I saw was his little face looking up at me. Smiling for the first time in days when I gave him that teddy bear. The way his face lit up.

"Actually," I continued, "I think Detective Patel might have it right. I always fall for the unavailable guys."

George leaned his head back and laughed, and I couldn't help but join in.

❧   ❧   ❧

"Detective Young." I looked around and saw the nurse from earlier.

"Thank you for the phone call," I said when she got near, "I'm sorry I couldn't get here sooner. I had to clean out my desk."

The nurse stopped dead in her tracks. "You were fired?"

"No, I took a transfer into a department with a lighter caseload. Stolen Property, actually. That way I'll have more time for Eddy."

A grin spread across the nurse's face, "That's good, because a lady from Child Services wants to talk to you." She pointed down the hall and I could see a woman sitting in the chair beside his door.

"Well. Talk about timing."

I should have felt nervous but I felt kind of relieved. It would be good to get this out of the way. I introduced myself as soon as I was close enough. I even shook the woman's hand.

"I know you're busy, Detective, so I'll get to the point. I believe you have taken an interest in young Edward's life. While we are grateful to have a continued police interest, I am afraid I must ask you allow us to take things from here. I assure you, despite what you might think, the system will take care of Edward."

I could feel myself wanting to intimidate her. I wanted her to know who was really in control. That her stupid speech wasn't going to stop me. But Eddy was close, and I didn't need him to hear raised voices.

"Thank you... however, I'm not here on police business. I'm here because I want to be. And I will be speaking to a lawyer in the morning to start jumping through whatever legal hoops your department has created to begin the adoption process." I smiled as sweetly as I could. "I will do everything I can to make sure Eddy never enters the system."

"You're serious?"

"Very." I looked over her shoulder into the room. I could just make out an Eddy-sized lump in the bed.

"Well, I can only see one option here, Detective Young." I looked back at her, ready to stand my ground if need be, but she looked... happy.

"I'll bring round some paperwork for you to fill out later tonight and send an agent over to assess your home, to see if you meet the temporary residence requirements until the adoption is finalised. They take a while, you know that right?"

"Yes," I said, knowing I had a stupid grin on my face. "I'm prepared to wait."

"Good. You should go see him, he has been asking for you."

Asking?

I didn't bother saying thank you or goodbye, I just barrelled into the room. Eddy hadn't spoken since the murder.

"Tor-weee," a little voice called from the bed. Eddy put his arms out for a hug.

I was happy to oblige.

The Other Side of Limbo

Claudia Osmond

"You will come back to chat some more, won't you?" Mildred called, her feeble voice swallowed up in the commotion of the airport crowd.

The woman walking away didn't seem to hear her. She just kept her nose buried in the book she was reading as she joined the back of the line to the women's restroom.

"Now, she was a nice young lady, wasn't she, dear?"

"Yes indeed she was. Reminds me a lot of our Annie."

"A shame she didn't stay longer. Shall we follow her?"

Mildred looked to where the woman was standing. Several others had taken their place behind her so now only her red hair was visible.

"Oh, no. I don't suppose we should, dear. Seems as though she doesn't need us anymore."

Mildred sighed. *Just like our Annie.*

She scanned the concourse. There were a few people arguing, a few sleeping on the hard plastic seats, a couple kissing in a corner, and a woman changing her baby's nappy right on the floor.

"Look at that," she whispered. "How dreadful."

She couldn't decide which was worse: the couple kissing or the mother changing her baby in public.

171

"Mind your business, dear."

Mildred didn't feel like minding her business. What she felt like doing was telling the couple in the corner if they weren't careful they'd end up precisely in the shoes of the woman who was changing her baby's nappy And they were far too young for that; they probably had even less sense between the pair of them than that young mother had on her own.

But as she thought about the time and effort it would take to stand up and walk across the concourse, she became distracted by a woman's shrill voice, just a few feet from where she was sitting.

"Is everything alright, Calvinsweetheart?" the woman called after a man who, it seemed to Mildred, was in an awful hurry to visit the restroom.

Calvinsweetheart. What an odd name. Ah, but to each his own; that's what Frank would say.

Mildred's heart gave a little flip.

Frank? Where is Frank? Her heart flipped again and started racing as she looked this way and that, searching for Frank. *This is what happens when I take my eyes off him…*

"Calvinsweetheart?" the woman called again, her voice so grating Mildred couldn't help but look her way. She called once more, but her husband had already disappeared into the men's room.

Ah, the men's room, thought Mildred, relief flooding her as she patted her chest. Frank must have just gone to the men's room.

The woman gave an exasperated sigh and plopped herself down, two seats away from Mildred. Mildred thought she looked like a nice lady: neatly styled hair, bright eyes, and a gorgeous tweed travel jacket Mildred would have loved to own herself.

Must ask Frank to get me one of those for my birthday. Of course, it will need to be quite a few sizes smaller.

Mildred cleared her throat. "Perhaps you would be so kind as to have your Calvinsweetheart check on my Frank," she said, reaching out a hand across the two seats that separated them. "Once he's finished in there, of course."

"Pardon me?" said the woman turning her head, but not pulling her eyes away from the men's room door.

"You see," said Mildred, "Frank has a heart condition and, well, I worry, although he always tells me to stop worrying, that nobody ever lived a day longer through worrying, in fact worrying, says Frank, can actually shorten one's life by literally years and, well, at our age we can't afford even one second, so Frank always makes sure that I stay on the positive side of things and mind my own business and—"

The woman turned and looked at Mildred in a way that made Mildred snap her mouth shut. She couldn't remember ever being looked at like that before. She shivered and retracted her hand as quickly as her ninety-year-old muscles would let her.

The woman, holding a steady stare, pulled something out of her jacket pocket and popped it into her mouth. It crunched.

Probably the remains of the last poor creature to cross her path, thought Mildred with a shudder.

The woman finally relented by pulling a compact out of her purse and touching up her lipstick.

"Well, I thought that perhaps…" ventured Mildred again after a few moments. Now that the woman was puckering and blotting she didn't seem so intimidating. More to the point, Mildred had to find out if Frank was all right. "Perhaps since your husband is using the restroom… perhaps…" Mildred stroked the arm of her crocheted sweater before lacing her shaky fingers together. She tried to steady her hands in her lap.

"My husband?" said the woman, looking at Mildred again. To Mildred it looked like she was trying to suppress a smile.

"Yes," said Mildred. "I heard you…" She trailed off and looked down at her hands.

Mind your business, Mildred dear…

"Oh, yes, well," said the woman. She recapped the lipstick, snapped the compact shut, and returned both items to her purse. "Yes." She started tapping the arm of her seat with one red polished nail.

"Well, as I was saying, I was just wondering… do you think that perhaps—" Before Mildred could finish her request, the woman stood up and marched towards the men's room. And then she walked right in!

"Oh my," said Mildred to herself. "She's going right in there and checking on Frank herself!"

Mildred shook her head, disappointed in herself for misjudging the woman; for suggesting that her pockets were stuffed with remains.

Frank always says to be gracious to people, and not to judge. Shame on you, Mildred. Shame on you for being so judgmental.

As she waited, Mildred once again spotted the young mother. Only now Mildred saw that her children—she counted four, no, five—were running pell-mell around the concourse. And their mother was just sitting, arms and legs crossed, doing absolutely nothing about it. Mildred shook her head.

She's got herself a brood of little hooligans. That's what happens when children barely out of nappies themselves have babies. I wouldn't be surprised to read about them in the paper one day.

Her gaze followed two of the little hooligans, pretending to be airplanes, dipping and diving and crashing into each other. After one such crash that ended in tears—it always does—her eyes flicked towards a sign that had Quick Stop Coffee Shop painted in green letters.

"What we need is some tea," she said and decided to start making her way towards the men's restroom so that when Frank came out they could go straight to the coffee shop together.

Mildred put the strap of her carry-on bag over her shoulder and pulled herself to a standing position, steadying her tiny frame with the arm of her seat.

"Whoa! Let me help you, there, comrade," came a voice from behind her.

Mildred's eyes flashed upward. The red-faced man looked familiar, but… oh, her memory wasn't what it used to be!

"Randall, Ms Mildred," he said, tapping his nametag. "Remember?"

She looked at the tag. "Oh, Randall. Yes, of course! Thank you dear. I was just heading to the men's room."

"You mean the ladies' room," Randall corrected, and blushed so his already red face became almost purple.

"No, the men's room," Mildred replied. "I need to wait for Frank.

Then we are going to get some tea." She pointed at the café logo embroidered on his apron.

"Well then let me help you navigate the land mines," said Randall. He took her carry-on off of her shoulder and slung it over his own.

"Oh, yes," said Mildred. "Thank you."

As Randall led Mildred through the crowds of people, Mildred shouted, "If we'd had a son, we'd have wanted him to be just like you." The noise level had risen to the point where Mildred was having a hard time hearing herself talk, let alone think. For Mildred, hearing herself think was very important.

Mildred spotted the woman with the tweed travel jacket coming out of the men's room. "Oh, Randall, dear, take me to that lovely lady wearing the expensive travel jacket," she said, pointing.

"Do you know her?"

"Oh, yes."

By the time Mildred and Randall made it to within a few steps of the woman in the tweed jacket, her husband had joined her. They were arguing, the woman jabbing a manicured, red nail into his puny chest.

"I see you found your husband!" Mildred shouted, even though she was standing right in front of them now.

Calvinsweetheart glared at Mildred, then at his wife.

Whatever was that for?" she thought, shaking her head. The younger generation these days…

Avoiding Calvinsweetheart's eyes, Mildred asked the woman, "Did you happen to see my Frank in there?"

"No," she replied, grabbing her husband's arm.

"Oh, heavens!" said Mildred. "Well then where–" She stopped abruptly, mid-sentence, and shifted her focus from their conversation to the men's room door. "Frank!" she exclaimed.

The woman's and Calvinsweetheart's heads turned, but other than a young child bouncing on the spot, pretending to be a frog, there was no one between them and the men's room door.

Mildred kept talking. "You know how I worry when you're not within earshot, you always tell me not to worry, and then you go and disappear like that! Next time you must tell me."

The woman in the tweed jacket looked back at the space between them and the men's room door. The frog-boy was gone. There was no one else there. She looked at her husband and rolled her eyes.

"Now, Randall, here," Mildred continued, changing the subject as she patted Randall's hand, "is going to take us to get some tea. Won't that be lovely?"

"Oh, yes. A lovely spot of tea is just what we need," Mildred answered herself.

The woman and her husband stood there staring. Randall smiled and shrugged and led Mildred toward the coffee shop, escorting her to a table. There was a man sitting there, an unlit cigarette hanging out of his mouth bouncing in rhythm with his leg. He was tracing the rim of his paper coffee cup with his middle finger. Randall cleared his throat. Small beads of sweat formed on his forehead.

"See this, soldier?" Randall tapped the blue sign screwed onto the tabletop. He outlined the engraved white wheelchair with his fingernail.

The man looked at Randall as if challenging him to ask another stupid question. Randall cleared his throat again and shifted his weight from one foot, then to the other.

"Don't let him bully you," said Mildred, looking up at Randall, patting his arm.

The man's gaze suddenly shot beyond Randall's shoulder, and without out a word he stood and hurried out of the coffee shop, knocking his empty paper cup to the floor.

"That's showing him who's boss," said Mildred.

"Oh, a fine job, indeed," she said. "We're proud of you, Randall."

Randall stood a bit taller and turned around. "And don't even think of lighting that thing hanging from your lip, private!" he called, but not loud enough for the man to actually hear.

Randall turned to Mildred and smiled, his face muscles twitching. "Rules are here for the good of the entire platoon and should be followed," he said. "Here now, Ms Mildred. Have a sit down."

He helped Mildred lower herself into the seat. He put her carry-on bag under the table and picked up the abandoned coffee cup. He wiped the sweat off his forehead with his apron before using it to brush the crumbs off the table.

Mildred straightened her skirt and shuffled her feet together. She looked up and noticed the man who'd been sitting in her seat was having a few harsh words with a lady in a blue raincoat. The lady looked like she was crying. The man gave her shoulders a shake and then took her arm in his. They walked a few paces and sat on the far edge of a concrete planter.

"Poor dears," said Mildred, shaking her head. "They must be distraught over the delayed flights. We know how they feel."

"Yes, we certainly do."

Randall put his hand on Mildred's shoulder. "Why don't I get you some tea, Ms Mildred?"

"Oh, yes, that would be lovely. We'll have chamomile."

"No, not chamomile," she corrected herself. "Peppermint. Let's have peppermint today."

"Lovely choice," she said. And then she smiled up at Randall.

"Peppermint it is. I'll be right back."

Mildred watched Randall toss the paper cup into the trash bin. As he walked toward the kitchen, he stopped to talk to a red-haired woman sitting on the floor reading a book—the same red-haired woman who had reminded Mildred so much of her own Annie.

Mildred watched them exchange words before the woman stood, shaking her head and brushing off her derriere. She picked up her bag, slung it over her shoulder, and started walking towards Mildred's table.

"You can have a seat with us, dear," Mildred offered as she passed by.

Mildred reached out to touch her elbow, but she was too far away. And it appeared she didn't hear Mildred, yet again. She settled on the opposite side of the planter to the man with the cigarette.

"She must be very busy," said Mildred.

"Oh, yes. Yes indeed," she replied. "Just like Annie."

Randall came back with Mildred's tea. "Bag in?" he asked as he put two cups on the table.

"Oh, yes please. Leave the bag in. We like our tea strong."

"So, where was your destination today, Ms Mildred, before the airline launched that nuke into your plans?"

"Paris. We were headed to Paris. For our grandson's wedding."

Randall knew Mildred wasn't flying anywhere. Just like she hadn't flown anywhere yesterday, or the day before that. Or any other day.

"Pass up our carry-on, will you Randall dear?"

Randall did.

Mildred unzipped an outside pocket and shuffled through it. "Here we are." She pulled out two airline tickets. "We do hope the delay isn't too long, don't we?"

"That's right, dear. We don't want to miss Henry's wedding."

"Randall, dear," she said, holding the tickets out to him. "Can you imagine? We've both forgotten our reading glasses. Could you tell us which gate we're to be at once they announce the flights have resumed?"

"Sure thing, Ms Mildred," said Randall, although she only had an crumbled paper ticket, the same tickets she asked him to read every day.

FLIGHT PA341 28/07/1996

BOARDING 10:35

"Have you checked in yet, Ms Mildred?"

Mildred put the tickets down. "Have we…" she had a faraway look on her face. "Why, no. No we haven't…"

"Well, it's a good thing, Ms Mildred, what with the way *Pangaean* shut down this morning," Randall said, tapping the *Pangaean Airlines* logo on the tickets. "Or else you'd have some time trying to get your luggage back."

"Pardon?" said Mildred. She felt like a damp cloud had just lowered onto her shoulders. She shivered. "But… but we thought the flights were only delayed."

"No, no. *Pangaean* just up and shut down," Randall said. "No warning, no apologies, no nothing. Just pffft! Shut down."

Mildred looked at Randall like a little girl whose balloon just floated away. "We would much prefer to go to Paris anyway," she said.

"Well, I guess… I guess you could re-book with Balder Air. Or *Ganda*. Or *Freedom*," Randall suggested. "I mean, if you really want to."

Mildred put a shaky hand over her mouth. The cloud swallowed her up completely. "No, thank you," she whispered.

A sudden commotion caught both their attention. A man in a dark jacket elbowed his way through, flashing a badge. He grabbed the man sitting on the planter, and they began to struggle.

"That's the same soldier who was sitting here!" exclaimed Randall. "I bet he tried lighting that lung-grenade!"

Mildred saw the familiar red-haired woman walking away from the scene. "Annie," her voice thin and low was lost.

She pushed herself to her feet.

"Where are you going?" asked Randall. "Ms Mildred, I don't think you should go over there right now. You'll be putting yourself right in the middle of a combat zone."

Mildred didn't hear him. She shuffled herself along the tiled floor toward the red-haired woman. Randall followed her and when he tried to take her by the arm, Mildred pulled away.

"No, thank you," she said.

This time Mildred wasn't going to let Annie get away. She grabbed a hold of the woman's wrist. "Annie," she said.

The woman jumped. Her eyes flashed to Mildred's cold hand clamped around her wrist and back up to her face.

"Annie," said Mildred again. "*Pangaean* has shut down. What should we do?"

The woman blinked several times. Then she looked Mildred directly in the eyes. "Regret nothing," she said. And with that, she pulled free and disappeared into the crowd.

"Do you know that lady?" asked Randall, who had been standing behind Mildred the entire time.

Mildred didn't reply.

"Ms Mildred," said Randall, trying once more to take her by the elbow. But Mildred just shuffled off.

This time Randall let her go. She'd be back again. She always was.

Mildred made her way through the crowd. There were still people arguing all around her, but Mildred didn't notice them anymore. She had been devoured by the crowd and only aware of her own thoughts and ragged breaths.

Regret nothing. That's what Annie had said. Mildred turned that phrase over and over in her mind.

"What do you think she meant by that?" Mildred asked aloud.

There was no reply.

"What do you think she meant by that, Frank?" she asked again, panic rising in her chest.

There was still no reply.

Mildred stopped, dread gripping her heart. She didn't realise it, but she had left the terminal building. She pulled her crocheted sweater tightly around her frail body.

"Frank? Frank!"

"Can I help you get a taxi, ma'am?" asked a young attendant.

Mildred suddenly felt a tightening spread across her chest and she was hit by a dizzy spell. "What about Paris?" she said as she reached out and steadied herself on a cold metal trash bin. "What about Henry's wedding?"

"The, uh … you'll have to check in if you're heading to Paris, ma'am," the attendant said. "Inside the building."

"Frank?" Mildred called again. "We must check in, Frank." She let go of the trash bin. *"Frank?"* She shuffled down the walkway, farther from the building.

"Uh, just shout if you need anything, okay?" the attendant called after her. "If… if you can't find Frank."

Mildred kept walking.

"We must check in, Frank," she said again. "We can't go to Paris unless we check in."

Mildred's heart raced and her body shook. She didn't know where to go, what to do.

Where is Frank?

"Ms Mildred, wait! You forgot your bag and tickets at the coffee shop! Ms Mildred!"

At the sound of her name Mildred snapped to and stopped, just as she reached the curb. The voice was familiar. It was coming from behind her.

"Frank?" she whispered.

As she turned around another dizzy spell hit her, this one taking the pavement out from under her feet. Her foot slipped off the curb as a taxi rounded the corner.

"MS MILDRED!"

The sound of screeching tyres. The sickening smell of diesel fumes. The sensation of being pushed, or pulled, or lifted; she wasn't sure. And then she went down, hard.

A cacophony of indistinct sounds surrounded her. A heavy weight across her shoulders made it difficult to breathe. Her eyes fluttered open, briefly. Through blurred vision she saw a man's face, right beside her own.

Frank? she thought, although had she had her wits about her, she would have realised he was too young. *Oh, Frank.*

Her head pounded, her vision faded a little more with each beat.

I'm afraid we might miss Henry's wedding after all.

Freedom

Laura Eno

"You couldn't even arrange for a direct flight home?"

Her husband continued the same lament he'd been repeating since they boarded the plane. Even though they were on final descent, Mary was sure he'd badger her about it through the final leg of their trip.

"It's only a one-hour layover. We don't even have to collect the luggage." She glanced sideways to see if he even heard her. No response, just his normal sulk. She sighed and stared out the window, anywhere but in his direction.

"Quit chewing your fingernails. It's bad enough being married to a nutcase, at least try to keep up outward appearances."

Mary dropped the hand that had made its way to her mouth. Silent tears formed under closed eyelids. Thirty-five years of marriage—a lifetime wasted. Why had she thought this trip would be any different? Dear God, she was tired. To be free of the constant criticism...

He leaned in closer, his hot breath smelling of alcohol and bad memories.

"It's your fault Kevin didn't spend more time with us, you know. If you'd just shut up and quit harassing him he might even move back home."

The flight attendant came around to collect drinks, standing next to George while he chugged the last of his bourbon. His leer as he watched the young woman walk away said it all. Mary wondered, not for the first time, if he was sleeping with other women. He never touched her anymore. She wasn't going to ask. He'd probably tell her the truth and she didn't think she could bear it.

They landed with only a slight bump on the tarmac and began the taxi toward the gate. Disappointment washed over Mary. A crash would have been an end to her troubles. Her face burned with the thought of wishing harm to the rest of the people on the plane.

The flight attendant thanked them for flying with a plastic smile on her face as they shuffled out. Mary noticed another attendant off to the side speaking urgently into a phone. She looked upset about something.

Bedlam greeted the passengers as they disembarked from the plane.

"What the fuck is going on here?"

George shoved his way through the restless, milling crowd. The noise level hurt Mary's ears as she tried to take it all in. The buzz sounded angry as people overwhelmed the gates of various airlines.

She slid between people, whispering apologies as she went. Making her way over to the airport map where George stood to locate their next gate, Mary glanced up at the departures board overhead. Bold red letters saying 'cancelled' flashed beside several flights. With a sinking feeling, she realised they all belonged to the airline she booked their flights on. George saw it at the same time.

"That's just great. A lousy finish to a lousy vacation. If you'd just booked a direct flight in the first place we wouldn't be having this problem."

"Maybe we can go collect our luggage and take another flight." She despised the timid sound of her voice but didn't have the energy to speak louder.

"Someone's going to pay for this," he said, as if he hadn't heard her. Mary wondered if that someone would be her.

She watched him storm off towards the luggage belts, not bothering to see if she would follow or not. Struggling to keep up, Mary trotted after her husband as if he held a leash around her neck. In many ways he did, she realised. It'd been a long time since she'd had the ability to stand on her own.

The luggage carousels didn't have their flight number listed. Mary watched George try to browbeat a security guard for information, finally storming back to her with a disgusted look on his face.

"He says I have to go to the airline desk and talk to them. Something about the company folding and the luggage still being on the plane. If that doesn't beat all. I'm going to sue the shit out of them when we get home."

Mary tagged along behind him as they made their way back to the desk. A mob stood in front of it without a single employee in sight.

"Can't we just go home? I'm sure they'll send our luggage to us in a day or two." Mary tried to diffuse the explosion she saw building on George's face. He already had a few drinks in him. She couldn't take any more trouble.

"I'm staying right here until I get some answers." He turned his back on her, not caring about her opinion.

"I'm going to get some tea at that restaurant we passed on the way here. Is that alright with you?" Anything to get away from him for a few minutes. Mary felt like she couldn't breathe. Her doctor told her to find a quiet place to sit down when she felt like this but it seemed impossible to do that here.

George ignored her question, although she was sure he'd heard her over the general noise of the place. She bit her lip, feeling overwhelmed by the situation. Hugging her purse close to her side, Mary turned around and walked away, stumbling slightly as her vision blurred.

The café would have been pleasant if it weren't so crowded. The décor promised a relaxed environment, somewhere to while the time away between flights. Mary ordered a tea and stood sipping it, as there weren't any vacant seats. She studied a young woman surreptitiously over the rim of her cup. The redhead sat reading a book, looking at ease, an air of self-assurance about her. Mary wished she could be as bold.

Taking the trip to Paris for their son's graduation had been her idea.

She hadn't seen him in so long and getting his doctorate was a milestone she hadn't wanted to miss. Her doctor had had misgivings about letting her travel, telling her he was still trying to adjust her medication and she wouldn't be in a position to get help if needed. He finally relented when he saw how much it meant to her.

She shouldn't have gone; Mary saw that now. Kevin was no longer the sweet boy she remembered. He was cold and distant, just like his father. Other than two quick dinners, they didn't see him at all during the week they'd spent there. He had other plans with friends, despite the fact that he knew ahead of time they were coming.

Mary watched the people around her talking into their phones, idly wondering how long the batteries lasted in those things. She didn't own one. George said there was no reason for her to have one since she didn't have any friends. It would be nice to commiserate with somebody right now though.

She set her cup down on the counter she stood next to and opened her purse. Reaching inside, Mary withdrew the bottle of little white pills. She clutched them in her hand, as she'd done so many times in recent days. She stuck them in her coat pocket and walked back to the counter to purchase a bottle of water.

Wandering through the crowded concourse, Mary tried not to think about the trip but couldn't get her mind to settle on anything else. Paris—the city of lovers.

How ironic, she thought.

They hadn't been back there since their honeymoon. So much had changed since then. What could have been a last chance to renew their failed relationship instead turned into a re-creation of life at home—she sat in the room and he sat in the bar downstairs. The one time she'd thought to venture out on her own had come to an ignominious end.

The taxi had meandered up and down the *Champs Elysees*, the meter clicking over as Mary sat in the back seat frozen in indecision about where to go or what to see. She'd finally had the cab driver return to the hotel, having seen nothing of the beautiful city.

Berating her for money spent on nothing, George had stormed out of the room and gone downstairs to claim his usual barstool, leaving Mary in tears. She spent the rest of the week sitting in the hotel room, staring at the flower patterns on the wallpaper. George only spoke to her at meal-times, and then it was only to correct her many perceived deficiencies.

Life had never been easy with him, but the last ten years had been the worst—ever since Lauren…

Stop. I can't go there right now. It's too much.

She left the dubious sanctuary of the café and walked out into the concourse and tried to peek into the different shops but they held no interest for her. The various sundries were the same, no matter what airport one was in. Mary didn't have an interest in the latest magazines or mystery novel; in fact, she didn't have much of an interest in anything lately.

Life had become nothing more than a treadmill for her, everything about her day orchestrated by someone else. Her hand strayed to the pocket holding her pills as she sat on the edge of a planter. The weight of the bottle comforted her. A woman plopped down on the seat next to Mary, exhaustion etched on her young face. Two children played tag with each other, running in circles in front of her. The boy and girl looked to be twins, probably six or seven years old.

"This is crazy. What do the airlines expect me to do with two kids and no luggage?"

"I don't know." Mary didn't want to be drawn into a conversation but she didn't want to seem rude either.

"Stop it and come sit down! You're bothering people." The kids trudged over to their mother and sat on the ground in front of her, cupping their chins in their hands like bookends on a shelf.

"They told us we could take a later flight on another airline but that our luggage wouldn't be on it. Is that what they told you?"

"I haven't checked into that yet," Mary said. "My husband hasn't come back from the airline desk."

"Well, you'd better hurry. The other flights are filling up fast."

The children were back to running around again so Mary took the opportunity to leave during the commotion. She wondered if George was looking for her and decided to go back down to the desk.

More police had arrived by the time Mary got there. She tried to make her way through the knot of people, being as unobtrusive as possible. She could hear shouting but wasn't close enough to see over the heads of the people in front of her.

As she got closer to the front, she could see security guards hauling away a man with his hands cuffed behind his back. With a sinking heart, Mary recognised George as the man being arrested. She pushed closer until she came up against a police officer barricading the section.

"Please, you have my husband in handcuffs. I have to get through."

"I'm sorry, ma'am. This section is off-limits. You'll be able to post bond for him tomorrow."

"Tomorrow? Why is he being arrested? What am I supposed to do?"

"Destruction of private property, ma'am. Now, please step back."

Mary watched helplessly as George continued to be belligerent as he was led away. With a sob, she melted back into the crowd, confused as to what to do next.

Finding a restroom, Mary wandered inside, gripping her bottle of pills in one hand and her bottle of water in the other. There was a line to use the stalls. As she waited, Mary saw the woman she had been studying in the restaurant again—the one who'd been reading.

She stood next to a woman in a blue raincoat, who was obviously upset, her face red and blotchy with tears.

This place was too crowded—too public. Unhappiness swirled in the air like a malignant fog. Mary needed to get away, go somewhere she could think without all the noise. She turned and ran out onto the concourse, breathing heavily. The spin subsided after a moment. Food, that's what she needed. It had been hours since she had eaten.

She walked in quiet desperation until she found the food court. It resembled an indoor bazaar, with people standing shoulder-to-shoulder, impatiently waiting their turn at the various counters. The angry sweat of people in close quarters assaulted her nose. A young girl with dark hair stepped out of the crowd, catching her eye. She looked so much like Lauren that Mary started.

"Ma'am… Ma'am? Excuse me, but are you in line?"

The irritated voice behind her snapped Mary out of her frozen state.

"No, I'm sorry," Mary whispered. She stepped aside, looking for the girl but she couldn't spot her in the sea of faces.

How long had it been since she'd gone into a trance? The accident replayed in her mind like a bad movie, taking her daughter from her once again, the years of therapy gone in an instant. Tyres screeching, the rending of metal as the car tore apart. Glass flying. Screams. The blood… blood everywhere. The ghosts were coming back. Mary walked back out, desperately seeking solace that didn't exist.

Bereft of support, she let the tidal surge of humanity carry her along until she stood among the kiosks for rental car companies. Spotting a young man standing behind a counter full of brochures advertising places of interest in the city, she wandered over.

"Could you make a hotel reservation for me?"

"Certainly. Are you looking for something close to the airport?" His hands hovered over the keyboard.

"No." Mary surprised herself by saying that but bolstered her courage as a plan formed in her mind. "No, and I'd like it to be a nice place, perhaps with a suite?"

"Let me take a look." His fingers tapped in rapid succession, finding a positive answer within a matter of moments.

Mary left in a daze, the address he'd written down clutched in her hand. The automatic doors opened at her approach, ushering her out to the lines of taxis waiting to take people on adventures. At least it seemed like one to her. The thought had its own exhilaration. She felt adrenaline coursing through her veins.

The driver glanced at the address and opened the door for her. "No bags?"

"No." She watched him shrug and climb into the driver's seat.

Now seated, Mary realised how much her feet hurt. It felt good to relax and not think for a minute. The radio added more noise, but it was better than thousands of grumbling people milling around her.

"Driver, I've changed my mind. Would you take me on a tour of the city first, before going to the hotel?"

"It'll be expensive, lady." He eyed her in the rear-view mirror.

"I have the money."

Fortunately, George had given her the cash to hold in her purse. She watched the cabbie nod and settled back into the seat.

The city streets flowed by as they drove, people strolling on the sidewalks with somewhere to go, shopping to do, lives that went on. Just like in Paris, Mary stared at it all but saw none of it. But unlike in Paris, there was no indecision. She stood apart from it now, carried along on her own course to arrive at her destination alone—somehow always alone.

After hours voyaging through the streets of the city, the taxi drew up to her final destination. She paid the fare and stood outside the hotel for a moment, marvelling at the façade. Its old-world charm drew her in, promising peace from her demons. Mary straightened and walked toward the waiting doorman.

"Good evening madam." He held the door open for her as she drifted towards the reception desk.

The clerk at the desk spoke with deference as he took her credit card. "Will you be staying just the one night, Mrs Fitzgerald?"

"Yes."

"If there's anything you need, just call room service. Your suite is on the tenth floor, room 1012. Just take the elevator up and turn to your right." He handed her the card key with a smile. "Please enjoy your stay."

"Thank you, I will."

The silence of the elevator soothed Mary's nerves as she rode it up to her room. The darkened interior of the suite welcomed her as a lover would after a long journey's end. She opened the curtains and watched the setting sun bring the city alive with bright lights before closing the world off once more.

Ensconced in lovely surroundings such as she'd never had occasion to enjoy before, Mary pondered what to do next as she removed the shoes from her aching feet. It was dinnertime and her stomach rumbled as a reminder, a banal counterpoint to the distress of the day. Reaching for the room service menu, Mary decided to live out this night in splendour.

She ordered food that George would have vetoed for being too expensive or frivolous—filet mignon, asparagus tips in hollandaise sauce, strawberries dipped in chocolate.

"And I'd like a glass… no, make that a bottle of merlot." She hadn't had a drink since the night of Lauren's death; George had blamed the accident on her one glass of wine with dinner that evening even though the police cited the other driver. The woman on the phone repeated everything back and asked if she could do anything else for her. Mary thanked her politely.

She pulled the small locket that held Lauren's picture out of her purse and opened it. The ten-year-old's smiling face shone out at her, full of love and sunshine. Mary smiled back. Her little girl would have been twenty next month.

"I miss you, baby."

A quiet knock announced the arrival of her food. Mary opened the door to let the gentleman push the cart in. She watched while he set it all out on the table and opened the bottle of wine for her, pouring a small sample into the glass for her approval.

"It's fine, thank you." She signed the bill and silently wished him a speedy departure. She wanted—needed—this time alone. Putting the do not disturb card on the door after he left, Mary carried the locket out of the bedroom and put it on the table beside her. She raised the glass of wine in a silent toast to Lauren, sipping at the blood-red liquid while deep in thought.

Mary couldn't remember a meal ever tasting better.

Perhaps it was the company.

She giggled at the thought, the sound so foreign to her ears that she looked around the room for the source before realising it came from her own lips. She wondered what George was having for dinner and laughed aloud. The release felt wonderful.

After dinner, Mary drew a bath, pouring a generous amount of rose-scented oil into the tub. She sank deep into the fragrant water, lying back while eating the chocolate strawberries. She reflected on the decision she had made, knowing it was the right path for her even as she wondered how she had arrived at it with no conscious thought. Maybe this was a

road she had been travelling for some time now and she just hadn't noticed it.

Too much thinking, not enough doing. Stepping out of the tub it
occurred to her that she had nothing clean to put on. Mary laughed
again, delighted at the happy sound. It didn't matter. She padded over to
the luxurious bed and slid between the silky sheets. She poured herself
another glass of wine and opened the bottle of pills that sat on the nightstand, shaking them out into her hand. The pills and the wine ran out at
the same time. As she lay down, the sheets caressing her bare skin, a feeling of peace stole over her. Mary smiled as she understood what it meant.

She was free.

Cobalt Blue

Jasmine Gallant

"Are you Sam Harris?"

"Yes."

"Who do you work for?"

"Airport Security.

My interrogator smiles and closes his eyes. A silence fills the room and nobody moves.

"What do you want from me?"

"I want to know who your employers are." His eyes are on me again, cool and steady.

"My employers? What is this—" I look behind me and realise a gun is trained on me. "What the fuck's going on?"

✯ ✯ ✯

"Another cup, Sam?"

Melissa, the tired and frumpy waitress, stands in front of me at the counter holding a pot of coffee by the handle, blocking my view of the wall- mounted television. A pretty but severe-looking woman tells me the airport faces more delays and overwrought passengers have nowhere to go as flights are grounded indefinitely.

Grounded indefinitely, huh? Join the club. Ten years. Ten years I've worked this shitty job and what do I have to show for it? A broken down car and a handful of debts. A few broken down relationships and a handful of regrets. I was meant for greater things than this.

"Yeah, why not?"

Melissa pours the coffee with a deft hand, hardly paying attention. I have no idea how long she's worked here, longer than the three years I've been coming here, with her worn red dress and frizzy hair always escaping the bun she ties it up in. I picture her, standing before a dusty mirror at dawn in heavy-duty support garments, the slow movements of a sleepwalker pulling her hair back for another day of her meaningless and monotonous life.

"You hear anything else about *Pangaean*?"

"Not a thing."

"Huh, sure is strange. What do you think must've happened for it to go bust so quickly?"

"I guess that's how it happens sometimes. Don't pay your bills and then… Still, nice to know it happens to the big sharks as well as us small fry."

"I think there's more to it than that," says the old codger at the end of the counter. He gestures up to the television with his fork. "Big airlines like that don't just go under. They've got—what do you call it—insurance and the like. Maybe they were being investigated for something…" He trails off.

"For what, tax evasion?" I snort. "Big companies don't have to worry about all that. They've got connections you can't even imagine."

"Oh yeah? You know that for a fact? Who the hell you work for?"

"*Are you Sam Harris?*"

"*Yes, for fuck's sake, I've told you that already!*"

"*Who do you work for?*"

"I'm a security guard for the airport. How many times are you going to ask me that?"

"Until we get the right answer. Now tell me Mr Harris, who do you really work for?"

❧   ❧   ❧

I ignore the old man and look back up to the television, hoping the conversation is over. It appears to be; I can see him out of the corner of my eye also looking up and concentrating on the weather report, chewing his steak methodically.

I wonder if he's right. I remember the scene, suits streaming into the baggage area and speaking to all the *Pangaean* staff. I made myself scarce, as it looked like it might kick off, so they'd probably want security to put in overtime. I saw Bull and Leo leave quickly, trying not to attract attention to the pack they were carrying. I was close to clocking-off and they're good guys; they'd already been shafted by the airline, I wasn't going to add to their worries. Or my own.

I pick up my paper and take another mouthful of coffee as I hear the door chime, but don't bother to look up. Chances are it's just another trucker or airport worker—I don't come here for the company. I like this time of day, the evening as the lights start to come on and the starkness of the day evaporates. I've been working early morning shifts for six months and it suits me, leaving behind the bustle of rush hour and industrious self-important people. It's quiet, with the television murmuring to itself and you can watch the planes rise and fall in the distance while you wait for exhaustion to come knocking.

She sidles up next to me at the counter, slightly out of breath. The scent of her perfume draws my eyes from my paper to her long dark hair, a little wet and tangled. She must feel my gaze because she turns and her blue eyes laser straight through me, sizing me up. I've always been a sucker for blue eyes.

The moment breaks when she glances back towards the booths, spotting Melissa playing matron to a family of tourists. The girl blows out a breath of impatience and slides into the seat next to me, looking up at the television. She exudes an air of controlled panic that arouses my curiosity.

"What can I get you, miss?" Melissa is in front of us suddenly, pad to hand.

The girl spots my coffee cup and orders one of her own. While Melissa fetches a cup and the pot, the girl removes her coat and I find myself glancing at her slim neck. I rustle my paper and hold it up to my face, pretending to read, stealing glances at her from the side of the page. I watch as she lets the coffee cool, lifting the cup and blowing across it, before placing it back down.

After a few minutes, she asks, from behind my paper, if I could pass her the sugar. She has a sight accent, but I'm not sure from where.

"Raining outside?"

"No."

She takes the sugar and turns back to the television. Well that's that then, I think to myself. I know when someone doesn't want company.

We sit that way in silence: her absorbed in the news and me pretending to read my paper. Suddenly she tenses and I look up to the television as well—more scenes from the airport, people with glazed eyes milling around like cows in a field.

"Everything alright?" She glances at me quickly before shaking her head, staring down at her coffee cup.

I watch as she looks back up at the television, her hair obscuring her features from me and I look up as well. A reporter is standing outside the chaotic crowds in arrivals, telling us all *Pangaean* flights are grounded and the airport staff are struggling to cope.

"I... can't find my brother." The words come out barely a whisper and I think I hear a catch in her throat. I lean in closer, matching her body language.

"Was he flying?"

She nods, staring down at her empty cup.

"*Pangaean*?"

Another nod. "We were meant to catch a flight together. To Dubai. But with *Pangaean* folding, and all the chaos, I can't find him."

"It's probably fine; he's probably grabbing a coffee like you. He'll call you."

"No it's…" this she does whisper and looks at me again, anguish darkening her eyes. "Never mind," she mutters and looks away again.

"What?"

"No, it's nothing."

"Listen," I lower my tone. "I might be able to help. I… know how to take care of things."

Her eyes search my face again, and I sense I'm being measured.

"I do a little work on the side, you know… Pays the bills." I give her a sharp smile and push back off my seat a little, offering a hand. "Sam Harris."

She returns my smile with a more demure one of her own. "Sam. My brother's name is Sam too. Sara Lidsmore."

    🐜   🐜   🐜

"Sam, we know who you are. We know you were here to kill the Prince and we also know the Pangaean mess stopped you from being able to leave."

She leans in close, her steely eyes narrowing. She slides the muzzle of her gun down my cheek.

"What? Prince? I don't know what–"

"The time for being coy is over now Mr Harris." Her companion stands behind me and places his hands on my shoulders. "Either you tell us who your employers are or we will kill you."

    🐜   🐜   🐜

"Do you think–" She stops, her brow furrows. "Do you think you'd be able to find out about a private jet that was supposed to have landed?"

"Sure, I know a guy that works air traffic control." A small voice whispers in my head to back off, stay out of whatever this is. But hey, what else was I going to do? Go home and stare at an empty room? I think she seems like a sweet girl and her brother's probably nothing more

197

than a jumped-up city boy with a bankroll. You got to have money to fly private? It wouldn't hurt me to help out his little sister, now would it? Might see a nice little chunk of change coming my way, just for being the nice guy, let alone what she might do for being the hero.

Sara mulls it over before saying, "Okay." She blows the hair out of her face and sounds decisive now. She leans in closer and my previous reservations blow away with the scent of her perfume. "Here's the deal: my brother was flying security with some very big Gulf financiers."

My face must've drawn a blank. She rushes on. "No, it's true—he called me yesterday, asking me to meet him here. He said he'd treat me to a holiday in Dubai. I drove all night to get here on time."

"Ah-huh."

"So do you think they're letting private jets in and out?"

"Huh?" I realise I hadn't heard a word she'd said. I was lost in those eyes.

"The jet my brother's coming in on. Maybe he's already left again?" Her voice rising with a panic.

"Without calling you? You think he just forgot?"

"His phone's switched off, I can't get in touch with him. I'm…" She stops and shakes her head. I watch her, lost in her thoughts and the words come out of my mouth before I can stop them.

"You're worried something bad has happened. Look… Let me call my friend Rusty, he might be able to find something out." I stand up, numbness in my legs and I stretch.

"Yeah?" She looks at me hopefully.

"Yeah, I'll go call him now. He might be able to find something out." I move past her, brushing her leg lightly as I go, trying to pass it off as an accident.

"Where are you going?"

"Payphone."

"Oh, why don't you use mine?" She starts rummaging in her bag and hands me her mobile.

I frown and hold it in my hand. "Any chance this is tapped?"

She throws her head back to laugh and I look at her slender neck again. She really is beautiful.

"I wouldn't think so! Who'd take the time to tap my phone?"

"Well with your brother…"

"No, I think it would be fine. Honestly, Sam." She rolls her eyes as I take the phone and head outside to make the call.

Around the side of the building in the shadows, I lean my shoulders against the stuccoed wall. The street light flickers and I close my weary eyes.

What am I doing, getting involved like this?

Telling her I can help, acting tough for fuck's sake?

Gulf financiers, security ops, private planes?

It's all something out of a bad detective novel, with warning bells ringing all over the place.

I'm throwing myself into the middle of it for a pair of cobalt blues.

"I'm telling you the truth. I work for the airport. That's all."

She shakes her head. "Stop lying, Sam."

"I'm not. I work at the airport, like Rusty. Ask him!"

She smiles and nods to the other man, who kicks open a door, revealing Rusty tied to a chair, slumped forward. A man standing behind him grabs Rusty's hair, and pulls his head up so I can see his face. In the centre of his forehead is a small black hole.

"We would, but Rusty stopped talking."

I remember the torment in Sara's eyes when she thought her brother might have left, and decide the only thing to do is to call Rusty. He'll be able to get me info on private flights. We can put this drama behind us and I can put Sara's mind to rest. He answers on the third ring, sounding slightly drunk.

"Rusty, it's Sam."

"Shit Sam, how the fuck are you? Haven't seen you since the snooker night at The Crown. You seen this crazy shit going down at the airport with *Pangaean*? Sucks balls to be a Hildebrand today!"

"Yeah I ducked out of there as soon as I could. Saw it on the news. You working today Rusty?"

"Night off, thank Christ. Why? Sounds like the circus kicked off down there." I hear the snap of a lighter down the line.

"Just wondering if you knew anything about private planes? Or if you could find out."

"Yeah, Jimmy's working—I'll ring him and see what flights are logged. In-bound or out-bound?

"Uh, both I guess."

"What's this about Sam?"

"Same reason as always," I sigh.

"Oh, a woman." I hear his sardonic chuckle in my ear. "Why don't you come by in about half an hour with 'your reason'? I'll have spoken to Jimmy by then."

"Sounds good. Hey Rusty, thanks." I hang up and rub a hand over my eyes.

When I push back the door to enter the café , both dread and a strange sense of relief fill me—she's gone! But no, there she is by the window staring out toward the airport. Fog is rolling in and the light from the control tower shines through the haze, looking farther away than it actually is. I stand beside and behind her, our silhouettes lit from the strip lighting behind us and our faces lost in shadow.

"My friend's going to try to get us some information. I told him we'd go round to his place."

I can't see her eyes, but I can feel them on me and we stand like that for a long moment, looking at each other without seeing. I'm getting in way over my head, but I can't stop now.

"Okay, let me just go to the toilet."

She turns suddenly and strides past me, to the back. I follow in her wake and grab my coat from the chair, downing the last of my own coffee. The television is still showing scenes from the airport and I watch as

I wait.

"You off then, Sam?" Melissa comes from the kitchen door, wiping her hands on a stained dishtowel. Sara returns from the bathroom and joins us.

"Yeah…" suddenly I don't want Melissa to see me leave with Sara, and I don't know why.

But Sara smiles brightly at her. "He's going to show me the way to a hotel so I can get some rest. I'm exhausted." Her lie flows so easily I'm momentarily stunned and nod in agreement.

"Right then, I guess I'll see you tomorrow." Melissa looks at me closely and her words seem heavy with hidden meaning.

"Sure, see you then."

The need to get away from Melissa's scrutiny propels me towards the door. I open it for Sara, who steps out and is swallowed by the fog. As we walk to my car, I hesitate—we haven't discussed how we're going to get to Rusty's.

"The Volvo's not yours is it?"

"It's a courtesy car. Mine's at the garage."

Sara nods and goes to the passenger side, looking at me over the roof.

"We'll come back and pick up my car later. It's just easier this way."

"Yeah, sure," I hear myself say, but wonder which one's her car. I wave this concern away, and unlock the doors. Pulling out of the car park and onto the deserted street, I find myself testing her story again.

"So, ah… Where are you guys from?"

"All over," she mutters, searching around in her handbag.

"So what do you do when not racing around, looking for your brother?"

"I'm in HR. I'm a trouble-shooter. Fix the mistakes others don't want to touch."

"You what, sack people?"

"Yeah, something like that."

Pulling out some cigarettes, she offers me one before lighting her own and sinking back into the seat. The glow from passing head lights flashes on the angles of her face, distorting it.

Beads of condensation collect on the inside of the windows. Low jazz plays on the stereo and we smoke without speaking.

We pull up outside Rusty's place, a sleepy-looking low-rise building. The engine ticks quietly as it cools and we both stare at the building in silence.

"He's on the second floor, toward the back."

"Well, let's go then." She opens the door and slides out quickly, slamming it shut behind her. Something in me starts saying I should just go home, but she turns and smiles, and those eyes take hold of me. I swear, blue eyes will be the death of me.

☯   ☯   ☯

"You fucks! You killed him!"

I start straining against the duct tape they've used to strap me into the chair, bucking back and forth. She glares at me and raises her gun.

"Last chance Sam, or I will kill you, too."

☯   ☯   ☯

We head for the stairway where a light flickers manically above our heads. Our footfalls echo on the concrete stairs as we make our way into the gloom of the building. We follow the sound of a television and stop at Rusty's front door, lying slightly open on the hinge and look at each other. Neither of us says a word.

Putting a finger to my lips, I reach out to push the door but she grabs my arm and pulls me back. She rifles through her bag again and I motion at her, frowning. Calling the police may be the right thing to do, but it might not be the smartest thing if she's got herself caught up in something dodgy.

And then she pulls out a handgun almost the size of her head.

I start to say something, but she motions me to push the door again, holding the piece steady in front of her. Slowly, the door opens and I step inside. The television's cold light dances along the walls.

She follows me, closing the front door behind her. With the gun pointing to the hidden recesses she checks the room. I stand stock-still. What is she doing with a handgun in her handbag and who exactly is she?

She motions me through to the dingy kitchen and a light snaps on revealing a man is seated at the small brown stained table, hands resting on the top. He is thin and austere looking, dressed in a dark suit and looking intently at me.

I realise Sara has moved behind me. Terror crawls down my spine.

"Hello Sam, nice to meet you," he says, his accent deep and dark.

"Who are you?"

"The real question is, who are you?"

Sara pushes me down into a seat.

"I think there's been some mistake."

"No mistake Sam. Unlike you, we don't make mistakes…"

👀   👀   👀

"Sam, we know who you are. We know you were here to kill the Prince and we also know the *Pangaean* mess stopped you from being able to leave." Sara leans in close, her steely eyes narrowing. She slides the muzzle of her gun down my cheek.

"What? Prince? I don't know what–"

"The time for being coy is over now Mr Harris." The austere man leans forward on the table. "Either you tell us who your employers are, or we will kill you."

The words freeze in my mouth with this threat and I feel ice slide down my spine, my mouth dries instantly. He eases back in his chair and watches me intently with his dark eyes; I see a little of Sara in them.

"I work at the airport, I don't know anything about a prince-"

"Stop lying to me, Sam!" Sara shouts.

"I'm telling you the truth! I work for the airport, that's all."

Sara shakes her head. "Stop lying, Sam."

"I'm not, I work at the airport, like Rusty. Ask him!"

She smiles and nods to the man, who kicks open a door, revealing Rusty tied to a chair, slumped forward. A moves behind him, grabs Rusty's hair and pulls his head up so I can see his face. In the centre of his forehead is a small black hole.

"We would, but Rusty stopped talking."

"You fucks. You killed him!"

Sara glares at me and raises her gun.

"Last chance Sam, or I will kill you too."

Her voice betrays no emotion, and the gun doesn't waver.

"You crazy bitch, I don't know what you're talking about!"

I hear a sound I've only ever heard in the movies until now—a gun firing twice.

My chest explodes in pain and I try to scream but no noise escapes my lungs. I fall to the floor, knocked backwards by the force of the gunshots. Darkness begins to press into my faltering vision. I see both Sara and the austere man standing over me. They are talking but I can barely make out their words.

"…the other bodies in the woods—make sure no one…"

"…he is? What if he was telling the truth?"

Sara leans in close to me, and I stare at her until the darkness steals those cobalt blue eyes.

The Strangest Comfort

Icy Sedgwick

The shit only hits the fan when you've devoted a sizeable chunk of your life to planning for it to not hit the fan. Take today, for example. If everything had gone according to plan, I would now be sitting in the departures lounge, reading a book and probably knocking back a Jack and Coke. Or two. Maybe I'd even be enjoying a giant Toblerone from Duty Free. But no. The crap started when I ran out of the house in a hurry, leaving my passport behind. On top of that, I got stuck in a traffic jam on the way to the airport after going home to get it. I could have handled that. Really, I could, but my plan didn't stretch far enough to include *Pangaean Airlines* collapsing and stranding its passengers all over the world.

This particular airport is on the verge of meltdown. I stop and look across the concourse to the crowded waiting area. It's crammed with harassed parents, bored children, and angry travellers. I've never seen the collapse of an airline before, and it's certainly not pretty. Every other word I hear is 'lawsuit' or 'unfair'. These people don't even think to question the logic of suing a bankrupt airline.

Off to my right, a woman stands at the check-in desk, verbally wrangling with a tired-looking blonde woman. I assume she's a representative of the company that handles whatever it is that needs to be handled when an airline goes bust. The argument revolves around the location of a bag. The would-be passenger is going to a wedding, if the conversation is anything to go by and it seems her dress has been impounded by the airline, along with the bag. Judging by the sobbing and shouting around me, hers isn't the only important bag swallowed up by the airline's collapse. I'm actually glad I forgot my passport, and I mentally thank the traffic jam that stopped me getting here on time. Half an hour earlier, and my bag would also be stuck in the now-defunct airline's inner sanctum beyond the desk.

As it is, my scruffy Union Jack holdall is at my feet. That bag has been everywhere with me. It's seen the aurora borealis, been soaked in the spray of Niagara Falls, and it even survived a riot in South America. Friends laugh at me, and tell me I should replace it, but why? It does the job. That bag is the most reliable thing in my life right now.

Scanning the departures board, it's clear that anything flying out today will be packed. Robert won't mind if I'm late. I'm not sure he'd notice if I never arrived at all. I grimace at the thought of Robert. The blonde woman beside me mistakes the expression for annoyance at the pandemonium around me and nods in agreement.

I move off the concourse and fish my phone out of my pocket. Robert might not care, but I'm pretty sure my publisher will. I'm supposed to be meeting her this evening. Well, her evening. I dial the number, cursing the time difference.

"PIPPA!" Melanie squawks down the phone at me.

"You're awake!"

"Ohmigod, I can't sleep, darling! Gerry woke me up when he saw the news about *Pangaean* on TV! And I thought to myself, just how is my favourite writer going to get here now? Are you okay, darling? Have you got enough money? Are the police there? Is anyone rioting yet? Can you see any blood?" I hold the phone away from my ear slightly; I don't want her to deafen me.

"I'm fine, Melanie. I'm just calling to say I might not be able to get a flight until tomorrow, or maybe later. Everyone's trying to switch to other airlines so it's a bit mental."

"Sweetheart, you just get here when you can, don't worry about the details. Pay whatever you have to. Oh, shoot, I'm getting another call—keep me posted, okay? Ciao!"

Melanie hangs up. I feel lighter knowing I'm in no rush. I decide to let the queues die down before I try to find another flight. I wander to one of the waiting areas. I spot a man far into middle age standing up to follow his implausibly attractive younger wife toward the food court. I stride down the row and slide into the vacant seat before a woman with three brats can grab it. She glares at me, marching away with the kids. I shrug at her retreating back.

The plastic seat is hard and unyielding, but I'm glad to be sitting down. Other people are perched in all manner of strange places, squeezed into gaps and hugging columns. A redhead with a paperback has taken refuge under one of the huge ferns dotted around the terminal. I ball up my jacket and shove it behind me as a makeshift cushion. I sit back and stretch out my legs.

Someone has switched the overhead TVs from flight information to one of the news channels. The sound is off, but I watch a report anyway. A young prince is due to arrive today; the name of the country flashes up but I've never heard of it. The picture changes from a generic newsreader to a scowling boy, shrugging away the hand of a bodyguard. The caption says something about a rare heart condition. The subtitles are slow to catch up, but I guess he's coming for some kind of medical treatment. The piece ends and the newsreader switches on a smile to discuss local sports. I lose interest in the TV.

My eye is drawn to the battered briefcase on the floor beside my feet. 'JR Coker' is scrawled across the white label stuck to the top left corner. A child's scrawl. Junior must be awfully proud of Dad. A quick glance at the threadbare suit and cracked leather shoes says that Junior must also be very poor. I sneak a look at his face. The heavy lines around his eyes make his dark brown skin look like crumpled paper. Grey lurks among his tight brown curls. He turns to look at me. His sad chocolate eyes make me think of a Disney puppy.

"Well, we've got a fine to-do here, haven't we? Ain't never seen nuthin' like this before." He raises a hand and gestures at the chaos around us.

"I know, I didn't expect this when I left the house. It's mayhem," I reply.

"Nawww, I seen mayhem afore, and I can tell you that mayhem is far worse'n this. This? It's inconvenient, that's all."

"You think?" The collapse of an airline strikes me as being more than inconvenient.

"Why, sure, child. We ain't never given more'n we can handle," he says. A faint thrill of unease tickles my spine. I know I've heard a phrase like that before.

"You're not from around here, are you?" I ask, trying to change the subject. I can't place his accent. I don't really care where he's from, but a little conversation should help to pass the time.

"Naww, cherie, I'm from New Orleans, or somewhere near it," he replies. He smiles, and wrinkles deepen in the papery skin around his eyes.

"Blimey, what brings you here?" I ask.

"Oh, I wander all over, so I'm always here. It's jus' 'here' changes."

"So you never know where you're going?"

"I jus' go where the Lord wants me to go."

I'm surprised he doesn't hear the clunk as my heart sinks. I kick my bag over so he can't see the Richard Dawkins book I bought for the flight. For a second, I wish that Fate was human so I could throttle her in person. These guys always try and convert me. The memory of my God-fearing grandmother beating my seven-year-old bottom with a length of leather strap thunders into my mind.

"There's a lot o' suffering in this world, child." He nods. The loose skin around his chin wobbles. I remember being locked in the cupboard under the stairs for wanting to be a Jedi, and the visits when I got left outside in the rain because I asked why the Bible had no dinosaurs.

"Yes… yes, there is." I try to sound neutral. I doubt he will consider the way that woman treated me as suffering. Some people think she was just trying to educate me.

"And those who can help… well I guess I think they should."

By now, I'm fiddling with my phone in my pocket, willing it to ring. Anyone. My mother. Melanie. My accountant. The crazy guy who keeps trying to sell me life insurance. Even Robert would be a welcome distraction.

"Tell me, child… have you ever met Christ?"

I stare at him. I wonder if maybe I misheard him, but he just looks at me with those big eyes, waiting for an answer like a placid bloodhound waiting for his dinner. At this point I would normally snort, laugh and walk away. I can't. For one thing, I don't want to give up my seat, and for another, he seems more earnest than they usually are. I don't want him following me.

"Err… have I met him in person? I don't think so. I mean, I thought he'd be kind of hard to miss. Though I guess he might blend in at a Bon Jovi concert. All that long hair and such."

"D'awww, no, child. Christ can enter your life in so many ways." He nods slowly, agreeing with himself. He gazes into the middle distance and I can't help but follow his gaze. I half expect to see the Messiah standing at the check-in desk. I bet he wouldn't have any problems getting his luggage back. He could probably turn his tattered old receipts into a new ticket.

"I dare say it'd be handy if he popped in here now, especially if he did his 'feeding of the five thousand' trick," I reply. The *Pangaean* staff started dishing out free airline food, but I can see more empty carts than full ones. With the coffee shops full and the food running out, the air smells of riots. I check the location of my bag with my foot.

"It ain't no trick, child."

"If you say so."

"I don't say so, child. I know so." He taps his left temple with a long, skinny finger. By this point, I'm starting to get annoyed. I decide to cut to the chase.

"I'm sorry, if you need money for your church then I'm really not the best person to…" I trail off. He's looking at me with those puppy eyes again. I can't bring myself to finish. I make it a point of principle to donate money only to charities involving animals or kids, but I'm not sure how to tell him that.

"I don't need money. None of us do, not really. We jus' think we

209

do. Naw, we jus' need to wake up to what's around us." His voice grows stronger as he leans closer, wrapping his fingers around my right forearm. A slight scowl settles into his features, like a thumbprint into butter. A quick glance around me tells me no help is on the way. Everyone is too wrapped up in their own dramas.

"So, Mr Coker, is it?" I try to sound cheerful. The dark cloud lifts from his face and he sits back. He releases my arm and smiles.

"I ain't been called that these twenty years together," he replies. "Most folks call me JR."

"Do you have any family, JR?"

"I do, but they're a long, long way away from here." He looks at the floor.

"In Louisiana?"

"Further away even than that."

"Do you have kids?" I know people love talking about their kids. I'll even pretend I'm interested if it keeps him off the Jesus crap.

"Naw, child. It's jus' me down here."

I look at the childish writing on the label. Maybe JR wrote it himself. He doesn't seem like the sharpest knife in the drawer. Or maybe he works with abused kids on his travels. If he does, then he should have opened with that. I'd be signing up to help right now.

"I know where I'm headed, but where are you going?" he asks.

"I'm supposed to be catching a flight to see my publisher about my new book. Well, my publisher and my boyfriend. Only I think my publisher is the only one who actually wants to see me," I reply.

"You write?"

I nod. "Novels, mostly, but I had a couple of books about photography published under a different name a few years back." I can almost taste the relief at not being recognised. I'm not sure that a travelling preacher will take too kindly to the kind of gory religious horror I tend to write. My grandmother never did.

"Creativity is a gift, child. I'm glad you're using it. So many just throw it away." He nods. He does that a lot, it seems.

"Yeah, I'm lucky to get paid for doing what I enjoy doing most."

"That's a very good attitude, child." He smiles. "So why don't you think your man wants to see you?"

"Just a feeling I've got. Each time I go to see him, it seems like he's less interested in me being there. We used to make plans to do things together, like the whole trip was this exciting event, and he'd even take time off work. But now he just does the same stuff he does when I'm not there, and it's up to me if I want to tag along or not," I reply. My level of honesty surprises me.

JR is about to reply when my phone rings. Robert's name flashes up on the screen. He is in the middle of a yawn when I answer.

"I heard about the airline." Typical Robert, not even a greeting. My father excuses him, saying he's simply being efficient by getting straight to the point. I find it rude.

"Yeah, it might take me until tomorrow or later to get a flight out," I say. "It's crazy here."

"Don't hurry on my account."

"Well I need to see Melanie, so—"

"Maybe this is a sign." A cold hand reaches into my chest and wraps its fingers around my heart. I've been waiting for this, but I kept hoping it wouldn't actually happen.

"A sign about what?" I try to sound nonchalant, but the tremor in my voice is bound to give me away.

"Us. Look, it's just not working. I'm not ready for anything serious. I've been thinking…and I guess what it comes down to is that I just don't love you."

I can barely hear him above the roar of blood in my ears. Darkness creeps into the edge of my vision and I worry I will pass out. I don't even notice that JR is holding my free hand. Is he murmuring something? I can't tell.

"But what about all those times when you said you did?" I know I sound pathetic. I might also be shouting, as other people in the waiting area look at me. A woman on the verge of tears must provide a welcome distraction from their own transport hell.

"I guess I just thought I did. I mean, I'd only just broken up with

Debs when you came along, and you just plugged the hole. You were so loving, and caring, I just got caught up in it." I can hear him crunching as he talks. I can't believe he's snacking as he dumps me.

"You what?"

"I got carried along by you. You know, these things happen, right? Look, I'm really sorry but I have to go. I'll leave your stuff with Melanie. You can pick it up from her whenever you get here. Hope you manage to get a flight at some point."

The line goes dead. I stare at my phone. I can't quite work out if that conversation actually just happened. I hear the voices of my characters all the time; maybe I'm just going mad. A look at my call register confirms that it did just happen. A peculiar vertiginous sensation washes over me.

"Are you alright, child?" JR leans close to me.

"I just got dumped over the phone by my stupid boyfriend, because he's too much of a coward to do it in person. I'm stuck in an airport and I have no idea when, or even if, I'll be able to get another flight, and I haven't had a cigarette in four hours. And you're asking if I'm okay?"

"It ain't nice about your boyfriend, but people like that get their due eventually. Believe me, I know, child," he replies. "As for the airport, things could be worse. And the cigarette? Well, see this as an opportunity for a fresh start."

He pats my hand and smiles. This is a bigger, warmer smile than before. Without wanting to, I smile back. I forget that I wanted a cigarette.

"Child, I meet a lotta people on my travels, but you? You're one of the nicest I met yet. You talked to me, when most people woulda jus' walked away, or told me to shut up. Maybe you're just bein' polite, maybe you're jus' humourin' an old man, but you've given me your time," he goes on. "Good things will happen to you, Pippa. Better'n you can imagine."

"You're just saying that to cheer me up."

"Maybe I am, maybe I ain't. But you're a strong soul, child. Even your grandma couldn't take that away from you. You'll be jus' fine."

There is some kind of commotion over near the entrance to the toilets. People are shouting and pointing in that hyperactive way that people get when they feel the need to be active. It doesn't feel like the beginnings of a riot. A row of men in identical black suits and sunglasses forms a barrier between the growing crowd and a heap on the floor. Even the people nearest the *Pangaean* desk jostle to see what's going on.

"Aw, I guess that's my cue to leave," says JR. "It was mighty nice meetin' with you."

He hauls himself to his feet and picks up his briefcase. He smiles at me, and shuffles off in the direction of the crowd.

"I think they've got a first aider there!" I call after him.

"It ain't first aid that boy needs," he calls back.

He heads across the waiting area, and I watch his small, awkward steps become the proud stride of a man on a mission. He reaches the crowd and slips between two tall, broad men. I lose sight of him among the press of bodies. Airport officials are already calling medical staff over the Tannoy, so I wonder what JR hopes to achieve. My narrow nasty streak wonders if he hopes to offer a last salvation to a heart attack victim. As I stare at the crowd, I realise I don't remember telling JR my name. Nor anything about my grandmother…?

Something flits above the crowd, and I wonder how a bird got into the terminal. A mental image of a pigeon using a revolving door makes me giggle. Moments later, JR reappears. The crowd seems to part easily as he emerges, leading a young boy by the hand. The boy looks about eleven or so, and is dressed in fine silk. I'm sure I've seen his face before, but I can't think where. No one has noticed them leave the crush of people. The boy looks up at JR, his mouth hanging open in awe. JR looks across the waiting area at me. He waves, and I realise I am waving back. They disappear behind a column, and are gone.

I sit down with a thump, the plastic seat bending under my weight. I wonder if I should tell anyone, but I can't see any security staff. I don't even know what I would say. Instead, my eye is drawn to my bag. There, sitting on my battered old holdall, a single white feather.

Lost and Found

Jen Brubacher

The public rarely noticed the ground beneath their feet, and thank God for that. It was awful: a laminated sheet of cream-coloured plastic stained brown along the regular routes. Each person in the airport was a stranger hoping like hell to be anywhere else as soon as possible, but together they were a ceaseless army of Nikes, Oxfords and Jimmy Choos. The crud they dragged in from the street and out of the planes smeared off their soles and onto the floor. But this wasn't the part of their debris Ashley Gardner was interested in, even though it was the part she spent the most time with, using mop and bucket, working the skin off her hands.

The skin cells fascinated Ashley the most, shed by the billion. She had heard the average person lost two million every hour, so even if your layover was only the run from one gate to another you still left a part of yourself behind on the floor and between the fibres of the grey carpet that soaked them up beneath the waiting room chairs. Not to mention the hair—about a hundred strands a day, so at least a few lost while you dragged your carry-on bag with its wonky wheels past *News Amuse* and into the bar. You might not remember the weather flickering through the thick windows or what flavour muffin you choked down while you waited to board, but the airport remembered you. It kept you, at least a bit of you, turning to dust beneath the feet of new strangers.

Even if Ashley spent the rest of her life sweeping up she'd never catch every cell. And she'd spent long enough. She'd worked at the airport ever since giving up on high school. Almost three years as an airport janitor meant over two trillion skin cells lost and one hundred thousand hairs. There was more of her in this impersonal building than in the apartment she called home.

☯   ☯   ☯

Ashley would have missed the ring if the woman hadn't looked at her so desperately. There was trouble at the check-in desks and the food court had exploded with angry travellers who weren't hungry so much as empty, unsatisfied and stuck where they had only meant to pause. Ashley had been ambushed. One moment she was sweeping cells in a lonely corner, and the next she was pushing through a hostile crowd, bumping shoulders with suit jackets and Hawaiian-print blouses.

The woman was almost in line. It was difficult to tell where the queue was with all the trudging and shoving going on, but she was near Hello Sushi! and infuriating someone behind her. The woman looked Ashley in the eye and a current flashed between them, recognition on the woman's part, panic for Ashley.

Duck your head, dodge right.

Ashley followed through with the thought and slipped past the line to the other side of the chaos where the woman couldn't follow. She was sure she didn't know her. She should have been content with that, but the flash of desperate recognition was blazing in her mind.

She neared the wall and nudged herself and her broom forward, using the long-handled dustpan to clear the way for her feet. The strangers let her go by. She was at the edge of the food court, beside the staff entrance to the back of the restaurants, when she heard the clunk of metal against the inside of the pan.

She leaned and saw a glint among the skin cells and hair she'd collected through the building. She reached thumb and finger into the mess

216

without any squeamishness, grasped the ring and brought it near her face.

For a moment she focussed only on its interior edge: the long gold curve where the remains of whoever had worn it last must be stuck, holding their evidence. Then she turned it and examined its scruffy sheen. It was a plain band and it had been worn for some time. Ashley was small, sometimes mistaken for a child, and the ring slipped easily onto her thumb. She couldn't tell if it was a woman's or a man's. She'd never worn a ring like this herself.

She looked around. For the first time she really saw the mess at check-in, *Pangaean's* desk drowning in angry strangers. There was just one person at the *Ganda* desk, dealing with overflow, and the girl looked terrified. The PA system repeated a message, unintelligible above the frustrated crowd. She saw Leon and that other guy, the slimy one who always hit on her, leaving the airport. They were baggage handlers. If they were fleeing it was really screwed up on the inside. Rats from a sinking ship.

The ring didn't tell her any more about its owner than the cells and hair stuck to it. She had to think, to escape the mess.

Ashley fisted her hand around her broom and pushed the security code into the keypad at the staff door.

The display panel flashed ERROR. Fingers slippery with sweat, she tried again. Again the keypad flashed ERROR. Her uniform, usually so loose, suddenly felt too thick and hot. She tried to concentrate on the security code, but the numbers swam around in her mind. Ashley basted in her own panic and glared at the keypad, her fingers hovering over the buttons.

Ashley hated that her first instinct was to call Zoe. She had a flash of her mother wrapping her in a thick towel, steaming hot from the drier.

Her next thought was of Mildred, the old lady who practically lived in the airport even though she didn't work here, and never remembered a thing beyond the last word you told her. Ashley felt guilty the first time she'd pretended Mildred was her mother. But it satisfied Ashley's needs, and made the old lady happy, and five minutes later she didn't remember it anyway, her indiscretion erased, existing in some other reality.

But Mildred wasn't in sight. Ashley could hardly see anything through the crowd of strangers and the ring had turned hot on her thumb. She started toward the bathroom.

A couple sat in the corner, kissing each other frantically. They weren't in her way but they distracted her addled mind. Ashley chanced a look and saw the woman wore a wedding ring. But the man? No. And he had slim fingers that might have fit Ashley's prize.

Had he lost this ring?

She imagined this man. He stood in line with a dozen others for a cup of coffee and shook out a packet of sugar and poured it in, stirred, took a sip. Too hot. He started, moved too quickly, spilled a slosh over his shirt, his hand. He moved the cup to his other hand and shook his wounded paw and there went his ring—through the crowd, to the ground. Late for a flight, for a meeting, he didn't even notice the loss. Until he met his wife, and it took her less than a second to see it was gone. An argument, a few tears. And then:

"It isn't the ring."

"What is it then?"

"I'm pregnant."

Years of trying and finally they'd have their miracle. The ring—forgotten. What did it matter next to this? Smile, sob. Kiss, kiss.

If this is their ring they don't need it anymore.

Ashley kept walking. The fantasy calmed her. She no longer felt the need for Zoe, which was good because that phone number was long gone, wrapped in a child's fleece pyjamas, and left in a hostel.

If the woman in the food court thought she knew Ashley, she was wrong. That was all. The trouble at *Pangaean* also had nothing to do with her.

Ashley breathed in, and breathed out.

All the strangers kicked up dust. Ashley breathed it in, absorbing the remains of the crowd into her lungs, tasting a hundred countries around the world. She might never see any of them but they were a part of her, just as she was a part of this airport. Letting the crowd move around her, she breathed deep and swept near her feet, letting her eye follow the glint of the ring on her thumb.

She saw shuffling feet and heard a delicate voice.

"Annie. *Pangaean* has shut down. What should we do?"

Mildred was gripping the arm of a nervous redheaded woman who stared back at the old lady. Ashley didn't hear her reply, but she felt something else: a tug of jealousy.

Annie was Mildred's daughter. She thought this redhead was–

Ashley turned away.

Don't think of Zoe. It doesn't matter.

She looked at the ring. Maybe it was Mildred's or her missing husband's. Or Annie's. Maybe they brought Mildred here, her husband and child, under the guise of taking her to Paris for her grandson's wedding. They'd create something big and amazing like that: a wedding in Paris. Something life-changing so she'd be distracted. No longer able to care for her, they brought her to the airport and they left her, hoping someone would take her in. And they left her the ring so she'd have a bit of them when she was lonely. So she'd think she wasn't abandoned.

But no one had ever adopted Mildred. They put up with her; sometimes they were kind to her. But that was all. She was still alone, and so she peopled the space around her with missing loved-ones.

The old lady had her loved-ones, imaginary or not, Ashley concluded. So she didn't need the ring.

She barely looked up as Mildred shuffled away.

Extra staff stood near the exits to the airport. Support staff, keeping the stuck travellers from doing anything stupid. Some of them looked even more official than the airport security uniforms allowed: black suits, thick jaws. Officers of something. They scanned the crowd but didn't look at Ashley.

She began to see how the dust of strangers, trivial on its own, could gang up on her: enough cells to make a foot, a leg, a shoulder. Someone tripped on her broom. She was jostled from behind. There was nowhere in the steady stream of agitated strangers that she could be still.

"Where is the manager's office?"

Ashley looked at the tanned face in front of her. He was at least a foot taller than her, and much older. Maybe thirty. He crossed his arms over his chest and she saw yellow stains in his armpits. She recognized the pressurized scent of airplane upholstery wafting from his crumpled clothes.

"Well? You work here, right?" He leaned forward.

For a second she was afraid she'd have to speak to him, but then she nodded and he seemed satisfied.

"So where's the manager's office? You know? The manager?"

Ashley nodded again and started walking through the crowd.

"I really need to see someone about this mess!" The man kept his arms crossed and he didn't shut up as he trailed behind her. He huffed, and Ashley winced, but then two children sped past and a woman's voice carried after them.

"Stop it this minute, you little devils! Come back!"

No longer the smallest person she could see, Ashley felt better.

"I can't believe it, after all these years of professional air travel." The man with the tanned face was losing steam, but he was becoming more and more interested in her response. Ashley knew this because he had taken to looking at her face rather than their route. They found the narrow corridor between the International and Domestic terminals. They had to skirt around a line near the bank of vending machines where someone had their hand stuck up inside a machine, and someone else was calling for help, but the man just kept looking at Ashley. He almost tripped her, trying to see her face as he talked.

"You'd think they'd have figured it out. Wouldn't you? Well, wouldn't you?"

Ashley nodded. There was a small staircase leading up from the corridor and she stopped beside it. Most strangers missed it because it looked like it led nowhere interesting. Once she'd found a pile of used tissues on the third step and wondered who had sat there, sniffling or weeping.

The man she'd led stared up at the grey door. "Is this a joke? Are you messing with me?"

Ashley shook her head.

He started to laugh and then choked it, his face turning purple beneath his tan. "This has got to be a joke. I don't want a goddamn janitor, I want the manager of the airport. The real one! There must be someone in charge of... everything. I'm a customer. I have rights."

Ashley shrugged.

He grabbed her arm, his fingers squeezing her uniform. She stared. His ring finger pressed tight against her skin and there was a pale line at its base, the ghost of something missing.

He shook her.

"What the hell are you doing?"

Randall, one of the coffee shop employees, had stepped from the flood of people passing and into the corridor. Ashley saw with relief that he was taller than the purple-faced man.

The man dropped her arm. Something like guilt swam over his blotched face. Then he said, "I need to see a manager."

The men stared at each other. There was a dangerous moment Ashley felt distant from, and then Randall slumped on himself.

"A manager? Do you know—do you have any idea at all what's happened here?"

"The goddamn airline shut down and stole my suitcase," said the stranger, but he made it sound like a question.

Randall closed his eyes briefly then gestured through the crowd. "Come with me, sir. Ashley, stay out of trouble, alright?"

As they left, Ashley thought if the ring belonged to the stranger he would have noticed it. So if it did, he didn't want it anymore.

She sat on the steps in front of the grey door marked JANITORIAL.

It was coming up to her ninth hour of work. She felt exhausted in every cell, as if she might fall to dust right where she sat.

She shifted on the hard concrete stair. It wasn't the worst place she had ever slept.

The worst was at home with Zoe.

Her mother was a smart woman who loved psychology. So she said.

Ashley would wake up to screaming. She'd open her eyes and see Zoe's huge face right near her own. Her mother would stop screaming and jump up from the bed and start coaching her.

"Okay Ashley! Stand up, stand up! Can you stand up? Fast as you can! Fast!"

And Ashley would stumble up on the mattress with her legs not yet working, arms flailing. Her face felt like a dough mask, sliding and shifting as her initial terror gave way to something else—a desperation to please her mother and show her she was game. But shaken from her dreams she could only hobble and fall. It took her so many wasted seconds before she was on her feet, long past when Zoe stopped coaching and watched with disappointment.

"Not great, Ashley."

She knew.

The last time it happened Ashley had felt her heart so hard and frightened in her chest she wondered if it was a separate creature, as trapped inside her body as she was inside her mother's house.

She hadn't intended to run away for good. Zoe always told her how important she was, how much she needed her daughter and the valuable—no, invaluable data gained from the experiments. Ashley didn't understand what the experiments were for, but she believed her mother when she said they were important.

So Ashley devised her own.

She figured if she disappeared there would be a search of some kind. Her photo would be printed on the sides of milk cartons and the front wall of grocery stores, solemn-eyed and pretty. And they would find her eventually. Her mother would search, and bring Ashley home.

It sounded important. More, it sounded like a psychological experiment from which important information could be gained.

But maybe Zoe hadn't liked her daughter's experiment.

Ashley snapped out of her thoughts. Randall hadn't come back. And she had a job to do. She stood and gathered her broom and dustpan and admired the ring on her thumb pressed to the wood handle. She swept her way down the corridor and evaluated the main lounge. The check-in desks looked no less chaotic. The food court dribbled grim travellers with take-away cups and sandwiches.

The dust, the cells, brushed off the floor and into her pan. Another moment, another dozen strangers collected together in her care.

The travellers in the airport boiled in their frustration. In the waiting area a woman with a child on her lap was shouting at another girl. Here was an experiment. A long queue winding through the giant room held its ground like a live thing, so those who walked by had to make their way right to the end before they could cross to the other side. This was psychology.

The cells and hairs in her dustpan told her nothing. The lives they'd been shed from had let them go completely, unknowingly.

An angry girl stood and struck the face of the woman in front of her. Ashley saw a part of the woman's cheek fall away to dust on the floor.

But she must have imagined it. It never happened that way. Not all at once.

She was just tired. Confused.

Ashley detoured around the winding line and neared the information desk. Past another line, this one tired and sagging, she reached a door marked LOST AND FOUND.

It was always unlocked. From time to time she brought in mobile phones and paperback books forgotten on chairs and windowsills through the airport. They were accepted with a resignation lacking any hope by a security officer who manned the desk inside the small room, waiting for a call that he was needed out on the floor.

Today, everyone was needed and the room was empty. There were two coats lying on the counter, waiting to be stored, and the rickety chair the officer usually lolled in had rolled right back to the wall, empty.

Ashley knew where small items were kept. If she was caught on the surveillance camera they'd know she was just leaving another thing for collection. So she didn't pause, walking around the counter and kneeling to open a low cupboard, drawing out a stack of shoeboxes.

They kept the books and magazines elsewhere. The crates were full of phones, the latest models right back to thick slabs of plastic from last year. One of the officers, trying to make conversation, told her people rarely returned looking for their things. At the end of every month they were either donated or thrown away. Going through the three crates, Ashley saw dozens of phones, maybe a hundred altogether. On the bottom shelf there was a shoebox, mystery babushka.

She slid off the cover and looked inside.

Jewellery. Bracelets, maybe the overlarge swoop of an anklet. Rings. Plain bands, wedding rings, even the shine of a diamond here and there. And necklaces woven through the lot. The tangle appeared organic and she imagined trying to remove one piece and dragging the rest in a gold and silver knot.

Lost and never claimed.

The ring on her thumb glinted. She squeezed her hand into a fist and closed the box.

It was better to be separate, to be distinct from the rest of the dust, the strangers. Even if it meant you were still lost.

Her fist held tight to her broom and dustpan.

She'd sweep, collect the shed cells, the hair. Detritus of strangers, brought together by her.

Enough dust to make a hand, a ring finger, a thumb. Enough for a whole girl.

Ashley walked out and closed the door to the lost and found.

Kanyasulkam

Annie Evett

"I should have taken my plane."

Ava applied lip-gloss, tilting the phone screen to catch her reflection. Finished, she threw the cosmetic in the nearest bin.

"It's in Canada for the ski trip." Louise's tiny face glared at her from the screen.

"My double gets better holidays than I do."

"Pouting causes wrinkles, an accessory no bride needs the day before her walk down the aisle," Louise blurted, wincing immediately at her slip.

Unconcerned, Ava changed the pout to her much practiced Monroe smile and tilted her head. "Tell me I look like Hilda Bosch in *Runaway to Forever*.

Her hand fluttered over an enticing gossip magazine on the newsstand, fingertips prickling at the thought of touching the glossy, fake Hollywood smiles on the cover. Ava clenched her fist.

"She was a real superstar. Not like the tramps nowadays." The smile dissolved. "Get my plane back, Louise. Tell Irving to fly here straight away. Tonia and her cronies can find their own way back from Canada."

"Mandy's plan…"

"Mandy can shove her plan. Who lets their therapist plan their wed-

225

ding?"

Silence.

Ava twisted the plain gold ring on her finger. Her eyes narrowed when they settled on an enamoured couple, limbs intertwined and oblivious to the airport crowds. "You should see this place—people touching things—each other." She gently teased the ring back and forth over a chafed finger. "Just get me on any damn flight now!"

"I'm booking you on *Ganda Airways*, business class. I'll text you the e-ticket reference number. It leaves in three hours."

"Three hours? I've already been here two."

Off came the ring, thrust quickly onto another finger, cruelly cutting into the raw skin.

"*Pangaean Airlines* has collapsed and everyone on those flights wants out. I know someone at *Ganda* who bumped the list for me."

An oversized tourist, heavily laden with luggage brushed past Ava's shoulder as the Tannoy droned incomprehensibly. He unfolded his well-worn map and stared bewildered at it. Ava stepped nimbly aside, weaving her way through the milling crowds and began to brush her shoulder vigorously.

"Track down who owns that shitty airline and threaten them with the biggest lawsuit my lawyers can dump on them. I can't leave this airport without my bag."

"I'm sorry, Miss Scott, the official response is they aren't releasing any baggage."

Ava put a finger delicately to her ear in an attempt to block out the rising argument from a nearby couple. She squeezed her way through to the seating beside the windows, the runway clearly visible from the pre-security lounge. Her heart lurched as she watched a continuous progression of planes taking off, mocking everyone still stranded at the airport.

"This is ridiculous. Don't they realise who I am? I need that dress. I don't care about the rest of the luggage, but I can't do without the dress. It's vintage Chanel. It's unique!"

"That's just it, Miss Scott, they don't know because of your... desire not to be known. You can't have it both–"

"I can have it any damn way I want! I'm Ava Scott." The gold ring flicked back and forth between fingers. "This is one of the most important journeys of my life. I'm stuck here and my dress is in some dark hellhole filled with rats." The ring caught on her knuckle. "I can't get married in some tacky resort-bought bikini."

Louise's hands tapped away on her keyboard and she murmured absentmindedly, "It was good enough for Pamela."

"Are you seriously putting me in the same league as her? I had three Oscar nominations last year alone."

Louise stopped typing and looked squarely into the screen. "Apologies, Miss Scott, I just meant a wedding is more than just a dress. I'll sort out alternative details while you're en route. I'll get one of our people to come to the airport and stand there till they release the luggage."

Ava breathed in deeply and glanced around at the seething crowds flapping their defunct airline tickets at one another.

"Mandy said she'd call you when you get to the island. She wanted to remind you that you're doing this journey for Beau and for you."

Ava wiped a small tear from the corner of her eye and rotated her ring with her thumb. "I am doing well, aren't I? I've hardly used the wipes and I've even taken my gloves off. Where's Beau?"

"He's about to board his flight. He'll be on the island before you now. It actually works out better with your delay. There's no chance the paparazzi will link the two of you, even if they do get a tip-off."

"Thanks, Louise. Where would I be without you?"

Louise smiled, her eyes lowered.

"I'll see you tomorrow. Remember what Mandy said. Wipes to a minimum, you don't need them. And keep positive. This experience is an opportunity for you to grow... really."

"Louise. I'm glad you're my bridesmaid... and my PA... not so sure about being a cohort to my therapist though."

The tiny face allowed itself a small smile. "The pleasure is all mine, Miss Scott."

"Why do I get the feeling you're enjoying this more than I am?"

Ava flicked the screen shut and tucked it into its designated spot in her handbag. She smiled a silent message at the backpacker whose large rucksack perched on the only spare seat in the vicinity. Wordlessly removing it, he pushed it between his legs and continued messaging on his iPhone.

Ava hesitated, looking at the seat before she sat. She pulled from her cavernous handbag a film-wrapped celebrity magazine. Not only did it double as good ammunition to stave off boredom and talkative flight companions, but it served as a cover should she be recognised by any fans. She flicked quickly through the pages, frowning at the meringue wedding dress the latest starlet had donned for her wedding.

With the noise and movement about her, Ava found it difficult to concentrate on the wedding scoop. She closed the magazine, laid it flat on her lap and smiled, taking in the pulsating mass around her. Crowded, busy places such as airports made perfect fodder.

With military precision, she zipped her handbag open again and selected a brand new pen from the line up secured along the inside flap. From another compartment, she pulled a notepad and flicked its crisp pages open. Ava preferred to take character notes longhand; she felt her thoughts couldn't be stolen this way.

She scanned the milling crowds surreptitiously, searching for character observations. It was her meticulous observations and the ability to fully integrate them into her characters that set Ava apart from her Hollywood peers. Ava saw the tiny nuances that made individuals unique, allowing her to portray characters with authenticity and empathy.

Despite her talent and work ethic, Ava knew she was overlooked for the really big roles because of her... habits. This fuelled her determination to continue with Mandy's plan: to dispel her anxiety and gain control over her obsessive-compulsive behaviours. If she could master these... idiosyncrasies, she could win back some of the directors she'd driven away over the past few years and ensure the thousands she paid her Mandy were worth it.

And thinking positively, as Mandy insisted she must, perhaps this enforced stopover would provide her with inspiration for her next role. She would focus on the people and not their hands or the germs they carried with them. With such a spectrum of raw emotions, she was sure to find a unique emotional build-up she could emulate for an Oscar-winning performance.

Two children shot past her, one grabbing her leg as he skidded around the corner. Ava looked in horror at the tiny mark he left on her white linen pants.

"Oh, I'm so sorry... Boys! Back here now!" Comfortably attired for a long haul flight, a young, tired mother with a baby on hip, flicked a look of weary apology toward Ava. She tucked a wisp of hair behind her ear. "Kids, hey?"

The boys screeched to a halt and shuffled their way back to the line of seats, mumbling their apologies.

Ava smiled. "It's nothing."

The woman gasped and stared. "You're Ava Scott? Oh, where's my pen? The girls at home won't believe me."

"Sorry, I'm not her. I get it a lot though—well either her or Hilda Bosch in her heyday."

The woman frowned in confusion, swaying side to side when the baby started to fuss. Ava held up the gossip magazine at the page where her double smiled in genuine enjoyment in the snow.

"Ava's skiing in Canada at the moment. Lucky her."

The woman blushed. "Sorry!" She grasped the magazine in one hand and stared at the skiing photos critically. "Do you think she's happy? I mean she's got the body, the looks, the lifestyle, that gorgeous boyfriend, the career. But is she really happy?"

She handed the magazine back and Ava stared at her double's convincing performance of throwing snowballs at friends. For once she didn't consider the contamination her magazine or trousers were suffering. Her only thought was to wonder what true happiness was.

Spare hand on hip, squaring her shoulders the woman slyly grinned at Ava. "I might not look like her but I wouldn't swap my kids and my life for hers." Then frowned again, staring at Ava. "Sorry—but you do look like her. It's the hair I think. Anyway, Ava Scott's a lot older than you."

"Lucky me, huh?"

Bored with the conversation, the boys shot up and extended their arms, flying personal bomber planes about the chairs, shooting one another as they went. With an extra burst of noise they raced off into the middle of the concourse.

"Josh! Henry! Come back here you little devils." And with that, the crowd too swallowed their mother.

Ava held her breath, but gave up, frowned and unzipped her handbag. She pulled out her antibacterial wipes and meticulously wiped her linen trousers clean. With another breath, she forced herself to throw the wipe away. She needed a coffee and a cigarette.

A discrete beeping sounded at her hip.

Louise.

Ava stood and, with her phone pressed to her ear, began to walk toward the food court.

"Miss Scott, an update on wedding details. This *Pangaean* thing is bad. I'm afraid some of your parcels travelling as freight on other *Pangaean* flights have been impounded also."

"What are you saying exactly?" The gold ring loosened and twisted along her knuckle.

"The handmade chocolates, the individual Bavarian crystal trinkets and your shoes. They won't make it in time."

"My handmade Italian satin shoes? But they're the only shoes which will go with my dress!"

"It's a beach wedding. Barefoot will be fine."

"I'm supposed to have a fairytale wedding; the dress, the shoes, the crystal—none of it's going to be there."

"Beau will be there and so will you."

"Louise, am I happy?"

"What? Miss Scott, you're a superstar. Which reminds me, I have a script for you to look at when you land."

"But am I happy?"

"You're about to marry a man Adonis would be jealous of. Of course you're happy."

Ava flicked the phone shut and pulled out a wipe, exploring each crevice in her hands, polishing and cleaning her ring, slipping it back and forth from finger to finger, before breathing with satisfaction when it settled on the correct finger then shut her eyes. The ravenous noises of panicked people bombarded her ears.

"Excuse me, Miss Scott? Ava Scott?"

Ava blinked and lifted her gaze to the desperate pale eyes of one of life's flotsam. Straw blond hair glued to a flushed forehead glistening with sweat. The damp patches under his arms announcing his struggle with the over-laden luggage trolley behind him.

She smiled and shook her head. "I'm flattered, but I'm not her."

Ava pulled out her magazine and tapped the photo of the skiing starlet.

He stuttered slightly but stared at her with insistent, feverish eyes. "It's your double. You do that all the time—to put people off—so you can find some private time. Not get swallowed up."

Ava caught her breath.

"I'm sorry," he flushed and cleared his throat. "I don't mean to intrude, it's just I'm a huge fan. Calvin. Calvin Smith. I never dreamed I'd ever be this close to you."

Ava's skin began to itch. Her eyes darted about seeking a minder only to remember she was alone.

"Just an autograph. Please? I know your face, your presence. I've watched all your films hundreds of times. I've even got a brand new pen. It's all wrapped up."

Ava didn't doubt this. She'd had plenty of fanatics forcing their way through her security. But this time she had to deal with it herself.

She smiled again. "It's very sweet of you, but really—I'm just an ordinary lass on her way home."

"Scene 15, *Where the Flag Flies*, 2003."

Ava hid a smile. He'd spotted her favourite line from one of her earliest films. Calvin fumbled at his breast pocket and retrieved a plastic-wrapped biro, thrusting it towards her.

"Calvinsweetheart, you just stormed off." The newly arrived woman's eyes pierced through the quivering man. His fragile bravado crumpled, shoulders sagging as he mumbled a reply. Her defensive face hardened further when she saw Ava. "Is this lady annoying you?"

Ava stared with professional delight, mentally cataloguing the neatly styled hair, bright eyes, and old-fashioned tweed travel jacket. The older woman reached out a clawed hand, resplendent with vivid red nails, and grabbed Calvin's arm.

Ava fixed a warm smile, ripping the plastic from the biro. "I'm afraid it's my fault. I was lost and your very considerate son saw my distress. And they say chivalry is dead." Ava quickly retrieved a tissue from a fresh packet in her handbag and scrawled her autograph on it, winking as she handed it to him. "Calvin. Thank you and I'm sorry to have kept you."

The woman's considerable bosom expanded, adding a saccharine smile as she petted Calvin's shoulder. "I do my best; as much as a poor, single mother can."

The blushing Calvin stretched his hand out, careful not to touch Ava's fingers, and accepted the tissue reverently. His hand shook as he folded it carefully and put it into his breast pocket. The shrewish woman narrowed her eyes at Ava, but was met with a cool, even gaze.

"We've a plane to catch. Come, Calvinsweetheart."

Ava marvelled at Calvin's delicious tormentor and stepped into the milling crowds to follow them, observe her in more depth. The masses swarmed about her and finally adjacent the food court, Ava conceded she'd lost them. Stopping Ava realised she was surrounded by snippets of conversations, fearful intonations and panicked gestures.

"–airline gone bust–"

"–picket line outside–"

"–everything impounded–"

"–shutting the airport down–"

"–bomb threat–"

"–trapped here–"

"–no planes leaving–"

Her heart hammered.

Was it true? Would all flights be cancelled?

She was bustled about as frantic travellers rushed along the concourse, a lone slender stick in the whirlpool of the airport. Ava was used to minders carving space for her and now a faceless piece of flotsam on a roiling wave of humanity in her anonymity, started to panic. She stood gasping for air.

A small contingent from the picket line she'd seen outside forced their way through the crowd, placards banging indiscriminately against each other, sights temporary set on food. Ava stood rooted to the spot as the gaggle approached. She squeezed her eyes shut, attempting to ignore their harsh tones and steeling herself for the intrusion they would inflict.

Then she opened her eyes. They had passed and only one body had brushed briefly against her. Ava fought the urge to wipe off their presence and shifted her ring frantically from finger to finger. Giving in, she tore an anti-bacterial wipe from her bag and stared at her jacket where she had been bumped into. She breathed out slowly and crumpled the wipe, throwing it in the nearest bin.

Shifting her ring nervously from one finger to the next, Ava could feel her nerve endings shrieking to cease with the ring, but she continued to pull it on and off, her palms sweaty and shaking.

The passionate couple from the pre-security lounge were in line for the sushi bar, but had resumed their amorous positions.

How long would that couple be together? Did they really love one another or was it all just for show?

Who was she getting married for?

The ring slipped on and off, passing fingers and onto thumb.

She needed to escape the noise and frantic energy enveloping her. She looked tentatively at the crisscrossed clamour of travellers in the food court. There was no director to call cut and no secluded caravan to escape to. She was alone. Ava grasped her ring and pulled it off her thumb, forced it onto her middle finger and began to twist and turn it, the skin screaming and tearing.

To the side of the crowds, Ava spotted a small figure, almost child-like, clutching a broom. Drawn by those sad, old eyes, Ava started toward her, entranced by her direct gaze and calmness set against the whirlwind of emotions, the ring poised in the air between two fingers. Ava stepped into the current and a large man collided with her. The ring jolted from her fingers and rolled through the trample of feet. Ava was incensed and waited for an apology, but his angry face contorted.

"Have you any idea who is in charge here. This disorganised mess is outrageous. I want answers."

Ava stood stock still and started to perspire.

"I want to speak to someone about this." He glared at her from his salon-tanned face, orange rather than a golden glow won with leisure time.

Ava took a deep breath realising he was more unhinged than she was. Drawing on the inner well she used when on set and jutting her chin out said, "I want answers too. My lawyers are already in the process of filing proceedings against the two-bit airline."

"Lawyers, huh." Ava watched something shift in his eyes, then he looked away, erratically taking in the people behind her. "Hey," he called out, focusing on someone further away. "Hey, where's the manager's office. I want to speak to someone." And he was off.

Ava remember the oasis of calm and looked for the girl on the periphery of the nightmare. But she had been consumed by the monstrosity of humanity.

Swamped by the clashing feeling of mourning for the loss of the girl and relief of having dealt with the orange-faced man, Ava grasped for her ring. Finding it missing, she felt each of her fingers desperately.

Nothing.

She threw her hands in front of her face, twisting them back and forth in horror. She searched the faces about her, looking for a possible pickpocket or thief. Ava trembled. Her fingers continually and frantically searched each other for the ring.

No meditation cushions, essential oils or masseur on hand to calm her. Even Mandy, who travelled everywhere with her, was in Canada skiing.

I need to get the hell out of here.

Close by, in a café , a beautiful redheaded lady dropped her notebook. The delicate pages fluttering to the floor caught her attention. A frail, elderly woman appeared and made a beeline toward the redhead, gripping her arm with ferocity. With keen ears, Ava heard their exchange.

"Annie, *Pangaean* has shut down. What should we do?"

The redhead blinked several times and appeared shaken. With the grace of a courtier, she drew a breath and looked deep into the old lady's eyes. "Regret nothing." With a twist, she escaped the old lady's grip and strode off through the thinning crowds toward the doors.

Ava's heart pounded. Her fingers clenched and released. Humanity pushed and pulsated around her, swarming and squirming. A plague of passengers threatening to overcome and suffocate her.

Her phone rang.

Louise. More bad news?

Regret nothing. Hilda's trademark line in every film she made. It was a sign.

The dress, her shoes, all the fripperies. They'd all be soiled now. Someone else having touched them, put their dirty marks all over them.

Whose idea were they anyway?

Whose wedding was it?

Was she happy?

Regret nothing.

The phone rang again. Louise. She turned it off.

Ava strode over to the premier check-in for *Balder Airlines*, where a few overstuffed suits loitered. Fixing her best mega-star look on her face, tempering it with a cool smile of haughtiness, she brushed them aside and snapped her fingers at the girl behind the desk.

"I want a first class ticket on your next flight to Aspen."

Not bothering to look up from her screen, the attendant answered in the tired monotone of someone having uttered the same phrase countless times in the past hour.

"Our flights are experiencing overburdening due to the situation with *Pangaean*. Unfortunately even our first class seats have–"

Ava smiled and tapped her platinum card on the desk, flipping a cream business card with her personal number toward the girl.

"How would you like an invitation to the Oscars with a seat for you and a friend in the main auditorium?"

The assistant gasped and gripped the business card and looked directly into Ava's eyes. She stammered as recognition dawned.

"Cer-certainly, Miss Scott. I have an opening on our next flight. Do you have any bags to check in?"

"No. No baggage. Not today."

Double Talk

Lily Mulholland

"Where the fuck is that lazy cunt?"

John Hildebrand's voice could be heard well in advance of his corporeal arrival. He stormed past the butler, throwing his hat and gloves at the vestibule table.

"I'm sorry, sir, but he's indisposed."

"Which one of his slags is in there with him?"

"Sir, he is sleeping alone this morning."

"Left already, did she? Well get up there and tell him to get his arse down here now. His airline's going down faster than one of his cheap conquests."

"Right away, sir."

The butler hurried up a structural glass staircase with as much grace as he could muster, happy to escape the man's surgical gaze. Hildebrand Senior was a tyrant with a fearsome reputation and a temper to match.

JJ stirred on the large bed, the sheets in disarray. His head thumped in time to the knocking on his door. He tried to speak, but the sandpaper in his throat abraded his voice to a croak. The door opened and Manfred peered around its edge.

"Your father is here, Mr Hildebrand. He wishes to see you."

"Time's it?" JJ slurred.

"It is past 10 o'clock, sir."

"Fuck! Whydinya wake me?" JJ struggled up onto his elbows.

"I tried, sir. But you were… ah…" The butler rotated his hands back and forth, as though he was trying to shape the right word.

"My head is killing me." JJ groaned and flopped back on the pillows.

"Sir, your father. He is insisting on seeing you. Something about *Pangaean*? What shall I tell him?"

"I'll be down in ten. Make him a coffee. Or something stronger, if he wants it." JJ knew his father's vices well.

"And bring me some goddamn pills." He started to drag himself from the king-size bed and stopped dead.

"Where's Keely?"

"Miss Jackson is not here. She left a message asking me to let you sleep. She has cleared your diary for the day."

The butler glided professionally out of the room, to descend like Dante into the waiting inferno. JJ watched him go, confident in Manfred's ability to placate his father. He paid the man a substantial salary and provided a large Christmas bonus each year; a little extra went a long way to buying absolute discretion in his staff.

Stepping into the ensuite shower, he struggled to clear the fog in his brain. Where the hell was Keely? And what was this shit about clearing his diary? He never took time off. Except to see his counsellor, but he had a good cover for that. He told his staff he was taking golf lessons down at the pro range. The psych obliged, ensuring she invoiced him using the golf course's official stationery he provided the receptionist with.

He towelled himself off and jumped into a suit. With no time to shave, he checked his face in the mirror, rubbed some product through his hair, and headed down to the kitchen.

"Father."

John Hildebrand Senior turned from the floor-to-ceiling window where he had been surveying the city and inventoried his son from head to toe.

"You look like shit, John."

Never 'JJ'. Not to his father. Hildebrand Senior viewed the Americanised version of his son's name with abhorrence.

"What's this about *Pangaean*?"

"I have placed the company into receivership."

JJ reeled as though his father had struck him.

"What right—"

"Shut up. I had no choice. She's taken it."

"Who? Taken what?"

"You don't have a fucking clue, do you? Your whore. The painting. My God, John. No wonder I still have to do every fucking thing myself." John Hildebrand spat words with the efficiency of a machine gun. "You're as useless as your mother."

"I don't understand." JJ's head spun.

He leant against the tiled wall, the cool porcelain soothing his throbbing head, trying to take in what his father was saying.

"Then let me spell it out for you. Judging from the look of you, that bitch slipped you something nasty before your little session last night. While you were impersonating Sleeping Beauty, Keely, or whatever her fucking name is, opened your safe, took the painting and made a run for the airport."

JJ's head shot up.

"And how do you know this, Father?"

"I have my sources."

"Sources?"

The two men faced off against each other like duellists.

"Surveillance, John."

"You have me watched?"

"Yes, I have you watched. You can't be trusted not to cock up everything I've been working for." Hildebrand Senior stared down at his only son, no emotion registering on his concrete face.

JJ concentrated on just breathing—he would regret anything he said at this point. Feeling desperately sick in every cell of his body, his mind shifted into overdrive, trying to grasp the enormity of everything his father had said. He sifted through the facts as his father presented them.

Keely was gone, and so was the painting.

She had gone to the airport.

Pangaean was in crisis. Why? It all came back to Keely.

Was she working for someone else?

"The painting. The safe is in my room. The only way you could know she took it is if—"

"There's a camera in your bedroom."

JJ blanched.

"Yes. I know all your dirty bedroom secrets."

Did his father know about the counsellor too?

Fuck, he thought, the diary.

"Quite frankly, I don't care what you do in your own time. Right now you need to get your shit together. The gutter press are all over us wanting to know why *Pangaean* is under administration. I need you front and centre to represent the family. Don't say anything—just stall for time. Tell them we've been hit hard by the global financial crisis just like every other fucking airline on the planet and the administrators are examining our cash flow options. I will have your precious company up and running again by tomorrow. For now, get your arse down to the airport. Carly has arranged a presser for midday."

Hildebrand Senior checked his chronometer.

"Better get your skates on, son. Time is money." He headed for the elevator, JJ hard on his heels.

"If I'm going to the airport, where are you going?"

"To get the fucking painting back."

Manfred appeared unobtrusively as the lift door closed behind JJ's father.

"Macchiato, sir?"

"Make it a double."

The machine hissed and spluttered as Manfred worked the machine with the finesse of a concert pianist. A sweet-sharp smell punctured the air as the near-boiling water contacted the Sumatran special blend. Making the perfect coffee was a skill highly valued by JJ.

"And shall I call for your car, sir?" he asked over his shoulder as he shot steam into a steel jug and brought up a dense froth in the imported Italian milk.

JJ nodded and picked up the iPhone the butler had left on the marble benchtop for him.

No messages from Keely.

He selected her number and pressed the dial wheel; after two rings it went straight to voicemail: "You have called Keely Jackson at Saxon Enterprises. Please leave a message."

Ending the call, JJ downed his coffee, grabbed the coat and hat offered to him by Manfred and headed for the elevator, jabbing the down button. He thought about the painting his grandfather had left him. It was a van Gogh, quite lovely, a still life done in thick, textural oils, but not the kind of art that interested JJ. His tastes were more modern, abstract—although, more truthfully, 'his taste' belonged to the interior designer hired to transform the apartment from a fusty wood-panelled den into a minimalist bachelor pad with panoramic views of the river and city. JJ's walls were adorned with Saville and Rothko. The fusty oil painting didn't suit his aesthetic, but he was forbidden from offloading any of it. Especially the van Gogh which couldn't even be hung, a precondition of his Grandfather's will. He wasn't allowed to sell it either. So it lived in the safe. Along with his diary.

"Oh fuck."

JJ raced back into the penthouse, ran up the stairs, his shoes drumming out a staccato beat, and into the master suite, where he flipped back from the wall a hinged Hirst and punched in the code to his safe. The lock released and JJ pulled the door open. The safe was empty and the entire security system was offline.

Traffic oozed like pus through the roads surrounding the strangulated terminal. Traditional black cabs were hard up against pragmatic minicabs; sleek Lexus and Beamers shared space with beaten up Beetles. The only things moving were motorbikes, scooters and the odd crazy cyclist. JJ slouched on the almond-beige leather in the back of his S-Class Mercedes, stuck in the logjam just like everyone else. The delay gave him time to think.

Keely…

He couldn't get her out of his head, nor could he believe she had just disappeared. He had sent one of his men around to her apartment. All her belongings were there, but of the woman, not a trace. It was as though she had never existed.

While there had been plenty of women after he left America, Keely had worked her way under his skin and turned his world upside down. What had seemed like a hard-won seduction capped with mind-blowing sex now felt like a game of chess, and he wasn't the king but a pawn.

And Keely, the Queen, had his diary.

JJ cursed the psych for convincing him to write the damned thing. He had hated it at first: introspection and reflection were just not his thing. A talented businessman, he knew how to drive down the opposition and back them into a corner. He brought millions of dollars of business into the family accounts and was being groomed to take over once his father retired, despite their frosty relationship—blood was still blood.

But it JJ's was desire to harm the women he fucked that worried him. It was as though something primeval took hold of him when he was pounding their brains out. And Keely had really flipped the switch in his brain. He did not want to hurt her, so he forced himself to overcome his prejudices about shrinks, and booked in with Dr. Whiting. She was recommended by his doctor—another staff member he paid handsomely. It was Dr. Whiting who made him dig into his past, to unearth his early sexual experiences, ones he preferred to leave well behind.

The buzzing of the iPhone startled JJ. Thumbing the screen, he saw there was a message from Carly: "Presser 12 sharp. What's your ETA?"

"Marco, how much longer?"

"Be another ten minutes, boss."

JJ sent a reply telling her to keep her pants on, he would be there in time. Too late he realised she might take his message the wrong way. Carly had been an early conquest and was not entirely happy she had not become a more permanent interest of Saxon's heir. JJ shook the thought out of his head. He needed to concentrate and work out his lines for the press conference.

> *Pangaean is in receivership. The administrators are examining cash flow alternatives. We will do everything in our power to see Pangaean back in the air as soon as possible. We thank our customers and loyal Gaia Club members for their patience and we apologise for the inconvenience.*

That would have to do; his father had not given him much else to go on. He had shut down the airline because of Keely.

Christ! How did he discover she was leaving the country with the painting? How far did his father's tentacles reach? And if he had suspected Keely, why did he not say something? Did he think I was in love with her?

"Boss, I'm taking you in through the back way. The public entrance is a shit-storm."

The burnished black car drew alongside a security point controlling a gate at the airport's perimeter. The driver swiped a proximity card and entered the access code. The steel gate slid open quietly, allowing the saloon to be driven onto the ring road inside the fence line.

❧   ❧   ❧

Several security checkpoints later, JJ walked into the secure area of the airport's main terminal building, a myriad of airline offices tucked away in a rabbit warren of corridors and glass dividers, a world away from the architectural ambience of the terminal's public area. He headed directly to the *Pangaean* suite, where he found two of his father's men guarding the door. They were expecting him and barely nodded at his approach.

Inside he found Carly speaking furiously into a landline handset while a mobile buzzed across her desk. She sensed his presence and threw him a beaming smile, rolling her eyes simultaneously. Always in her element during a crisis, JJ knew she would be expecting a bigger bonus this year.

He strode into his office, trying not to notice the empty desk in the adjacent one where Keely should be waiting for him.

I'll deal with that later. Right now I've got an airline to save.

JJ picked up his phone and hit the top button on the speed dial.

"Kevin, it's JJ. Come on up."

The managing director of *Pangaean* Airlines was an old university friend. An odd couple, they had bonded when JJ returned from the United States, where he had spent his teenage years during his parent's messy divorce, to complete his education at Cambridge. JJ's father was a Trinity man—he graduated with first class honours and a Full Blue, so naturally it was incumbent on JJ to do likewise. Kevin was at university for only one reason: his father was a don. He'd never taken his studies too seriously, preferring instead to further intercollegiate relations with the New Hall undergrads. Walking into the office, it was clear he was not a happy man. He started babbling before JJ had the chance to acknowledge his arrival.

"I don't know what to say, JJ. The books are fine. Our cash flow is steady. Down on previous years maybe, but we're okay. I turned up at work this morning and the goons were here waiting for me," he said, motioning toward the front door. "Rex has got the front of house under control, but it's getting pretty ugly out there. I don't know how long we can hold the line. Some of our club members are getting pretty shitty about their luggage, never mind the fucking flights."

He slumped down on a swivel chair opposite JJ's desk, eyelids heavy and two days' stubble on his face, despite the crisis being only hours old. Apparently he went to water under pressure.

No bonus for you this year, mate.

"They're my father's men."

Kevin looked up. "I thought they were from the receivers? I've been waiting all morning for the auditors to arrive."

"Kev, go home. This won't be resolved today—there's nothing more you can do. I'm about to self-sacrifice out on the concourse. Watch the six o'clock news; yours truly will have a starring role."

"Hey, that's why you get paid the big bucks, right? I'm 'only' the MD."

"Don't take it personally. This isn't about you or *Pangaean*. This is about my father. I'm not sure what he's up to, but I intend to find out—today. *Pangaean* will be back in the air tomorrow. So, go home and rest up, because sure as shit, I'm not getting any sleep until this mess is sorted."

Kevin's face flooded with relief. He was a good man: reliable, methodical, and he could do the accounts blindfolded. But he wasn't a Hildebrand—he didn't have the balls for big business or its intrinsic gamesmanship. And Kevin's father was nothing like John Hildebrand Senior. That was enough to prepare anyone for a lifetime of playing hard and fast.

"Well, if you're sure…"

"I am. Now piss off and let me get some work done." JJ smiled. Kevin threw his hands in the air in an act of surrender and left the office.

JJ called out to Carly.

"When do we rock and roll?"

"Yesterday. Let's go!"

"That went well." JJ had a smile stapled to his face as he and Carly were ushered away from the media scrum, which continued to hurl questions as they retreated.

"Hey, you managed to say a lot without saying anything. You're a true professional, JJ." They were escorted away from the terminal's public area, back into the airline offices.

"Trained by the best, Carly." He doffed his hat at her. "What next?"

"Media release needs to go out, and it's over to the receivers. By the way, where are they? They should be here by now."

"They're probably over at Saxon. I'm sure they'll be here soon," he lied. "Dying to get their hands on our accounts, no doubt."

"And I'm dying for a drink. I might head into Zebrano and drown my sorrows before I start looking for a job. Join me?"

"I'll have to take a raincheck. I need to go and see my father."

Carly looked disappointed as he helped her into her coat. He turned her around and placed his hands on her shoulders. She tipped her face up and he could see the distress creased into the fine lines around her eyes.

"Carls, stop worrying. As long as Saxon is in business, you'll always have a job. You're almost part of the family. Now, turn your phone off, go and have one of those shite milky cocktails you insist on drinking, and relax. I'll have this in hand by tomorrow."

He watched her as she sashayed out the door. She was a nice kid and he almost regretted banging her.

Checking his phone for any messages from his father as he walked into his office, he nearly missed the package on his desk. JJ stepped back. Whatever the item was, it was in a paper bag from the terminal bookshop. There were no other identifying marks.

Picking up the phone to call security, he thought better of it and replaced the handset before the call connected. He grabbed a pen and poked the parcel. The object inside was hard. He ran the pen over the top of the package. It felt and sounded like a book.

Someone bought him a book? Someone who had access to the office. Keely?

He ripped open the bag. Inside was his diary.

"Jenkins!"

One of the burly guards came in through the glass door.

"Yes, Mr Hildebrand?"

"There's a book on my desk. How did it get there?"

"Sir?"

"It wasn't there when I left so you tell me how the fuck a book appears on my desk when you fuckwits are supposed to be guarding the door."

The man was unfazed. He'd worked for Hildebrand Senior. JJ's incivility was on a par with polite conversation compared to his father.

"I don't know. The only person who came in when you were out was the cleaner."

Cleaner? Keely was here dressed as a cleaner?

"Cleaner? Did you check her ID?"

"Of course. She had a legit airport identification card."

"What did she look like?"

"Small. Mousy. She had a mop and a bucket."

Not Keely. Is she still in the airport?

Hell, she could have been in the crowd surrounding the media scrum. But why had she returned the diary? He picked it up and flicked through, pausing at the last entry. Not his handwriting.

> *JJ, I'm sorry. For many things, as it turns out. You're not the person I thought you were, and let's just say I'm not the person you thought I was either.*
>
> *By now you will have worked out that my name is not Keely. I am not a personal assistant. I was hired for the sole purpose of locating the painting and returning it to its rightful owner. My employer chose me not only for my skills in that area, but because I am 'your type'. He knew I would be able to use sex as my weapon of choice. He pegged you as some kind of little rich deviant and I believed it. We have both been played JJ.*
>
> *If I had known who you really were, if I had done more research, I would never have taken this job. I know this probably won't help, because the damage is done… the damage was done all those years ago at school. The only possible thing I can do to help improve this situation is to tell you that your enemies are closer than you think. Look to Paris. You won't find me there, but I think you will know what I'm talking about.*

JJ, I cannot undo what has been done, but I am truly very sorry.

I wish you well,
Carrie.

JJ sat frozen at his desk, a sudden, diabolical headache surging through his frontal lobe. Massaging his temples with his fingers, he tried to make sense of what he had just read.

Keely is Carrie?

What the fucking hell is going on here?

Look to Paris?

Who the hell is in Paris and what do they have to do with the painting?

What does she mean my enemies are closer than I think?

For the first time since he was fifteen, JJ did not know what to do. He could not trust his father, his mother would not understand and he had no one else to turn to now Keely was gone; she had been his confidante. No wonder she had been able to get hold of the combination. He had let his guard down with her—twice as it turned out.

He read the entry one more time.

Look to Paris.

Mother?

JJ's mother was in Paris, hunting down missing entries in the family tree. She had been on a genealogical bender since turning sixty. He had thought nothing of her fierce interest in France. Until now.

A steel core hardened inside JJ. He called his father.

"Where are you? We need to talk. Now."

EPILOGUE

Earlier this morning…

"Hello, I'd like to report a theft please."

"When did this theft take place?"

"In the early hours of this morning. It was a painting. Priceless."

The police operator took a sharp breath in, having expected a wallet, or maybe a car. This was out of the normal Monday morning routine.

"Can I take your name please, madam? Are you the owner of the stolen painting?"

There was a pause, before the voice continued. "I'd rather not give my name. But I'm calling on behalf of John Hildebrand Junior, the owner of the painting. The thief will try to remove the painting from the country."

"Can you provide a description of the painting?"

"I'm afraid I've never seen it. Nobody has. Until this morning it was kept in a secure location in John Hildebrand's residence. If you want a description, I suggest you contact Mr Hildebrand directly."

❦   ❦   ❦

May 1st, 1944

Walter Hildestein stood in front of the small canvas, admiring the intense colours applied liberally with free brushstrokes.

"Simply breathtaking," he muttered, as he stepped closer to examine the picture. "The brushwork, the exquisite colours…"

A strangled moan made him glance towards the broken and bleeding man at his feet.

"Still breathing?"

He slid his Mauser from the holster and pointed it downwards. It barked once, then silence. Hildestein tapped the smoking barrel against the ornate frame.

"We have much in common Herr van Gogh. We are each artists." He looked down at the neat black hole in the centre of the forehead of the crumpled wretch beneath him. "Each in our own way, of course."

"Hauptsturmführer Hildestein, we must leave, the American infantry is approaching!"

Hildestein nodded at the agitated Sergeant.

"A shame to leave such lovely things to the Jew-loving philistines…"

"Then take it, herr. Who will know?"

Hildestein laughed, and grasped the frame, tearing the painting and hook from the wall.

"Very true. Who will know?"

❧   ❧   ❧

April 14, 2000

"I thought Mom would be there."

"That woman had no place there. It was a family funeral."

"Mom is family."

John Hildebrand Senior snorted. "Only by marriage, John. My father was right, she was never worthy of the Hildebrand name." He pushed his son into a chair in the boardroom, then sat beside him.

"Sit here boy, keep quiet, and learn. You're part of the business now. Just as I was my father's heir when he ran Saxon, now you're my heir as I run Saxon. You are a Hildebrand. That name carries a lot of weight and respect in the business world. You were born with it, now it's time to prove you are worthy of it."

Hildebrand Senior was interrupted by the grating buzz of the intercom. "Yes?"

"Mr Walsham has arrived, sir."

"Send him straight through."

John Senior rose as the door opened. "Fenix, how did it go?"

John Senior's right-hand man entered, carrying a package under his arm. "Swiftly, as expected, sir. My condolences on the loss of your father."

John Senior nodded his head.

"The will has been filed in probate court, it leaves everything to you. All the relevant papers have been lodged. You are now officially the CEO of Saxon Industries. Congratulations."

John Senior smiled warmly and shook Fenix's hand. "Promotions all around then! How does it feel to be part of the world's leading corporation, Fenix?"

"Pretty damn good, sir."

Hildebrand Senior took a silver case out of his jacket pocket, and opened it. The Hildebrand crest engraved on it was tarnished by years of wear. He took three cigars, clipping the ends off each before lighting one. Thick acrid smoke billowed around him, as he passed one cigar to Fenix, and the other to his son.

"To my father, and the Hildebrand name." He lit Fenix's cigar, then offered the lighter to John Junior.

"Fenix, you remember my boy? I'm bringing him on board. My apprentice if you will."

Fenix held out his hand, and John Junior shook it. "I remember you, but it's been a few years. Welcome home. I have something for you."

John Senior raised an eyebrow. Fenix placed his package on the table in front of JJ. "A bequest from your father's will, sir. A present for his grandson."

JJ opened the package and stared at the carefully wrapped painting.

John Senior gazed at it thoughtfully. "Ah. That one." He glanced up at Fenix. "And the usual conditions?"

Fenix nodded. "Yes sir, the will is very specific. The painting must never be sold, nor publicly displayed. A bit of a waste of good artwork if you ask me."

"Nobody did." John Senior turned and walked towards a window looking out over the sprawling metropolis. In the far distance he could see the sun glinting off of the planes taking off from the airport. He considered how many of them would be garbed in the blue livery of *Pangaean Airlines*. It had taken over a decade to establish *Pangaean* as one of the major forces in global aviation. Now the airline virtually ran itself. A good place to start…

"Do you like aeroplanes boy?"

JJ and Fenix looked up at John Senior, who remained staring out of the window.

"Uuh, I guess I do."

John Senior turned. "Good. *Pangaean*. It's yours. Nothing like throwing you in at the deep end to start your training."

3rd November, 1979

The staccato of American jazz filled the room with a levity belying the austerity of Karl Menschikow's East Berlin apartment.

"John, sit, have coffee. I even have the good stuff, French."

"No, Karl. I'm not staying."

"Oh? Not a social visit mein Freund."

"I've come for the papers."

Menschikow placed his coffee cup on the desk and sighed. "So we enter the endgame at last. MI6 attacks the heart of Russia's European stronghold, and her queen falls."

He walked over to his bookshelf and took down a copy of *Das Kapital*, opened it, and removed a small envelope.

"Here you are *mein Freund*, the microfilm."

John took the envelope and slipped it into his pocket. "And the manuscript?"

Karl returned to the bookshelf and cleared a row of philosophy texts. He tapped the exposed wooden panel, which tilted forward, enough for him to reach his hand behind it. On withdrawing his hand, he held a slim, bound volume.

"I would destroy this now John. The microfilm will be easier to smuggle out of the country." He held the manuscript out to John, who snatched it away. "And speaking of smuggling things out of the country, what are the arrangements to get Alex and I to the West?"

"There are no arrangements, Karl. The *Stasi* know about you, and are on their way now to arrest you."

Karl blanched and staggered into his seat. "*Mein Gott*! How? We were so careful, John."

"Because I told them."

"You?" Karl's eyes widened in disbelief. "No, John. Not you. Not my friend John."

"I'm sorry, Karl."

"But… why?"

"You know too much. About the painting. And the past."

Karl laughed, without humour. "You condemn me to death because I know about a painting?"

"Yes. I should never have shown it to you. I know now why my father insists it is for Hildebrands only."

"John, I would never have said a word. We all have a connection to the war. Things were complicated…"

"As you can identify the picture, you can expose my father…" John turned to leave, pausing at the door. "If it's any consolation, I'll get Alex out, make sure he's looked after." John turned and stared hard at Karl. "But breathe a word about this, and I swear I'll have him killed."

1st May, 2000

"Madame Hildebrand?"

"It's Goldberg now. Since the divorce."

"Apologies, Madame. Here is the documentation you requested."

Cynthia took the file and frowned. "There's not much."

"Many records were destroyed in the war, Madame. This is all we have left."

She thumbed through the files. A filed report from Captain Thomas of the US 1st Infantry, detailing the devastation encountered at Chateaux Briand and the discovery of her grandfather's body. The final line caused a chill to run down her spine: Beaten then executed.

"Do they know who killed him?"

"They suspected the SS officer in charge of the region. A Captain

255

Hildestein." He placed another file in front of her. "This is what we have on him. He disappeared in 1945, presumed dead in Berlin."

Cynthia looked at the photograph of the young German. She stared into his cold eyes and her heart began to pound.

"He didn't die in 1945."

"Madame?"

Tears stung her eyes as she stared, seeing too much of her son in the photograph.

"This man died last month, his funeral was only two weeks ago."

She held up the photograph or her grandfather's killer. "This was my father-in-law, Walter Hildebrand."

❧   ❧   ❧

12th March, 1980

"I fear this will be the last time I get to see you my boy." Karl sat opposite his son, separated by steel bars. "They will not let you visit again."

Alex Menschikow reached through the bars, and gripped his father's hands. He tried to speak, but the words were choked in his throat.

"How does John treat you?"

Alex cleared his throat before answering. "Old Suze? He treats me good, I guess. He got me in here to see you didn't he?"

Karl nodded his head. "Yes, he is a… good friend."

Alex glanced around, mindful of the presence of the prison guards, before whispering in hushed tones. "Mr Hildebrand told me that he destroyed your manuscript, so there's no evidence now. Surely without the evidence you could be–"

Karl laughed, leaning back in his chair. "Evidence doesn't matter in here, only perception. So long as they think you are a knight, they will treat you as such, even if you are merely a pawn." His eyes narrowed and he squeezed his son's hand tightly. "Never be a pawn son. Remember what I've told you about the monkeys. You remember?"

Alex shut his eyes, blinking away tears. Always those monkeys. Every day of his childhood had been about the monkeys. And now the first time he had seen his father since that awful night, he wanted to talk about the monkeys again? He understood the lesson. But his father was obsessed with it.

"Yes Father, I remember."

Karl patted his son's hand, and released it. "Never forget. Even when surrounded by people who treat you well. Always judge good people by what I've taught you. Even John…"

"I've brought my chess set, if you feel like a game?" Alex reached down to a bag at his feet, and pulled out the small wooden set that his father had taught him to play with. He placed the board on the table, and began to set up the pieces. The sight of the board brought a smile to his father's face.

The rattle of keys in a lock interrupted them. An iron door swung open on rusty hinges, and two members of the East German military marched in, escorting John Hildebrand.

"We have to go, Fenix." John touched Alex gently on the shoulder. "They won't allow us to stay any longer." He gazed at the old man in the cell, who returned the gaze. There was no malice there, only a deep sorrow, and for a moment John felt a short pang of regret. But only for a moment.

Alex began to protest, but one of the guards grabbed him by the arm and dragged him down the corridor. "Father! Wait, I want to stay, please…" His cries faded, until they were cut off by the slamming of a door.

Karl grasped the cell bars, tears streaming down his face. He glared at John, and for the first time in years John felt threatened.

"Look after him, John. Look after him well. Remember your promise!"

"I will, Karl. I owe you that much."

Karl nodded, and pressed his fingers to his lips. "Alex said you did as I asked, destroyed the manuscript. With that gone, and my silence, you're safe. And so is Alex."

John Hildebrand walked away without answering. The iron door slammed shut, and Karl was once again alone.

His silence, the pain, whatever fate the authorities had planned for him; all were a small price to buy his son's freedom.

@ @ @

30th June, 2008

"Have you spoken to your operative?"

Richard Stourbridge held the phone away from his ear. Cynthia Goldberg's voice had been a shrill and annoying presence in his life every day for the past week. If she wasn't paying a very large sum of money, he'd hang up on her and have the number disconnected.

"Yes Ms Goldberg, but I have to say she was rather, shall we say… perturbed by your request."

"If she has qualms about that then I'm afraid she's no use to me."

"No, she acquiesced in your request. We checked. Natural blonde, as you specified. Though I don't see what difference—"

"My son will know the difference. She has to be blonde, and she has to be naturally so. If she's going to fuck him, she has to be the type."

This was the one part of the plan that made Richard uneasy. It was too personal, and personal carried risks. "Ms Goldberg, we could simply send in an infiltration team, without the need for these games. I'm not running an escort service here."

"What I've asked you to acquire cannot be gained by mere thieves, Mr Stourbridge. It must be taken by guile. If my son doesn't trust her implicitly, and doesn't desire to punish her, then she'll never even get close."

"Understood. What you're asking won't be quick. It could take years for her to build that level of trust."

"Stourbridge, I can wait longer. The prize is worth it."

"All this for a painting?"

"You wouldn't understand Mr Stourbridge. This is family business. Good day."

Cynthia put the phone down, with just enough force she hoped it would cause Stourbridge to jump.

A painting?

No, not just a painting. Her family's painting. Her family's honour. Both stolen by a sociopath in a uniform who saluted a madman. And they were all so proud of the name Hildebrand.

She would destroy the thing most precious to them. Not their honour or their pride or their bank balance. But their name. The world would know soon enough the truth behind the Hildebrand fortune. How it was built on the war crimes of Walther Hildestein.

And it would end just as it started.

With a stolen painting.

THE END

Acknowledgements

Thank you Paul—come hell, highwater and all the other stuff in between you're there. How about we do it all again next year? I've got the jumper leads.

Thank-you Dave and Dylan—you know me better than I know myself and even though it means you go without me for huge chunks of time, you never begrudge me this path. I love you both and look forward to some quality time now the insanity is over for the year.

Thanks to the following people for their help and support: Kate Campbell, Wendy Stamp, Ron Cleghorn, Lisa Tregae, Karen van Harskamp, Annie Evett, the luscious ladies of literature featured in the Yin Book, Susan Talbot, Kerry and Steve Townsend, Kim Falconer, Cyrus Webb, Greg McQueen, The Logan Writers' Group and all my writing friends (too numerous to individually mention) on Facebook and Twitter. Lastly thank-you to Stacey Larner—proof reading extraordinaire.

A huge thank you also goes to Lucas Clevenger who, probably against his better judgement in retrospect, agreed to do our covers, producing three amazing covers under a relentless deadline.

The final tip of the hat goes to the guys I've been stuck in the airport with for the last nine months—Paul S, Chris, Tony, Dan, Dale, Jon, Rob, Richard, Jason and Ben. Thank you for 'getting it.' You took a crazy concept and made it work. I've grown and matured as an editor more than you could imagine this year—all compliments to you. It is a wild adventure and I'd do again with you all, but only if you promise we never have to again go into an airport toilet.

Jodi Cleghorn

Firstly, thanks to Jodi for having my back when the editorial chips were down. That we have an anthology at all is down to her patience, determination, and a herculean disregard for the human need for sleep.

Thanks to Julia for putting up with nine months of mood swings, procrastination, late nights, and the existential dreads of an editor who thought he couldn't edit, and a writer who thought he couldn't write. Thank you for putting up with being a writer's, editor's and publisher's wife!

Thank you to all my family and friends who promised to buy a copy of the anthology—time to make good on those promises guys!

And thank you to the ladies of the Yiniverse, without whom there would be no anthology—Emma, Carrie, Tina, Claudia, Laura, Jasmine, Icy, Jen, Annie and Lily—take a bow ladies, you have all earned your time in the sun. Thank you for populating the airport from hell with an array of flawed, funny, cruel, brave, fragile, and above all human characters.

A special thank you to Lily Mulholland and Paul Servini, whose stories provided the essential elements to tie two opposing realities together.

Throughout the time I edited the Yin Book stories I was kept company by a mischievous, irascible, and irreplaceable little gecko called Dooya. She was one of a kind, and I still miss my beautiful monster.

Paul Anderson

MEET THE
AUTHORS

Jodi Cleghorn
Brisbane, Australia
www.jodicleghorn.com

Jodi never planned to be an editor. She's learnt these 'never' statements (akin to, "I don't write sci-fi" or "pirate-adventure stories") are surreptitious magic spells which sneak up and manifest in the most unlikely ways. She is the editor of *The Red Book, The Yang Book, Deck the Halls and Nothing But Flowers*. In between dates with the 'beautiful razorblade' Jodi can be found gestating the next crazy idea for eMergent Publishing or penning eclectic fiction, inspired by the voices in her head. She is the Deputy Editor at Write Anything, cares for a young family in the leafy southern suburbs of Brisbane and dances like no one is watching.

About "Prologue"

A lot rides on your shoulders when you write the opening story. This time around I had to write an interesting story, one to hook the reader, but one which set the scene up the diverging sliding doors moment. In a lot of ways I felt like someone sketching a colouring-in book page, creating outlines for others to fill in. And what a job they did!

I only knew one thing about Medae when I first wrote the prologue—she would do anything to fulfil her contract. Left of centre for me, I chose to show this element of her personality through sex. She 'gives in' to her boss's advances completely aware of his penchant for rough sex and allows herself to be brutalised to steal his painting. Sex on page one—what the hell was I thinking? Yet so much ended up coming of it, so I am grateful for taking a risk and being amply supported in doing so by Paul and the writers who came after me.

My greatest creation though—the man in the cobalt suit. Did you work out who he was and what he was doing?

Paul Servini

Dole, France

www.merewords1958.wordpress.
com

Language and languages have always been a major interest and Paul ended up taking a degree in French and German only to marry a German and go and live in France. But only after trying out a number of other countries first. Paul takes great pleasure in seeing his students make progress in communicating in English. Language is also a means of creating and exploring, a journey Paul started on several years ago when he joined a local writing group. Other interests include reading, classical and Celtic folk music (did he forget to say he's Welsh), singing and rugby.

About "Three Monkeys"

I started out with a story about a female art thief and ended up with one about Fenix, a man in his early thirties heading straight for a crisis. A pretty big leap I'll admit but please don't ask me how. I couldn't answer you. It's all part of the mystery of writing. Sometimes, the story takes over from the writer and dictates where it wants to go. But fans of female art-thieves needn't despair. While he's going about having his crisis, he's actually chasing the art-thief half-way across western Europe.

The story poses a question fundamental to our own existence as Fenix is forced to wade through a choir of voices past and present trying to determine who he can actually trust. By sheer coincidence, in his pursuit of Medae he spots a news story about his own family's past that rocks his faith in Suze to its core. The question is only partially answered by the end of the story, for just as in real life, once you discover some people aren't worthy of loyalty, you have to begin the search again. Can Fenix trust this new voice in his life? That's a question the readers will have to answer for themselves.

Christopher Chartrand

Addison, USA

www.christopherchartrand.com

Christopher works in the non-profit sector by day and writes weird stories by night. While he is drawn to the western genre, he tries to keep his stories character driven. He has been known to throw his cowboys into fights with robots, vampires, and the ambiguities of purgatory. Chris lives in Addison, Maine with his high school sweetheart, three daughters, four horses, two goats, one lazy dog and sometimes a cat.

About "Three Rings"

I first met Mackenzie in a completely different story. She was a victim; weak and easy to manipulate. My mistake was soon clear, she is no victim.

There's a story that makes the rounds in my family. It's about a young me and my late Grandfather. The two of us somehow became separated in a store. I recall a man asking me my name and telling me to come with him, he would help me. As we walked out of the store and without warning, the man flew backward landing in a heap and my Grandfather and I were running to the car. Perhaps the man was trying to help but my Grandfather always swore something was wrong. Rather than take a chance he punched the man in the face and we left.

Mackenzie is not much different from my Grandfather or from any parent except she has killed before and has no problem doing it again. In fact she wants to kill now more than ever but she must control her rage to save her son. *Three Rings* is a no holds barred look at how far we will to go when a child is threatened.

Tony Noland

Philadelphia, USA

www.tonynoland.com

Tony is an avid reader who took up writing fiction in 2006 by successfully completing the 50,000 word NaNoWriMo challenge. As with most things in his life, he started off by diving into the deep end. His fiction ranges widely in genre and tone, with stories that are funny or scary, inspiring or disturbing. It was a stroke of purest luck that one of the first stories he posted on his blog is the one that caught the eye of the eMergent editors and led to the invitation to participate in this anthology. Nobody is laughing at that rabbit's foot now, that's for sure. Tony is happily married, with two sons, two daughters and one dog.

About "Dogs of War"

Some sights are so common, some people so familiar, they become background props without stories of their own. A couple of businessmen traveling together in the airport—the natural assumption is because they're coworkers, they're also on friendly terms, or at least collegial.

But what if they aren't? What if they dislike, even despise each other? In *Dogs of War*, Gene Thompson, a rising young star in the company, is paired with Vincent Guerrero, a canny old bastard. Gene is eager to prove himself; Vince is adept at crushing the competition. The high-profile meeting they've been sent to is a venue that can send a man rocketing up the corporate ladder or bury him forever.

There's a saying: youth and enthusiasm are no match for age and treachery. Sometimes that's meant metaphorically, but not in this case. When two dogs are fighting over the same bone, bet on the old dog.

Dan Powell

Gütersloh, Germany

www.danpowellfiction.com

Dan writes stories of various shapes and sizes. His work has been published all over the place, including in the pages of Metazen, Litsnack, 100 Stories for Haiti, The View From Here and Up The Stair-case Quarterly. His story "Half-mown Lawn" won the 2010 Yeovil Literary Prize for short fiction. When not writing he teaches, takes care of his three young children and blogs.

About "This Be The Verse"

Writing as part of the Chinese Whisperings family has been a uniquely satisfying experience. There is nothing quite like watching other writers craft their stories, reworking them in collaboration, each intersection of character and situation adding depth to the project as a whole as well as the component parts. The writers to a man and a woman left their egos at the door and allowed anyone and everyone to stick their sticky fingers into fictional worlds usually so closely guarded by their creators. I have loved playing with other people's characters while watching others take my creations and add to them in ways I could never have anticipated. I am a better writer for taking part in this project. You can't say fairer than that.

Dale Challener Roe

Raleigh, USA

www.dcroe.com

For nearly twenty years Dale Challener Roe has been a computer programmer and a writer for somewhat less than that. Although he has previously had a handful of stories published in now-defunct e-zines, this is his first foray into print. He lives in Raleigh, North Carolina with a non-fixed number of four-legged friends, where he spends his time collecting odd hobbies, designing websites for his friends, and chasing an increasingly fickle muse. He occasionally maintains his own website and for several years has contributed his lack of wisdom at Write Anything.

About "Providence"

For obscure, personal and entirely unimportant reasons, *Providence*, both the title of the story and the destination of the characters was easy to come up with. Everything else about this story felt like pulling teeth. After reading the initial drafts of the preceeding stories, I wanted to go in a different direction. The initial inspiration took the form of a story made up solely of dialogue.But after discussion with Jodi we both decided it might be cumbersome to share the story using only dialogue.

So I wrote the first draft. I hated it. Jodi was kinder, but grudgingly admitted it lacked something. The second draft, similarly left us cold. Finally, Jodi, slightly exasperated urged me to try a format that wasn't only dialogue, but very close to it. Along the way I lost Lilith's voice. Luckily, Jodi seemed to find it, refining it during the rapid-fire edit-counter-edit session, whileI kept control of Math. The entire time, I'm still not sure either of us knew how it would end.

J. M. Strother

St Louis, USA

JMStrother.com/MadUptopia

J.M Strother writes fiction, essays, and poems from his home in Missouri. He experiments on his blog, Mad Utopia, with new approaches to writing. He is the creative spark behind the Twitter meme Friday Flash (#fridayflash), and edited *The Best of Friday Flash – Volume One*. Jon enjoys gardening, cycling, chocolate, and reading. He has a Beagle affectionately known as Psycho Pup.

About "No Passengers Allowed"

It's not often inspiration strikes like a bolt out of the blue, but that is exactly what happened with *No Passengers Allowed*. I no sooner read the premise when I knew exactly where I wanted to go with my contribution. I asked permission to use (or abuse) one of the characters from that first piece, and once given the go-ahead dove right in.

No Passengers Allowed was a blast to write. My main character, Sam Harris, was like no other I had ever attempted before. I thoroughly enjoyed developing him, getting inside his head, exploring his inner workings, motivations, and reactions. I knew it would be a challenge to write someone like Sam and have the reader build any kind of empathy for him. I hope I succeeded in that, but only time and reader reaction will tell.

Sam proves the point, you never know who might be standing in line next to you, and perhaps serves as a reminder—it may be unwise to unduly annoy the people around you.

Rob Diaz II
Hamilton, USA
www.thirteenthdimension.word-
press.com

Rob Diaz is primarily a writer of science fiction, fantasy and comedy. He draws from his experiences as a busboy, waiter, computer systems consultant, software engineer, pointy-haired manager and horse stable cleaner to write stories and plays about the inherent goodness of coffee and its ability to help people overcome their troubles with life, love, aliens and zombies. Rob finds inspiration in his vegetable garden, his trumpet, the occasional cup of coffee and the number thirteen. He lives in central New Jersey with his wife, two children, two dogs, two cats, tropical fish and an absurd number of houseplants.

About "Thirteen Feathers"

I didn't intend to write a story about feathers or paranormal, New Age mysticism. I planned to write about the kidnapper in Chris Chartrand's *Three Rings*. However, no matter how many airplanes I put him on, his story kept bringing me to Larissa, his sister-in-law. She believes in the paranormal; needs the para-normal. She forces her world to fit into the definitions and explanations she gleans from the paranormal in an effort to explain the confusion and anger she feels. Her world has become the very nightmare the dreamcatcher she and her husband made on their honeymoon was supposed to protect her from.

In a lot of ways, Larissa is the person I want to be: trusting, honest and absolutely certain the world is inherently good. She takes the mysticism a bit far, perhaps, but after everything has been taken from her, it is almost understandable. But she never loses faith or thinks Fate will let her down. I'd like to think I could persevere through such hardships and come through with my world vision still intact; I don't think I'm there yet, but I'm working on it.

Richard Jay Parker

Salisbury, England

www.RichardJayParker.com

Richard was formerly a TV script writer, script editor and producer for British TV. His fiendishly dark thriller novel STOP ME, about a killer who describes and threatens to kill selected victims if a SPAM email isn't forwarded, was published in 2009 and shortlisted for the coveted Crime Writers' Association John Creasey (New Blood) Dagger Award. There has already been TV interest in adapting it. He is currently working on his second novel.

About "One Behind The Eye"

I was attracted to the project because of its dark edge and the notion that the writers involved could enjoy great freedom as well as the challenge of feeding off each other's stories. With *One Behind The Eye* I took a splinter of a true event and used it as the twist for my story. I wanted to write something dark and uncompromising but still have a rich vein of humanity running through it. Paying off the bizarre experiences my main character has was very important to me because I've read too many stories that intrigue but ultimately cop out.

Short stories are just as challenging to write as a novel because you have to introduce a reader to your imagination, get them sitting comfortably and nail an idea in a very short series of paragraphs. No mean feat. I hope "One Behind the Eye" achieves this and resonates with readers of the book for many nightmares to come.

Jason Coggins
Melbourne, Australia
www.moultworld.com

Jason has no noteworthy accomplishments... which in itself is kind of noteworthy. Plucked from obscurity by eMergent Publishing's editors in 2009, *Something Mean in the Dream Scene* was his first published work. He is a regular contributor to Write Anything's [fiction] Friday and publishes assorted weekly serials on his website. World building is his passion. Moult World is the first fruits of this labour.

About "Chase the Day"

Chase The Day came as a real surprise to me. It marked a turning of my back on the plot driven speculative fiction pieces in which I am comfortable and the writing of something much more character led. That's when a young girl called Quiche came along.

Admittedly, I originally called her Quiche whilst I waited for a better name to come along; but the girl in the military boots with satchel swinging around her ankles did more than just grow into that name... she took it, tried it on, liked what she saw and thanked my sub-conscious for christening her with the name she had always wanted. And in return I got to see the world through her eyes for a bit.

Lessons learned from *The Red Book* saw me in good stead with Jodi's editing process. In fact I was a bit jealous on the working relationship she struck up with Quiche. In fact, I have only just learned that the two of them enjoyed an inebriated long weekend draining Martinis in the name of a team building exercise... but I allow them this deceit because I am happy enough to have worked on *The Yang Book*.

Benjamin Solah
Melbourne, Australia
www.benjaminsolah.com

Benjamin Solah describes himself as a Marxist horror writer and lives in Melbourne, Australia where he works full-time in an office but prefers to dedicate his energy toward writing and political activism. He sees horror as an accurate metaphor for the world we live in and is involved in struggling for a less horrific world, even if it means less to write about. He can be found at most left-wing protests and poetry open mics in Melbourne as well as online—sometimes at the same time!

About "Somewhere to Pray (Kurush)"

When I think of airports today, I cannot ignore how things have changed post-9/11. I think of people's paranoia, the over-the-top security and the racial profiling.

With my character Kurush, I wanted to show readers this environment through another set of eyes often ignored. How does this fear affect the people you're scared of? I wanted to show that they're much more afraid of you. I wanted to show the reader what it's like to be a Muslim in the West in the age of the War on Terror. I've been trying to tell Kurush's story for years and finally think I've gotten it.

I also wanted to show how this fear is manufactured by using the children in the story. They're innocent and haven't yet been polluted with societies prejudices so whilst Kurush's story is a tragic one, there is a glimmer of hope in the world, I think.

Emma Newman
Somerset, England
www.enewman.co.uk

Emma drinks too much tea, has too many ideas and writes too many stories. Only one of these is true. According to her grandmother, Emma started writing stories at the age of four. She wrote fiction throughout her childhood until she penned a short story that won her a place at Oxford University to read Experimental Psychology. It was another ten years before Emma summoned the courage to write again, in the meantime distracting herself with such things as becoming an information architect for websites, dabbling with being a designer dressmaker and working for a magazine publisher. She even went to such lengths as becoming a Psychology teacher for four years in the madness of convincing herself that she wasn't a writer. Her debut novel 20 Years Later is now available to buy, with the second and third books of the trilogy now dominating her life.

About "The Guilty One"

Is it possible to live a life like Medae's and remain in touch with one's humanity? If one has to be tough and strict all of the time just to survive, isn't there a chance one could become brittle? I considered the rules Medae would have to live by to cope with deception, pressure and the constant fear of discovery. Being timid in real life, I'm often filled with an envious curiosity when I think about ruthless people.

I wanted to explore that, and the potential breaking point—that moment of brittleness—when those rules were challenged. I put her in a place forcing her to examine herself and her actions in a way I suspected she would never choose to do—self-reflection would be useless at best, destructive at worst for a person like her.

Carrie Clevenger

Austin, USA

www.carrieclevenger.com

Carrie worships Maynard and dreams of cephalopods on trains among other oddities in Austin, Texas. To say that she is busy with her two daughters, two cats, and a saintly jar-opening husband is an understatement, but the creative Muse (he goes by M) tends to insist on proper attention—often at the most improper times. Initially an avid non-fiction reader and occasional poet, she discovered the power of the Storyteller when she happened upon the horror/thriller genre. These books became kindling to a whole new passion. She didn't start the fire; she's just brought the gasoline.

About "Baggage Check"

As the second in line for the Yin Book, I was striking fairly fresh ground for *Baggage Check.* I wanted my story to contain a little bit of humor and a little dose of tragedy. Out came the two characters Bullwick and Leon. Best friends since childhood, they are two completely different personalities. Inspiration came from Shaun of the Dead's Shaun and Ed, although the story is nowhere near the cult-hit zombie-fest. I chose baggage handlers because I have always been comfortable in a support role.

While the entire airport is livid chaos, these two employees are completely ignorant of the goings-on but witty enough to dig through baggage, and thus happen upon 'The Painting'. The item costs Bullwick's life in a huge misunderstanding, but Leon is empowered that much more against his domineering girlfriend, (whom he probably would have married) Mindy.In my story, this 'stupid piece of art' takes wings and begins its whirlwind journey through the next eight stories. And the women's panties? You'll see them again.

Tina Hunter

Edmonton, Canada

www.tinahunter.ca

Tina writes primarily in the Science Fiction and Fantasy genres; however she's been known to dabble in horror, general fiction and women's fiction. Tina broke into print in 2009 with four flash fiction stories published in two anthologies and a short story in *The Red Book*. Tina currently lives in Edmonton, Alberta, Canada with her husband and two dogs, River and Masey.

About "Where the Heart Is"

It was while reading Carrie Clevenger's story I thought about writing a police officer being sent to the airport to investigate a crime. But I wanted it to be more than just another crime story.

Detective Tori Young came to me fully formed in a dream a few nights later. She was a complete workaholic with a god-complex but she secretly wanted to have a quiet life. So I created an event that caused her to really look at that secret desire.

Tori turned out to be the easy part.

You see, I also auctioned off a character in my story for a fundraiser event put on by the Rare Diseases Foundation in British Columbia, Canada. The winner of the auction wanted the character to be his mother, Anita (Neets) Patel.

I took the information he gave me and crafted Tori's police partner. I wanted to do it in a manner that respected the real woman, while making sure the character did what she was supposed to do to move the plot forward. It was a lot of hard work, but I really love this story and I hope you will too.

Claudia Osmond

Toronto, Canada

www.Claudia-Osmond.blogspot.com

Claudia is an only child, wife, and mother who loves caramel apples, hates snakes, stands for social justice, sits at the feet of her Muse, reads voraciously, writes passionately, sings only when no one's listening, and admits that she wrote her very first novel in a closet—both literally and figuratively speaking. As she believes there is more to this world than the eye can see, she has a tendency to place her characters in precisely the spot she wishes she could be: with both feet on the boundaries of the unseen.

About "The Other Side of Limbo"

I had the pleasure of meeting Jodi Cleghorn during the summer of 2009, via Twitter. She told me about the Chinese Whisperings *The Red Book* project that she and Paul Anderson were spearheading and I was completely fascinated by the concept. What an utterly appealing and unique initiative, I thought.

I followed the tail end of *The Red Book's* publication journey all the while imagining what it would be like to be part of a collaborative writing project like that. So the moment Jodi and Paul invited me to be a part of their 2010 Yin Book adventure, I jumped on it! I was thrilled and filled with anticipation. Mostly, I was dying to find out which character would jump out at me and shout, "Write me! Write me!" Well, my dear Mildred didn't exactly jump out at me; it was more like she shuffled up to me, pulling her crocheted sweater tightly around her frail body, and whispered, "I'll tell you why I'm here, dear, if you'd like." And by the look on her face, I knew I had to hear her story.

Laura Eno

Florida, USA

www.LauraEno.blogspot.com

Laura has a pet from the Underworld named Jezebel and a skull called Mr. Fluffy who help her write fantasy novels late at night. Her work has been published in various places, both in print and online, including *Twisted Dreams*, *The Monsters Next Door*, *Flashes in the Dark*, *10Flash*, *House of Horror*, *The New Flesh*, *Everyday Weirdness* and *MicroHorror*. Her main thrills include writing, reading and practicing Tai Chi.

About "Freedom"

My story reflects on what happens when the comfort zone of daily routine is gone. How do people react when forced to deal with the unexpected?

Haunted by a tragic past, the main character has lived a life where decisions are made for her. Now, she is able to see her life for the first time in years, without having to read it in the reflection of another's eyes. This story examines the choices she makes when left to cope on her own. Whether you agree with her or not, it is a celebration of original decision that defines a person as an individual and not part of a collective.

Jasmine Gallant
London, England

A natural procrastinator with visions of greatness, Jasmine overcomes her laziness to produce works that she can be proud of—often at the last minute. An avid reader and a writer since grade school, her stories try to focus on the darker aspects of human nature. *Not My Name* is her first piece of published fiction and hopefully a start to a long relationship with the editors at eMergent Publishing. Most of her stories try to tie in an element of surprise for the reader in the last act and touch on the idea of personal identity.

About "Cobalt Blue"

I really wanted to reach with this story and to write something completely outside my comfort zone.

The thing about my main character Sam is… he got away from me. I wanted him to be this hardnosed cynical son-of-a-bitch and that's how he began. But then he turned into this love-sick puppy sniffing after Sara as soon as she walked into his life. I completely rewrote their relationship to remove this but… it lingered.

With some constructive editing and some time spent playing with time and structure, I think I've managed to write something I can hear my own voice in, whilst being a piece worthy of the other writers involved in the project. Or perhaps I've bitten off more than I can write!

Icy Sedgwick
London, England
www.icysedgwick.com

Icy is part office manager, part writer, part film academic and part trainee supervillain. She hails from the frozen north of England. Icy dreams of Dickensian London and the Old West. Icy can't pin down what genre she likes the most, and she subsequently writes all kinds of nonsense about telepathic parrots, Cavalier ghosts and steampunk automatons. Find her ebooks, free weekly fiction and other shenanigans at her website!

About "The Strangest Comfort"

I read all of the stories written before mine and thought, "Well now, young Icy. Just what on earth are you going to write about?" Luckily writers, by and large, are a fairly narcissistic bunch and we do love to cast writers as our main characters. When looking for a reason why someone would need to be in an airport, it seemed obvious—a writer needed to go somewhere.

Thus Pippa walked into my head and started telling me her story. Parts of her are me, parts of her most definitely aren't (I don't drink or smoke, for example). JR Coker, on the other hand, was inspired by a man I sat next to on the tube, except for a changed consonant in his name, it might as well BE the guy I sat next to. A lot of the other (very excellent) stories deal with themes of the darker side of human nature and I suppose I wanted to add bring some light to the table. It's not like me to be optimistic, but I chose to write about redemption and hope.

Just how calm can a person can be when an airline collapses?

Jen Brubacher
London, England
www.jbrubacher.blogspot.com

A librarian who believes there aren't yet enough books in the world, Jen writes mostly mystery and suspense, but has also tried spy novels and the supernatural. She has participated in National Novel Writing Month for six of the last eight years and also writes books that take longer than a month. Her stories can be set anywhere, and her pet themes work worldwide: home, trust, and forgiveness. The best stories are universal. She currently lives in London, England, but was born in British Columbia and is Canadian right through.

About "Lost and Found"

Collaborative writing intimidated me. I didn't want to wreck the world that so many other writers were using, and I didn't want to wreck any of the characters that previous writers had created. But when I read Laura's story, particularly the moment when her main character thinks she recognises a young girl, Ashley Gardner instantly appeared in my mind. The lost girl, trying to stay invisible, unlikely to wreck anything.

But what was the rest of her story? Where had she come from, and how did she get so lost? I have a wonderful mother who has been a great support and inspiration to me throughout my life. She can't be held responsible for any of the characters I create, particularly those whose parents have messed them up completely. Ashley is a little bit of me, but a me with a very different history, someone with my own curiosity of the world—and my own tendency to over-think things, particularly the things that other people leave behind—but without the support I occasionally take for granted. I like to think Ashley ends up at peace with herself and that despite her past she truly leaves the 'Lost and Found'.

Annie Evett

Brisbane, Australia

www.annieevett.com

Pure scorpio, Annie lives enthusiastically and passionately; often not appreciating others don't keep up. Annie draws on years teaching and traversing the corporate landscape to infuse her eclectic writing with life experience, sharing her journey as woman and mother, attempting to stuff her time with kids activities, teaching, writing collaboratively for non-fiction and fiction projects with an occasional short stories created. Mild mannered grade teacher during the day, Mystress Weaver of tales by night, she occasionally sleeps.

About "Kanyasulkam"

Whilst there is a theme of misunderstood individuals through-out my work, I have to admit I silently begged all weirdoes, psychopaths and potential bombers to leave me alone while I read the prologue for *The Yin and Yang Book,* seeking a character to become immersed with. I think deeply when giving my stories titles, attempting to assist the reader by giving an insight into a twist or motivation for the characters. "Kanyasulkam" is no different. It is a derogatory term loosely meaning 'bride price', with its true roots in slavery and the loss of innocence.

Initially delighted to be struck by a young bride-to-be who may not make it to her own wedding; I'd thought those dramas alone would populate my story and looked forward, as I wrote, to how she found a way to join her true love. I soon discovered in her single minded goal to achieve fame and stardom she had sold her last threads of self. Her body, through its rejection of its environment was pleading for her to stop, take stock and reclaim her life.

Who says that art imitates life?

Lily Mulholland

Canberra, Australia

www.lilymullholand.com

Lily is an Australian writer of short stories and flash fiction, which have appeared in more than a dozen online and print publications, including the *Best of Friday Flash Volume One, Bewildering Stories, Miscellaneous Voices #1* and *Antipodean SF*.

About "Double Talk"

Coming late into the project, I had to get up to speed fast and quickly devoured about 16 story drafts before going back to the prologue and teasing out what I thought were the major themes and threads. I had Yin stories and Yang stories swirling around my brain, sifting facts, narrative arcs, time spans and possible trajectories. The diary entries Emma Newman constructed for her JJ character gave me a window into his world and he hadn't really been explored in any of the preceding Yin stories. As he was central to the prologue set-up, it became obvious to me I would have to find a way to bring JJ back into the picture.

Glimpses into JJ's psychological make-up got me thinking about how he could be a successful businessman yet have such traumatic markers from his childhood. I was also intrigued by the mystery of the painting, which felt almost like a second main character to me. I knew my story had to develop JJ and his links to the painting. I also needed to get JJ to the airport. Those three elements pretty much set me up and my story grew organically from there.

Paul Anderson

London, England

www.paulanderson.org.uk

Paul is a Scottish writer living in the westernmost suburbs of London with his wife Julia, a one-eyed gecko called Dooya and an old typewriter with a slightly wonky 'U' key. Paul served as joint editor as well as a contributor to *The Red Book*, and somehow along the way earned the reputation as the 'nice' editor. That of course was before the issue of Em-dashes and En-dashes got brought up! His main genres are urban fantasy and steampunk, although his preferred genre would be 'something that sells'. Paul is the co-founder of eMergent Publishing and Managing Editor of the Write Anything website.

About "Epilogue"

How do you bring two completely divergent storylines back to a common point? The answer is luck, espionage and Nazis. On re-reading Jodi's *Prologue*, I realised Medae hadn't simply been sent to steal a painting; she had been sent to steal what the Hildebrands valued most—their name and reputation. Paul Servini's *Three Monkeys* and Lily Mulholland's *Double Talk* provided the backstory to the family. Teasing out hints from the other stories created a family steeped in dirty deeds, willing to stop at nothing to preserve reputation and honour above all else.

Walt Hildebrand, the beloved founder of Saxon Industries, built his empire on the pain and suffering of others. John Senior is clearly aware of this, and goes to great lengths to cover up the truth: betraying a friend; killing employees; almost ruining his own son. John Junior is in many ways an innocent victim, but as with the rest of the family, his innocence is tainted. He may be ignorant of the family past, but he's not a nice man either. And so the anthologies end just as they started. Yin and Yang comes full circle.

CHINESE WHISPERINGS
The Red Book

In a small North American university town ten lives are intersecting.

Miranda reaps what she has sown

Mitchell understands there is no resisting fate

Clint dreams of forging a violent destiny

Elizabeth is about to make a discovery

Robin hides a terrible secret

Simon hasn't slept in ten days

Sam is pursued by nightmares

Susie has lost everything

David has just been found

Jake atones for past evils

Ten ordinary people struggling to keep their sanity in an insane world.

Featuring: Jason Coggins, Annie Evett, Paul Servini, Tina Hunter, Dale Challener Roe, Jasmine Gallant, Rob Diaz II & Emma Newman. Edited by Paul Anderson and Jodi Cleghorn

*What is perhaps most striking about The Red Book is the fact that,
on finishing the final tale, it leaves the reader with a desire
to return to the beginning and experience the various threads
of plot and character again, certain that a second read
will unlock deeper complexities of connection.*
DAN POWELL, 2010 2010 Yeovil Literary Prize winner (Short Story)

E.J. NEWMAN'S
From Dark Places

Abby finds a creative solution to her father's problems. Ben makes a pact with the Devil for a new Mum. Katie is pursued by unrelenting voices. John just found his colleague's hand in a strange girl's lap. Jarvis is falling apart on his wedding day. Rosalind comes face-to-face with her number one fan... and that is just the beginning.

E.J. Newman's debut anthology is a dark and twisting journey across the urban landscape, mining the rich seam of human frailties with insight and humour. The stories traverse the magical and the mundane, where supernatural beings are indistinguishable from their mortal counterparts in their complexity and complicity.

"Newman is unafraid to explore the darker side of fiction and, by extension, life. The stories are by turns touching and funny and heartwarming. And dark. In places very, very dark. Leave the light on."
DAN POWELL, 2010 Yeovil Literary Prize winner (Short Story)

"Gods, demons and angels inhabit these pages, as much at home as the cheating spouses, spurned lovers and ugly, foul-mouthed orphans. Newman is a powerful emerging voice in dark fiction. I'll be watching out for more of her stuff. You should too."
ALAN BAXTER , Author of "RealmShift" and "MageSign"

LITERARY MIX TAPE'S

Nothing But Flowers

an eMergent Publishing community project

Amazon UK and Canada #1
in Science Fiction Anthology and Fantasy Anthology

In a devastated world, a voice calls out through the darkness of space, a young woman embraces Darwin, a man lays flowers in a shattered doorway, a two-dimensional wedding feast awaits guests, a Dodge Challenger roars down the deserted highway…and that's just the beginning.

Inspired by the Talking Heads' song of the same name, the anthology explores the complexities and challenges of love in a post-apocalyptic landscape. Poignant, funny, horrifying and sensual, this collection of short fiction leaves an indelible mark on ideas of what it means to love and be loved.

Featuring stories by Sam Adamson, Jim Bronyaur, Jen Brubacher, Adam Byatt, Christopher Chartrand, Carrie Clevenger, Jason Coggins, Janette Dalgliesh, Rob Diaz II, Rebecca Dobbie, Rebecca Emin, Laura Eno, Annie Evett, Susan May James, P.J. Kaiser, Maria Kelly, Lily Mulholland, Emma Newman, Dan Powell, Dale Challener Roe, Icy Sedgwick, Paul Servini, Benjamin Solah & Graham Storrs. Edited by Jodi Cleghorn

All profits from the sale of this anthology go to The Grantham Flood Support Fund.

100 Stories for Queensland

an eMergent Publishing community project

"One hundred beautiful stories. Our stories. When so much was lost
or destroyed, this was created. That's something that
can never recede or wash away."
Kate Eltham – CEO of The Queensland Writers Centre

100 STORIES FOR QUEENSLAND has something for everyone, from slice of life to science fiction, fantasy to romance, crime to comedy, paranormal to literary fiction. Heart-warming, quirky, inspiring and funny, the stories between these covers will lift readers to higher ground.

100 stories donated by authors from across the globe, including best selling authors Janet Gover, Anita Heiss, Sue Moorcroft and Sean Williams.

All profits from the sale of this anthology go to the Queensland Premier's Flood Appeal.

www.100storiesforqueensland

CPSIA information can be obtained at www.ICGtesting.com
Printed in the USA
BVOW030155031011

272305BV00001B/48/P